Katherine lost one hero in the line of duty — can she risk loving another?

Katherine Pelham's fiance was a police officer, shot and killed during a robbery. Left with a house she can't afford, she must rent out the first floor to solve her money woes. Before she can finishing putting up the For Rent sign, along comes a man who seems interested in more than just the apartment.Fireman Jack Connelly is in a bind: he's rescued a dog, and his lease doesn't allow pets. The new apartment would be great. The new landlady, even better…

Books by Christa Maurice

Drawn to the Rhythm Series
Satellite of Love
Heaven Beside You
Waiting For A Girl Like You

Arden FD Series
Three Alarm Tenant
Struck By Lightning
Spark of Desire

Weaver's Circle Series
Secrets Everybody Knows
Long Memory

One Ring to Rule
Melody Unchained

Published by Kensington Publishing Corporation

Three Alarm Tenant

Arden FD Series

Christa Maurice

LYRICAL PRESS
Kensington Publishing Corp.
www.kensingtonbooks.com

Lyrical Press books are published by
Kensington Publishing Corp. 119 West 40th Street New York, NY 10018

All Kensington titles, imprints, and distributed lines are available at special quantity discounts for bulk purchases for sales promotion, premiums, fund-raising, and educational or institutional use.

Special book excerpts or customized printings can also be created to fit specific needs. For details, write or phone the office of the Kensington Special Sales Manager:
Kensington Publishing Corp.
119 West 40th Street
New York, NY 10018
Attn. Special Sales Department. Phone: 1-800-221-2647.

Kensington and the K logo Reg. U.S. Pat. & TM Off.
Lyrical Press and the L logo are trademarks of Kensington Publishing Corp.

First Electronic Edition: May 2010
eISBN-13: 978-098241-707-2
eISBN-10: 0-9824170-7-1

First Print Edition: May 2010
ISBN-13: 978-1-61650-892-0
ISBN-10: 1-61650-892-2

Printed in the United States of America

To Jackie for great info, great convo, and great lunches, and to the guys of the Dodge Street station who haven't minded my stalking.

Chapter 1

Katherine Pelham hefted the hammer and pounded the For Rent sign into the frozen ground.

"Happy Val-En-Tine's Day," she emphasized each syllable with a thwack. A truck slowed on the street, but she resisted the urge to look. She'd probably smash her thumb. Already this morning, she'd stubbed her toe, spilled hot coffee, and ripped a hole in her skirt getting it out of the dryer. Going back to bed sounded ideal.

She stepped back to admire her handiwork. The sign wasn't crooked and the post hadn't snapped. The perverse Ohio weather that transformed her yard to concrete had warmed the air until she only needed a sweatshirt. With the apartment done, she needed a reliable tenant. Then she could handle the mortgage, the credit cards and her leftover college loans. She started toward the front door and stopped. It wasn't her door anymore. Her apartment opened from the side.

The servants' entrance.

Oh, she could have taken the first floor, but it still would be half the house. And the half closer to the basement spiders. She walked around the side and up her new steps. As she reached for the door, a car pulled into the drive.

A truck actually. A green pick-up. A tall, broad-shouldered man climbed out. He looked as if he'd stepped out of an action adventure movie.

"Hi. You have a place for rent?"

His warm tenor voice worked its way through her ears and made straight for other parts of her body. She nodded.

"Do you take pets?"

"What kind of pets?" she asked.

"A dog."

A dog. She'd never had a dog and envied people who did. When other girls wanted ponies, she'd wanted a puppy. How wonderful would it be to have a dog romping in the back yard? How wonderful would it be to have this gorgeous man romping in the backyard with the dog? "What kind?"

"A big mutt." He held his hand two feet above the ground. Katherine wondered if that meant head height or shoulder height. Either one wasn't bad. Plenty to play with.

"Sure."

"How much is it?"

"Six hundred." Everybody said it was too low, but it sounded high to her. It covered the mortgage payment, freeing up her paycheck for other non-essentials like food.

"Plus utilities?"

She shook her head. "I cover utilities, but I control the thermostat."

He nodded. "What's the deposit?"

"One month's rent."

"And the pet deposit?"

Katherine bit her lip. Should she charge extra for pets? How much damage could it do? She supposed that depended on the animal, but the landlord book hadn't mentioned that, and she didn't want to take advantage. "Even for the dog."

He blinked. "Wow. Can I see the place?"

"Now?" Katherine's mind reeled. She'd just hammered the sign in the yard. She hadn't even put a notice in the paper yet. Everyone warned her it might take a month or, God forbid two, before anyone answered her ad. The book said she might show it dozens of times before an acceptable tenant came along. She'd braced herself to show the apartment until summer. This could be another annoyance in an already bad day, or a sign her luck was turning.

"If you've got time," he added.

"Of course." She walked back down the steps and tried to get a better look at him. Did he look crazy? No, he looked nice. Tall, well-proportioned, dark blond hair. His expression seemed to settle into bright-eyed amusement, as if life entertained him. He filled out his blue fleece jacket nicely. She caught her breath as she stepped past him to the door, wanting to run her hands over his fleece to see how soft and warm it was. What had gotten hold of her? His height? She didn't know many adult men anymore. Most of the males in her life were high school boys, or high school janitors who acted like juveniles.

"My name is Jack. Jack Conley," he announced, holding out his hand.

She caught his gaze sweeping up her body. He was checking her out. For a split second it annoyed her, but pleasure swamped that reaction.

She waited until his eyes met hers before shaking his hand. His eyes were extraordinary. Golden brown and smiling even when his face was serious. He had a good grip, firm, not crushing. His touch spread a liquid shiver up her arm.

"Katherine Pelham. Pleased to meet you," she said, struggling to keep the tremor out of her voice.

"Pleased to meet you, too." He raised one eyebrow.

She unlocked the front door. The foyer still looked strange with the stairs blocked off. It seemed cramped even though she'd painted the walls a pale tan to make it appear larger.

"The back door lets into the yard. This is the foyer, and there's the living room." She gestured through the archway as he pushed the door closed. She jumped away at the soft click. Her nerves hummed, but the sensation wasn't unpleasant, which confused her more.

"What?" he asked. His hand rested on the doorknob.

"Nothing." She stared at his hand. His fingers were long, graceful and ringless. She forced herself to meet his eyes.

He searched her face—his lips tightening to the closest thing she'd seen to a frown on him. "So. This is the foyer?"

Katherine forced herself to take a deep breath. She was acting like a fool. She couldn't deny a certain sense of tension around him, but it didn't feel like the tension of a scary situation. More like a warm ache she remembered feeling once or twice, a long time ago.

"It could be anything you want. It was the foyer before we divided the house. Through here is the kitchen." She started down the hall, pointing to another door. "This leads to the basement. This is the bathroom." She pushed open the bathroom door. "The shower's behind the door. It's very small."

He crowded behind her to peer into the narrow bathroom, which she'd painted mint green to brighten the windowless space.

Katherine found herself leaning toward him rather than away. He smelled good. His firm jaw came to the top of her head.

And he was looking down at her with those amused eyes.

She frowned, but didn't move. "It's very small," she repeated.

"It's fine."

She fled to the kitchen and waited for him, swearing she would gain control over this interview right now.

"This is the kitchen. The bathroom used to be part of the kitchen, so it was much larger. There's plenty of room in the nook for a table, but the floor gets cold in the wintertime. I don't think there's any insulation under there."

She'd loved the big kitchen when they bought the house. She considered it the heart of the house. Now it was the smallest room because she'd had to carve out space for the bathroom. "Through this door is—was, the dining room. I suppose it would make a wonderful bedroom." She blushed at the image of this room as a bedroom with him in it. She was developing some sort of obsession. Too many nights with a book and a bowl of soup. Nothing to do with the way he looked at her. Or the way she hoped he looked at her. She pushed open a door and stepped through it.

Jack crossed the room and peered at the inset china cabinet. He ran his finger along the dark mullion windows, studying the uneven glass. "Is this original?"

"As far as I know. The house was built in nineteen thirteen, and it was very fashionable back then to have built-in cabinets." Katherine tried to pull herself together. First time in a long time around an attractive man, and she started babbling like a schoolgirl in a chance encounter with the captain of the football team. So what if he was handsome? So what if she could almost feel his strong hands gliding down her spine?

She clenched her teeth and walked out of the dining room, acutely aware of him behind her. "There's another little room back here. We used it for storage. It's not insulated. Anything you put back here has to be able to take huge temperature fluctuations." She tugged open the French door leading to the storeroom. It popped open and she stepped through. "That's the back door. You could put in a doggie door, then your dog could get out if he needed to."

"Archer would like that."

Katherine found herself trapped between Jack and the door, struggling with the bolt. Blood rushed in her ears, and she couldn't remember when she'd last taken a decent breath. She seized the doorknob and yanked.

The door burst open. She stumbled backward. For an eternal moment, Jack's arms wrapped around her shoulders. Heat rushed to her face as she felt his hard chest through his coat. She wanted to sink into his embrace and stay there.

"Sticky door," he said, setting her on her feet. His hand trailed up her arm.

Katherine tried not to sound like a breathless fool. "It's worse in the summer when the wood swells." She pushed through the storm door and took a large step away to gain some room. Unfortunately, two feet of porch wasn't enough to slow her pulse or clear her mind. "This is the backyard. It's fenced and it goes all the way back to the alley." She pointed to the tree line.

"Big yard."

"We loved it when we bought the house, but we never got around to working on it. Our neighbor has a beautiful lawn. I have moss. Feel free to look around." She hurried inside and perched on what remained of the stairs.

Not long ago, these two steps had led to a landing and another nine steps to the upstairs. Now they led to a wall. On the other side was her front door, amputating her new home from what she'd always considered its heart. The symbolism was ironic. Katherine leaned back, trying not to think of Jack Conley, who she could hear walking around the kitchen and dining room.

It would be nice to have a tenant by the first of the month and to have a guy with a dog living downstairs for security purposes. That the potential tenant was gorgeous and that she'd been alone too long had nothing to do with the choice. This was business.

"Mrs. Pelham?"

Katherine looked up. He was admiring her legs. A giggle gathered in her throat. She stood, commanding those legs to hold her. "Ms."

His eyes swept up her body again. Low heat developed in her belly. "Ms. Pelham, then. It's a great place. Do you have an application?"

"Oh yes. Give me a minute, and I'll get it." She spun around to dart upstairs, checking herself before she ran into the wall. This chopped-up house would take getting used to. "I'll be back."

Katherine slowed to a walk as she stepped off the porch steps. Why was she running? It was business. Just because he looked at her like a woman and not like a teacher, or a friend, or a conquest didn't mean anything. She walked to her door and opened it. The applications lay on the steps. Without the wall, she could have handed him one through the banister. She heard Jack walking around, but knew she wouldn't be able to hear him upstairs. If she wanted to spy, she'd to have to sit at the bottom of the stairs. Or position herself at one of the heat vents.

Katherine shook her head. Why was she thinking of spying on her tenant? She didn't even have a tenant yet. She picked up one application, took a deep breath and went back around the house to the first floor. He waited in the foyer studying the cracks in the ceiling.

"Here you are," she said. "Drop it off in my mail box anytime."

"Thanks." Jack folded the paper and slipped it into his coat pocket. "You live upstairs?"

"Yes."

He nodded. "I'll have this back today."

"In a big hurry to move?" Katherine tensed.

"It's Archer. I just got him, and I can't have pets at my apartment. My landlord wants him out by the end of the month."

"I see. Well, you can drop the application off in the mailbox whenever."

"Thanks." He held out his hand. "Nice meeting you."

"Nice meeting you, too." She kept her composure when his hand enveloped hers, but it wasn't easy. "Good-bye."

He grinned. "See ya."

Katherine locked the front door as he backed his truck out of the drive. She'd forgotten to tell him about the garage and the basement, but it hadn't gone too badly. Chances were excellent he wouldn't bring the application back, and if he did, that he wouldn't be a good tenant. The book specifically discussed researching prospective tenants. Once they moved in, getting them out was impossible. She suspected evicting Mr. Conley would be the least of her troubles.

Living in half the house felt strange. Back in her own apartment, she turned toward her kitchen at the top of the stairs. This had been a four-bedroom house. Now, one was her bedroom, another her living room and the third room was her kitchen. Only her office stayed the same in the fourth bedroom. Her office didn't have bad memories attached to it, so she hadn't changed it.

She wandered back into the hall and studied the pictures on the wall. She didn't know why she hadn't taken them down. Photos of her 'happy' life with a hero. Getting engaged, college graduation, buying a home on a police force mortgage assistance program. All quite dandy until Gary was killed, leaving her with a mortgage she couldn't afford on her teacher's salary. And all Gary's cop buddies lost interest in his not-quite-widow. Four years later, she only rated an occasional drive by.

That mistake she wouldn't make again. The next time she married, if she married, she refused to marry a hero.

* * * *

When Jack got home, he greeted Archer, cleaned up the newspaper Archer had shredded all over the apartment, and had sat down to fill out the application when the phone rang.

"Hello?"

"Jack. It's Kevin. There's a place for rent on Jefferson."

"On Jefferson? Did you get a number?" Jack frowned. He hadn't noticed another For Rent sign on Jefferson, but all the way home, his eyes had been full of Katherine Pelham.

"No number on the sign."

"White Colonial?"

"Yeah."

Jack nodded. "I looked at it on the way home."

"And?"

"Nice. Big fenced-in yard, and a door that lets into a little room at the back. She said I could put in a dog door."

"And the deposit?"

"One month's rent. Nothing extra for Archer. I don't think she's done this before. It's cheap. I want to get the application back to her today." Jack scanned the next question. Employer. While he talked, he wrote in 'Arden Fire Department.'

"Are you sure there's nothing wrong with it?"

"I'm sure. She's just new at this. I looked the place over thoroughly. It needs work, but I'll talk her into letting me do it."

"Or you could buy a house, and then you wouldn't have to ask."

Jack shot the receiver a dirty look, knowing his friend expected one. "It takes a long time to buy a house. I need a place for Archer now."

"The landlord is a woman?"

Jack felt a spark of desire he hadn't felt in a long time. "Yeah." Definitely a woman. Long auburn hair. Great curves. Sparkling chocolate brown eyes. A little formal, but vulnerable too. Just his type.

"Good looking?"

"Oh, yeah."

"Anybody we know?"

"I don't think so. I haven't seen her around. It's only a couple blocks from the station." He wondered about the other half of her 'we'. Was it an old family home? Or was she divorced and saddled with a house she couldn't afford? Or did some other little tangle cause the tenseness around her eyes?

"So you can run home when you forget your St. Florian medal." Kevin chuckled.

"Very funny." Jack shifted to read the next line of the application. References. "Can I use you as a reference?"

"She asked for references? I guess so. Do I have to tell the truth?"

"Only if it's good."

"Should I tell her what a hero you are? How you run into burning buildings to save kitties who have already vacated the premises?"

"That was a long time ago, and I thought the woman said *kiddies*. You're welcome to tell her how much you admire me for my sheer masculinity though." Jack filled in Kevin's name and number on the last line. Mrs. Wilson would give him a reference, and Dale was so happy he'd taken Archer that he'd sell Ms. Pelham on Jack without encouragement. Still, he'd give them both a call to let them know.

"You know you can't date the landlady, right?"

"Ha ha."

"Hey, you coming over to help me with my plumbing tomorrow?"

"Okay if I bring Archer?"

"Sure. See ya tomorrow."

"See ya." Jack hung up and double-checked the phone numbers. Then, he called Mrs. Wilson and Dale to make sure they didn't mind being his other references. Mrs. Wilson was happy to help, and Dale promised to convince her Archer was well behaved.

Jack inspected the application, wondering how to skew the decision in his favor. The apartment was perfect. And the landlady wasn't anything to sneeze at.

Archer put his big head on Jack's leg. Jack looked at him. He looked like a Rottweiler, but he didn't have the typical markings and his face was longer and leaner. He couldn't be happy in this little apartment. The apartment on Jefferson would be big enough for him to move around without bumping into things and had lots of yard to chase squirrels in. "What do you want, boy? Do you want to go meet the landlady?"

Archer's ears perked up. All he heard was 'go.'

"All right, come on. Let's go."

Archer danced around the tiny kitchen, crashing into the cupboards and the table. Jack grabbed the leash and his keys. She'd seemed interested in the dog. She might like the idea of having one around. Maybe meeting him would convince the lovely Ms. Pelham.

Aw, who was he kidding? He wasn't going back to drop off the application as soon as possible, or so she could meet Archer. He was going back so he could see her.

* * * *

Katherine gathered up the graded quizzes and put them into her book bag. She hadn't assigned enough homework last week. She'd finished grading, and the weekend wasn't halfway over. What was she supposed to do with the rest of it? She grimaced. Maybe she should devote time to her bustling social life. Why, she had two books checked out of the library. That alone was a huge time commitment. She moved away from her desk and studied the room.

She'd lined the walls with shelves constructed of milk crates and boards. Most of the shelves bowed under the weight of books. Shortly after they bought the house, she'd talked to the school janitor about building real shelves, but Gary nixed the idea. He said he'd make them himself. He never had. Time ran out.

Katherine hung her book bag on the doorknob. Maybe she was wrong. Maybe the office did have bad memories. She wandered to her living room, trying to think of some way to waste the rest of the weekend. Her friends told her to move on. It had been four years. Get out and date. Have fun. Start over. The whole idea made her feel ill.

She'd never been outgoing, and the notion of hanging around a smoky bar trying to meet a nice, intelligent guy who wasn't trying to get himself killed for a living didn't sound like fun. She'd rather live alone. There had to be other ways to meet men who weren't heroes, teachers or, heaven forbid, school janitors. Maybe one would move in downstairs.

Like the guy she'd shown the apartment to this morning. He seemed nice and looked even nicer. She could recall the clever glint in his eyes and the timbre of his voice. Wrapping her arms around herself, she remembered how it felt when he caught her after the door burst open. The way his arms supported her. If he brought back the application, she'd know about his job. And if he moved in right downstairs, something might happen.

A vehicle pulled into the driveway. Jack Conley's truck. What was he doing back already? Was the apartment that much of a bargain, or was he desperate to move? He climbed out, pushing something back inside, and closed the door. Immediately, a dog's head poked out of the open driver's side window.

Archer. At least that's what she thought the name was.

He was big and black. Exactly the kind of dog a guy like Jack would have. And exactly the kind she'd always wanted to play with and have patrolling the backyard.

The sharp knock at the door startled her, even though she'd expected it. Katherine took a deep breath. A gorgeous man with a great dog, and he wanted to rent her first floor so much he'd returned the application before the ink was dry. Perfect, right? There had to be a catch. This was *her* life. There was always a catch. She answered the door trying to appear calm.

"Hello."

He stood holding the paperwork out. "I filled this out. I thought I'd see if you were home."

Katherine took it without looking, her heart fighting up her throat. "Thank you. Is that your dog?"

Jack glanced at the truck. "That's Archer. You want to meet him?"

"Sure." Katherine tried not to sound eager, but failed.

Jack led the way down the steps. Archer's face swiveled from one to the other, his long pink tongue lolling out of his mouth. Jack scratched his ears and the dog closed his eyes, leaning into Jack's hand. "Archer, this is Ms. Pelham. Ms. Pelham, this is Archer."

"Call me Katherine." She clasped her hands behind her back, afraid of what they might do given the opportunity. He was wearing the blue fleece jacket again. She wanted to pet him as much as she wanted to pet his dog. Maybe more.

"Katherine." He grinned, leaning against the side of the truck with his hands in his pockets. "You can pet him. He doesn't bite."

She reached out to the dog cautiously. She'd been bitten before, but this dog didn't look as if he would. As the tips of her fingers touched his head, he twisted and licked her hand with his sloppy tongue.

"Oh, thanks." She wiped her hand on her jeans before trying again. This time Archer allowed her to stroke the top of his head. His short fur felt smooth and slick under her fingers. "He's very pretty. Did you say you just got him?"

"A friend of mine had a kid. They were afraid to have a big dog around a baby."

Katherine rubbed Archer's ears. "I'm sure he'd be fine. He looks so gentle. He'd be like Carl in the picture books." As if to emphasize the point, Archer pressed his cheek against her hand and whimpered. Katherine laughed.

"My friend's wife wasn't so sure, so I said I'd take him. My landlord isn't as happy about the arrangement. I have until the end of the month to get rid of Archer or find a new apartment."

"So little time?"

Jack shrugged. "He doesn't want the dog in the building." He fished his keys out of his coat pocket. "Well, we shouldn't keep you. You probably have Valentine's plans."

Katherine pursed her lips. "Not me." Although walking up to the grocery store and buying a quart of ice cream for dinner sounded like a great idea.

"Really? I'm not doing anything either. You want to grab dinner? Nothing fancy, Wendy's or something."

"Are you serious?" Katherine warmed at the idea of seeing Jack again today. She didn't know the appropriate words to describe how much she wanted to have dinner with him, fast food wrappers and all.

"Sure." Jack shrugged. "Us singles should stick together."

"I don't know. We just met." Katherine reined herself in. What was going on here? Did he want the place that much?

"I don't bite, either. I can't stand to see a beautiful woman alone on Valentine's Day." Jack glanced at his watch. "Listen, I have to take Archer to the park, but I'll drop him home by about five and pick you up around six."

Katherine looked up at him. His expression didn't give her any real hints. This morning he hadn't known she existed and now, based on two short conversations about an apartment, he was asking her to dinner. What if he didn't need to move? What if he did think she was beautiful? And if he didn't think she was beautiful and wanted the apartment, did it matter? She didn't want to spend this holiday with Ben and Jerry's again. She scratched behind Archer's ear. "Okay. I'll be ready at six. We'll go Dutch."

"Dutch? What does that mean? It's not something rotten in the state of Denmark, is it?"

"Each pay our own way." Katherine stifled the urge to giggle. He couldn't possibly know a Shakespeare joke would win her over.

"If that's what you want. I'll see you then."

Katherine stepped back so he could climb into his truck. While she waited, she skimmed his application. When she got to the employer line, air vanished from the atmosphere. "You work for the fire department?"

"Yeah." He pulled the door closed. "I work up at nine."

"You're a fireman." She said, hoping he wasn't, but pretty sure it didn't matter. He was one of the brotherhood. They were all heroes, or wanted to be.

"Firefighter," he corrected.

"What?" She looked up from the traitorous application, blinking.

"Firefighter." He smiled. "I'm not actually on fire, and I do my best to stay that way."

"Oh. Firefighter. Right around the corner, you say."

"Up on Garfield Street where Worcester dead ends."

She nodded, but her head didn't feel attached to her neck. Naturally. The moment she saw him, she'd hit it in the head. The reason he looked as if he'd stepped out of an action adventure movie was because he had. His whole life was an action adventure movie. Cue soundtrack. Would this be the sweeping hero's theme or the ominous danger variation? Perhaps the comedy music. "I know where it is." Drawing a deep breath, she pursed her lips. "Well, I guess I'll expect you at six."

"I'll be back at six. See ya then."

"Yes." She stepped back until her shoe bumped the bottom step. A firefighter. Even better than chasing armed bad guys, he ran into burning buildings. She must have a tattoo on her forehead, Heroes Only—normal guys need not apply. Wasn't there one normal, intelligent guy in the entire city who would cross her path long enough to make an impression? Jack backed his truck down the driveway, pausing at the bottom long enough to wave before driving off. Katherine waved back. A firefighter. They were probably worse than cops.

Still, he might be a good tenant. He made enough money, judging by Gary's city salary. If he was noisy, he'd be at work for long shifts. And he had a great dog. Who said they couldn't be friends? Maybe he had friends who weren't firemen—firefighters.

Katherine snorted at the likelihood and turned back to the house. At least now she knew what the catch was.

* * * *

"What just happened?" Jack asked Archer.

Archer looked at him.

"One minute she's all for going out with me and the next, Wham! She's gone. I thought she'd walked back into the house and left her body behind."

Archer snuffled.

"I like her, buddy." Jack chewed his lip. "I wonder if she's always stiff or if it's nerves. She's too cute to be snooty."

Archer looked out the passenger window.

"Some help you are." Jack sighed. "Well, she liked you. She said you were pretty. What do you think about being pretty?"

Archer ignored him, demonstrating his entire opinion of his prettiness.

"Maybe if she likes you enough, she'll give me a chance, too. What do you think?"

Archer stood up on the seat still looking out the passenger window, offering Jack a view of his docked tail.

"Thanks a lot, pal." Jack patted the dog. She'd been adorably pleased to see Archer, but a little suspicious of his dinner invitation. He knew he'd rushed it, but the delighted flush on her cheeks was worth the risk, and she'd agreed. He'd have to remember the word she used. Dutch. He might get another blush if he worked it into conversation.

Then, she'd looked at the application, and her eyes went big as saucers. What had she seen?

He had one whole dinner to figure it out. After that, he might never see her again. Providing she didn't call off the dinner.

Now he wasn't sure which he wanted more, the woman or the apartment.

Chapter 2

"So, do you think I should go to dinner with him?" Katherine twisted her office chair back and forth. She could picture her friend Pam leaning on her kitchen counter, arms folded with the phone wedged between her ear and her shoulder, puzzling out Katherine's question. Katherine had decided a long time ago that she trusted Pam's judgment so much because they were so different. Pam was as opposite as possible without being a man, and if she came to the same conclusion, then it was probably correct.

"Wait a minute, I thought you were about to rent the downstairs to him. Why wouldn't you go to dinner with him? Honey, don't do that." Pam scolded one of her kids. "In a minute. I'm on the phone. Did you call his references?"

"Well, yes. I called his landlord. He's been living in the same place for seven years. Always on time with the rent. Quiet, polite. No damage the landlord knows about. Usually fixes things himself when they break. The way the guy moaned about losing him, I wondered why he didn't change his rule on pets." Katherine tangled the phone cord around her finger.

"Did you ask?"

Katherine heard banging on the other end of the line. "Yes, he said if he bent the rule for one, he'd have to bend it for everybody."

"Then there's your answer. This Jack is obviously a good tenant. You said your instincts were for him. Honey, stop that!"

The banging stopped.

"He seemed like a really nice guy. And he said he works at the fire station right around the corner."

"Really? Right around the corner? He sounds like a great catch. For a tenant."

"I can't go through another Gary." Katherine's jaw tightened at the thought of living that life again. Lonely and anxious when he was on duty and lonely when he wasn't. No, she couldn't go through another Gary.

"So don't. Listen, you're renting an apartment to this guy, not marrying him. A little perspective, huh?"

"But should I have dinner with him?"

"You're going Dutch treat, right? It's dinner with a friend. A new friend. Honestly Katherine, you need to get out some. Meet new people. Going out for fast food doesn't mean you're committed to marry him or sleep with him, or even kiss him goodnight for that matter."

"I don't want to lead him on."

"You're not. Friends go out to dinner all the time. You'd go out to dinner with me once in a while if I didn't have the rugrats to deal with. Take it easy and enjoy being single. You got engaged out of high school. Be free for a while. Gary's been gone for a long time. You've got to let him go."

"It's not that. I mean, he's gone and nothing's going to bring him back. I know that. It's not Gary at all. I don't feel strange about going out to dinner with a man. I feel strange having dinner with this man."

"Strange like your intuition is trying to tell you something, or strange like you've lost all your one-on-one social skills?"

Katherine thought for a minute. For no apparent reason, she'd trusted Jack immediately after she'd gotten past being alone with him in the house. And she'd thought about that, too. When the door clicked closed behind him, she hadn't been afraid of what he would do. She'd been more afraid of what she might do.

"I don't think he's an ax murderer if that's what you mean."

"Okay. Just remember that this guy is a tenant, not a roommate. Get me?"

"I get you." Katherine bit her lip. She didn't want to get Pam, but she did.

"I gotta go before the kids tear the place apart. Are you going to give him the keys?"

"I want to call his employer first. The book said to check all references."

"Okay, you do what the book says and call me tomorrow. I want to know what happens tonight. Bye."

"Good-bye." Katherine hung up the phone and finished the game of solitaire she had on her desk. She wasn't sure she'd gotten what she wanted out of Pam. She'd called her brash friend hoping for some kind of set answer, not a 'see what happens.' But then earlier, when she'd called his landlord, she'd hoped to find out he always paid his rent late and trashed the place. And before calling Pam, she'd called all his personal references hoping for something she could use for a reason to keep him out of the apartment. He acted rashly, took chances, didn't keep house well, something. Instead the first one, Kevin Marshall, had said he was solid and reliable and he knew how to do plumbing. The second had been an old lady whose plants he cared for when she went to Florida to visit her niece. She claimed her plants were healthier when she returned than they had been when she left. The last one had been Archer's former owner who assured her Archer was well behaved, except for a tendency to tear up newspapers, and a good watch dog.

They should have been things she wanted to hear. So why was she looking for reasons not to rent to him, and even better, not go to dinner with him?

He was too good to be true. Just because he had friends who would vouch for him, and a landlord bemoaning his fate at losing him, did not change the fact that he was a glory hounding firefighter bound to get himself killed and leave her alone again. But that shouldn't matter because he would just be a tenant, right? If something happened to him it would be sad, but not the end of the world. She'd just have to find a new tenant.

Katherine swept the cards together and rubber banded them together before dropping them into their place in her desk drawer. If she was going to dinner with a friend, she should get dressed.

She went into her bedroom and looked over her closet. Her clothing choices went straight from school clothes to weekend sweats with no lengthy stops in between. Her school wardrobe would be too dressy for fast food, even on Valentine's Day. What would Jack think if she turned up in a dress for this not-date? She hadn't bothered to keep a decent casual wardrobe since Gary died. As things wore out, she got rid of them. It didn't seem important when she never went out.

In the end, she chose a black chenille turtleneck and the least worn jeans she owned. This was as dressed up as she was willing to get for fast food. Running a comb through her hair, she cast a longing glance at her makeup. No, no makeup. Not for a non-date with a potential tenant. Even though the magazine she'd just gotten out of the library claimed that a little definition to her eyes would change her whole look. She reached for the eye liner.

At that moment she heard a knock at the door. Katherine glanced at the clock beside the bed. He was prompt, too. She picked up her purse and coat and headed down the stairs.

"Hey! We match." Jack announced as soon as she opened the door.

The soft navy jacket was back over a pair of excellently fitted black jeans. The V of the jacket revealed the round neck of a gray knit shirt, making her wonder how much time he'd spent on his wardrobe. Shrugging into her black wool coat, she said, "It must be the season. I bring out the black in my wardrobe."

"Here, I'll get the door." He hurried to the passenger side of the truck while she locked up the house. "So where do you want to go? We've got every fast food joint known to man within fifteen minutes of here."

"Wendy's is fine with me." Katherine climbed in. The truck smelled Armor All clean and the dashboard gleamed in the cab light. She didn't even see dog hair on the seat. Did it always smell that way, or had he taken the time to clean it out? And if he had, what did that mean? That she probably should have put on eyeliner.

"East or west?" He closed the door and spoke through the open window.

"West." From that side of town, she reasoned, it would be easy to get a bus home if she needed one. She wanted to be prepared for anything.

"West." He went around the front of the truck and climbed in the other side. "There are two out that way."

Katherine sighed, biting back frustration. None of his references had mentioned this facet of his personality. "There are? Are you an aficionado of fast food locations?"

"I did some overtime out there, so I paid attention to what was around in case it caught fire." He turned to her in the dark cab. "So, which one? The one that's further away is newer and seems to have better service, but the one that's closer is quieter. That I did learn from eating too much fast food." He winked.

Katherine's breath caught in her throat. She couldn't remember why his incessant questioning had annoyed her. He sat an arm's length away. The last time she'd been in this position, she'd leaned over and kissed the driver. She bit her lip and leaned back against the door to check the impulse.

"I don't care. Either one."

As soon as the words were out she regretted them. She didn't know how far out this other restaurant was, or if the buses ran there. At worst, she decided she could get a taxi, but she didn't know how much it would cost. Assuming he would, for some reason, abandon her. Then he certainly wouldn't get the apartment.

"So," Jack said.

She turned to him. He sat looking at her for a minute. His hair caught the light of the street lamp. A lock of it lay oddly and Katherine had to concentrate on not reaching over to brush it back into place. She smiled tightly.

He smiled back and involved himself with backing the truck onto the street.

She sighed and waited. It wasn't a date, she told herself. They were new friends commiserating about being alone on Valentine's Day. But if that was the case, why were they sitting in an awkward, first date silence? Katherine shifted and tried to think of something to say before her jaw locked up and she couldn't say anything at all. "So how was your afternoon in the park with Archer?"

"Great. He gets pretty wound up when I'm on duty. I work twenty-four hour shifts and he's cooped up in the apartment the whole time."

"Twenty-four hour shifts. That must be difficult." Katherine folded her hands in her lap before she forgot herself and laid the left on the seat between them where he could lay his over it. As if he would want to.

"It's not so bad. We're really just waiting most of the time."

"Waiting?"

"Waiting for runs. We usually get three or four a shift, but it's not always an emergency. Occasionally it's a prank, sometimes it's only somebody overreacting. Sometimes they decide they don't need us after all. In between, we do maintenance, physical training, and white board sessions." He shrugged. "What about you? What do you do? Besides rent an apartment."

"I teach high school English."

"Oh. I guess I better watch my language."

Katherine grimaced. Every time someone asked her what she did, and at least once every parent-teacher conference day, she heard that joke. They never seemed to understand it wasn't funny after the first dozen times. Of course, she reminded herself, it wasn't old to them. "Well, I promise not to grade you too hard," she answered by rote.

He chuckled, and the sound of it banished any annoyance she'd felt. It went straight to her knees, turning them to rubber and making her glad she was sitting down. "I bet you get that a lot," he said.

"Yes." Katherine hoped she didn't sound as breathless as she felt. What happened to friends? No one reacts to their friends like this. Maybe Pam was right, and she'd lost all her one-on-one people skills.

"Well, I promise not to say it again if you promise not to say 'where's the fire.'"

"I think I can manage that." She opened her purse and started digging through it for Chapstick. Suddenly she felt as if she needed to occupy herself, particularly her hands. Out the window, familiar landscape slid past. It felt reassuring. Traffic seemed light for a Saturday, but then everyone probably had some place to go, and had gone before now.

"So do you like teaching?" he asked, a little too loud.

"Sometimes. It has its rewards and its challenges." She found the tube rolling around in the bottom. Without flipping down the visor, she applied it. It gave her a moment to gather herself. And then he chuckled again.

"You probably have a bunch of students like I was. Bad kids who sit in the back of the room and don't finish their homework."

"I tend to move them up front and ask them questions. Sometimes they start doing their homework to keep from being humiliated in front of the class, and then sometimes they decide they like knowing the answers and getting good grades. Sometimes they hate me more." Katherine closed her purse, folded her hands together and wished she'd stayed home tonight. She really didn't know how to do this anymore, if she'd ever known.

"Really? My teachers gave up on me most of the time." He stopped for a traffic light and looked over at her. "As long as I was quiet and didn't interrupt the kids who were trying, they didn't care if I fell asleep."

"I don't like to give up on anyone. But then that's how I ended up here." Katherine grumbled before she remembered where she was and who she was talking to. Her jaws clicked shut too late. Not only had he heard, but he'd been looking at her when she said it.

He blinked, a little taken aback. "Well. Seen any good movies lately?" The light changed, and he focused on the road.

Katherine stared at her hands in her lap. No wonder she never went out, she wasn't fit company.

"Seriously, seen any good movies? We have a guy at the station who's a big movie buff. He'll watch about anything. Old movies, foreign movies, B movies. It's kinda neat the stuff he brings in. I think he's got a deal with the little video store on McKinley so he can rent a bunch of stuff and return it late without having to pay a fee. He brought this one in a couple of weeks ago…"

Katherine let him babble on about movies, half listening and glad it was dark. Did he think she meant here as in here with him? Should she explain she'd always believed the police force would bail her out if she needed them, and by the time she'd realized they wouldn't, she'd been in over her head? Would that make her look even more silly and pathetic to someone who lived by the same code? Or would he be able to make her understand why they left her the way they had? Pam never understood why she felt so betrayed, but maybe Jack would. If she only had the courage to ask him. But how much of herself did she want to expose on this first not-date?

They passed the Wendy's she knew. Only half the tables were taken, but she suspected fast food wasn't the dinner of choice for most couples on Valentine's Day. Last Valentine's Day, she'd sat at her desk with one light on and the heat turned down as low as she could stand to save a couple of bucks while she added up the state of her debt and graphed her decline into bankruptcy.

"So." Jack cleared his throat. "Have you seen any good movies lately?"

"I don't see many movies. The last thing I saw was Laurence Olivier in Hamlet when I showed it to the class." Katherine looked out the windshield at the strip malls on either side of the road. This whole area had expanded since the last time she'd had extra money to shop with. At least she hadn't blurted out how her DVD player had started eating DVDs nine months ago, and she'd given the TV to the school janitor in trade for some work he'd done because she ran out of cash.

"Is it any good?"

"It's restrained." Katherine focused on the film, forcing thoughts of strip malls, cops and Jack's easy smile out of her mind. "Olivier plays Hamlet as a very tightly controlled character. The kids have an easier time with the Mel Gibson version because he plays it more tortured."

"Why didn't you show that version to your class?"

"I couldn't get a copy. The district only has one and somebody else got to it first. Fortunately, I have my own DVD of To Kill a Mockingbird for when my sophomore class gets to that point in the Spring."

"I read that in school. It was great."

"It's one of my favorites. I teach it every year." Katherine looked out her window and noted a bus stop. So buses did run out here. Now the question was, why was she so sure he would strand her?

"Doesn't that get boring? Teaching the same book year after year?" Jack flipped on his left turn signal and angled the truck into the turn lane.

"No, I teach it to a different group of students every year."

He turned onto the access road to the Crossroads Plaza. "I don't read much. I used to read those military mystery novels, but they all started to sound the same after a while. You know, militant nut decides to take over the world and the hero has to find him and stop him before he can succeed. Maybe you can turn me on to a new author or something."

"Maybe." Katherine licked her lips, tasting the cherry Chapstick she'd put on. The phrase 'turn me on' caught in her mind and changed context. Turn him on? Certainly. Just say when. Then she realized it sounded as if he were making plans for the future with her. That probably meant he wasn't going to desert.

"Here we are. The new Wendy's." He turned into the parking lot.

She surveyed the area. This had been an empty field the last time she came here. Now there were a couple of restaurants and a jewelry store. She felt as if, after years of living in a cave, she'd emerged into a new century. Of course large portions of last summer had been spent in the basement, which was as close to a cave as she ever wanted to get. "I didn't know there was anything new out here."

"It only opened last summer. Nothing but the best for us."

"Well, it is Valentine's Day, I guess beggars can't be choosers." She stepped out and took a deep breath. The air smelled like fried chicken and melting snow. A cool breeze caressed her cheeks. Suddenly her stomach growled. Jack stopped at the front fender and stood waiting for her, watching her.

"It's still warm. I feel as if something's terribly wrong if I'm not wading though knee deep snow until April. We're on parole from winter," she announced to cover her odd pause. She hurried to the building, hoping the latest blush would fade before he noticed.

"I know what you mean, this weather has been really weird. Not that I don't like it, I'm waiting for the blizzards to come back." He opened the door for her.

"I hope this doesn't mean it's going to be a hundred and ten all summer long. Last year, I spent most of the summer in the basement battling the spiders and working on the foundation. I don't have another job like that to keep cool this year." She fought the urge to touch his coat as she passed him. It looked almost too teddy bear soft to resist.

"What's wrong with the foundation?" he asked, following her inside, almost on her heels.

"Nothing now." Katherine stepped into the queue. She knew what she was going to get. She always got the same thing so she would know how much it cost. "The mortar between the cement blocks had started to rot and I had to scrub it out and replace it. I warn you, the basement is inhabited by giant, fast, black spiders that are almost impossible to kill."

"Impossible to kill?"

She shivered. "Unless you smash them between two hard surfaces like a concrete floor and a big dictionary, they keep running. And they crunch if you step on them."

"Maybe I'll have to get a dictionary."

"I don't think they bite. They're just scary." Katherine hugged herself more to keep track of her hands than to secure herself.

"You really hate those spiders, don't you?" Jack grinned at her.

"Well, let's just say if you hear a lot of screaming and banging from upstairs, assume the spiders have moved in with me."

"I'll protect you."

Katherine studied him dispassionately. He looked so good and seemed so nice, why did he have to keep reminding her how inappropriate he was?

"I knew you would," she grumbled.

She stepped up to the counter and ordered. She held out the exact change before the cashier gave her the total. Jack ordered while other employees got her food, and she used the opportunity to study him out of the corner of her eye. He chatted with the cashier who, of course, glowed under his attentions. Then he started digging through his pockets for money. He pulled out a Swiss army knife, a set of keys, a dog whistle, two mangled Band-Aids and a handful of change. Frowning, he patted his other pockets.

"It's here some place. I had it when I left the apartment." He started through his pockets again. "Ah ha. Here it is." He pulled a battered wallet out of his fleece jacket and, grinning at Katherine and the cashier, sorted through his money.

Katherine collected her tray. She stopped at the condiment station to survey the seating choices while Jack gathered up his belongings and joined her.

"So, you have a firm idea on where you want to sit?" Jack raised an eyebrow.

"Yes." After the litany of questions on where to eat, she wasn't leaving this to debate. She picked up her tray and headed for a corner table by the window.

He followed, sitting across from her at the two person table. "Good choice. What do total strangers talk about over dinner?"

Katherine unwrapped her sandwich. "I have no idea. This was your suggestion."

"Oh yeah. I forgot. Well, what did you do this afternoon?"

"I called your references." She focused on arranging her fries on her sandwich wrapper and getting her straw unwrapped and into her cup. She didn't want to look up at him, because if she did, he might smile at her, and then she would lose her resolve to not be attracted to him. She felt like a moth telling itself 'don't look into the flame, don't look into the flame.'

"And they told you I'm a serial killer wanted in seventeen states?" He looked at her for a moment before leaning across the table. "It was a joke."

She cocked her head to one side and studied him. He had a faint smile on his face that almost enticed her more than the serious stare he'd been giving her when she showed him the apartment. As she watched, his expression turned a little uncertain, as if he'd realized he'd gone a tad too far. The longer she hesitated, the more uncertain his smile became and even that was endearing. "I know. I was trying to decide if it was funny enough to laugh at."

Jack cringed. "Ouch."

Katherine smiled. She'd forgotten how it felt to chat. "They were all complimentary. I want to contact your employer before I make any decision."

Jack shrugged. "Okay. I've worked for the department for twelve years. They know who I am. How long have you been a teacher?" He bit into his burger.

"Five years. I was engaged for eight." Katherine bit her tongue. She hadn't meant to say that. Why wouldn't Gary stay away?

He nodded as if she hadn't answered more than he asked. "Did you always want to be a teacher?"

"Yes. It's a very reliable, safe profession. Society will always need teachers."

"And it doesn't involve burning buildings," he added, dipping a French fry into her ketchup.

"Most of the time, no. We frown on burning down the school. I think that would result in a lot of detention. Possibly expulsion." She tried to remain serious and thoughtful, but part of her wanted to giggle over the fact that he'd stolen her ketchup. Pam was right. She had lost her one-on-one people skills.

He laughed. "I bet. I don't think I'd mind detention though."

"Why?"

"If I got to stay after school with you." His molten eyes turned very serious, sending a thrill down her spine.

Katherine looked down at her fries to hide her blush. "You must want that apartment quite a bit."

He shrugged and didn't answer.

* * * *

"That was stupid," Kevin announced resting one hip against the bathroom counter.

Jack leaned out from under the sink, wiping off the wrench. "Why?"

"What were you trying to do? 'If I got to stay after school with you.' It looks like a line. It sounds like a line. It must be a duck. Have you ever been subtle in your life?" Kevin shook his head.

"I like her."

"You like her, or you like her apartment?"

"I like her," Jack repeated. He'd spent most of last night dwelling on that question. He wanted to believe he loved the apartment and liked the landlady, but he hadn't woken up in the middle of the night with the bright, airy foyer on his mind.

Kevin brushed his hand through his dark hair. Jack knew that gesture usually indicated a lecture on the way. "Are you about done there?"

"I've been done for fifteen minutes. You're the one who wanted to hang out in the bathroom." Jack closed the tool box. He'd have preferred to have something else to work on, both to avoid the lecture and to keep his mind off Katherine Pelham. "Besides, it couldn't have been that bad. We had a great time. She's really funny, and really smart. I don't know. She runs hot and cold, though."

"What do you mean?"

"When she found out I worked for the department she closed up, but then she went out with me, and we had a great time."

"But, she paid for herself. You didn't exactly get a date with her." Kevin walked out of the bathroom. "I don't think it's a good idea to be trying to date a woman who might end up as your landlord."

"Might save time. She'll already have a key to my place."

"Ha ha. What if it ends badly? You'll be out a girlfriend and a place to live. Your track record isn't great. Remember Cynthia?"

Jack shuddered. Cynthia had been fun and a little wild. He hadn't realized her 'little wild' would turn into 'little crazy' on such short notice until too late.

"You still have scars from the ashtray she threw at you."

"So I stopped dating smokers." Jack fingered the crescent shaped scar on his chin.

Kevin grumbled, leaning into the fridge to fish out two cans. "And Evelyn who kept 'visiting' you at the station."

"She was obsessed. I broke up with her because she was suffocating."

"And Maureen."

"Hey," Jack shook his finger at Kevin. "Maureen dumped me." Then he paused, realizing that might not be a selling point. Being dumped by Maureen had been awful. He'd thought she was the one, and she'd thought he was the one of the week. She had been the first and last time he'd thought he found true love. At least until yesterday. Evelyn hadn't been the one even though she thought she had been. Cynthia just liked to fight and throw things. He couldn't imagine Katherine screaming or pitching glassware at his head.

Jack popped open the can Kevin gave him without looking at it. He smiled thinking about her laughing over dinner. Her eyes twinkling at him across the table. That big black sweater she'd worn made her look very dramatic. The sexy curves revealed by her sweater had been intriguing, too. And she had a nervous habit of licking her lips that was cute and sexy at the same time. Once she relaxed she was fun. Quick witted, throwing back snappy comment for snappy comment. Except for that one about detention. Then she'd coughed and become very interested in her sandwich. And even that seemed cute and wonderful.

"Wipe that silly grin off your face," Kevin ordered. He walked into the living room, leaving Jack in the kitchen.

Jack followed Kevin and dropped onto the couch next to Archer. Archer lifted his head long enough to look at Jack and yawn before flopping onto his side to go back to sleep.

"Listen. I'm your friend, and I don't want to steer you wrong, but I think it's a really bad idea to date the landlady, no matter how sexy her voice is." Kevin settled into the easy chair. "It might be fun, but it's going to end, and when it does you're going to be back where you started. Looking for an apartment that'll take Archer because you won't buy a house."

Jack wondered what her voice sounded like over the phone, but in person, the sound of it made his temperature rise. "So you think she has a sexy voice?"

"Did you hear a word I said?"

"I heard you." Jack frowned. He respected Kevin's opinion. Kevin was his superior at work, and he wasn't dim. Generally, once he'd thought something through, he had good advice. And he was right. There was more at stake here than a couple of dates. If she was an Evelyn, he couldn't make her stop hanging around him if they were living in the same house. If she was a Cynthia, she could really give him scars. And if she was a Maureen? Could he stand seeing her every day, knowing the relationship wouldn't progress beyond fun? He'd had to stop going to the places he'd gone with Maureen because the memories were too painful. "I guess you're right."

"Of course I am. And that doesn't mean you can't be friends with her."

"Yeah," Jack muttered.

"Stop mooning like that."

"If I didn't need the apartment so much, I'd just try for her. She's so much fun." Jack combed his fingers through Archer's fur, dragging it against its natural grain so it stuck up. "But that apartment is great. Good size, big yard, basement, she even said there's a washer and dryer in the basement I could use. She also told me I could park in the garage. And it's so cheap. I'm worried somebody else is going to snatch it out from under me."

"You said she was going to call the department tomorrow."

"She has some book on being a landlord, and it says to check all references, so she is. She probably would have given me the keys last night if it wasn't for that." Jack put his feet up on the coffee table.

"Hey, I did my best. I didn't tell her what a dingbat you are, or that you'd forget your head if it wasn't screwed on. I hope I don't go to hell for the lies I told her."

Jack glowered at his friend. "Why do I hang around with you again? I forget."

"To fix my plumbing." Kevin grinned and took a swig out of his beer can.

* * * *

Katherine hung up the phone and stepped out of the privacy booth in the gloomy, airless teacher's lounge. Her search to find a reason not to rent to Jack had been fruitless. He was the nicest guy on Earth, polite, handy, and heroic. Worst of all, heroic. Pam was sitting at the table slurping her soup and waiting for Katherine to deliver the verdict. Katherine crossed the room and sat down in front of her own lunch. "He's an exemplary employee. He was even decorated for something. Although the first person I talked to said 'Oh him', before she connected me to the right office."

"What was he decorated for?"

"They didn't say. I guess the record only said he was decorated two years ago."

"So he gets the apartment."

Katherine shrugged and studied her sandwich as if it might start talking back. "I guess so. Nobody else has stopped to look at it or called, and I really need the money."

"Yesterday you said you had a great time with him. You said he was funny and sweet. Saturday you called all his references, and they love him. You just called his employer, and he's been decorated. Why don't you want to rent to him? What is the problem? If you don't eat that now, you're going to be down here in your free period digging change out of the couch for a candy bar." Pam nudged Katherine's lunch closer.

Katherine picked up her sandwich and bit into it. What did she have against Jack? He was funny and sweet, handy around the house, decorated. He was even prompt.

He was also a firefighter-slash-hero, and the first man in years to make her heart do handsprings.

The school janitor dropped into the seat next to her and flashed his former football star grin at her.

"You wanted me," he said in a low tone she assumed was meant to be seductive.

Katherine felt her shoulders tighten. "Your temporary fix on the garage roof is coming undone. I need you to come by the house and fix it."

Randy seemed to think she would eventually bend to his boundless charm. The fact that she hadn't in the entire time he'd been hanging around her house doing the remodeling didn't sway him at all, even though she'd insisted on paying him market value for the work.

"Is that all?"

She raised one eyebrow. "Yes, that's all."

Randy leaned back in his chair, shaking his blond hair off his face. "I was thinking about that apartment. It's a pretty nice place. I might be interested in it."

"You have an apartment."

"Yeah, but your apartment is bigger and nicer, and has such quality workmanship in the remodeling. We could commute together." He winked at her as if his double entendre was clever.

"She already has a tenant, Randy," Pam announced, packing her Tupperware in her lunch bag.

Randy sat up. "No way. How'd you do that?"

"Someone stopped to look at the place right after I put the sign in the yard Saturday. He seems reliable, so I think I'm going to give the place to him," Katherine said.

"Him? Oh. Well, great." Randy's mouth twisted with what looked like disgust. "So when do you want me to come over and fix that roof?"

"I want you to fix the tarping. I can't afford to fix the roof right now."

Randy leaned toward her, smiling. "I work for trade."

"I have nothing left to trade. You already have my TV, and I don't think you're interested in my hardback mystery novels, are you? Just stop over as soon as you can and fix the tarp."

Randy stood up sighing. "All right. I can't come over tonight, but maybe Wednesday. Will that work?"

"As long as it gets done before the garage roof collapses."

"I told you. Your joists are fine. You've got a long way to go before the roof caves in." He shoved the chair under the table. "You worry too much, Kath." He swaggered out of the teacher's lounge.

"So, do you think he's ever going to get the message?" Pam asked.

"I don't think his receiver is working." Katherine glanced over her shoulder. He might be thick as a plank, but she didn't want to hurt his feelings if she didn't have to. "He wouldn't be so bad if it weren't for that raging ego. He's not bad looking, and he is kind of handy to have around."

"You forgot dumb as a post."

"Oh yeah, raging ego and dumb as a post."

Pam slid her lunch bag into her book bag. "So what is wrong with Jack the fireman? He doesn't sound stupid, rude or egotistical. What's the catch?"

"I don't want to get mixed up in another Gary thing."

"So don't." Pam shrugged as if it wasn't so difficult to resist Jack. "It's probably a bad idea to date your tenant anyway. Doesn't it say something in that book of yours about not dating tenants? What if you get into a fight, and he stopped paying the rent? What if you split up, and he wrecked the place for revenge?"

"Oh. I didn't think of that." Katherine shuddered. She couldn't afford to get the place fixed up again. She had maxed herself out on all sides just getting by for the last few years and she owed Randy money, yet.

"Hey, snap out of it. This is all going to work out great. You're going to have this nice guy living downstairs with a great dog. You're going to catch up on your bills and who knows, maybe you'll be able to get a TV in time for summer reruns." Pam pulled out her lesson plan book and fished out a couple of worksheets to copy before class. "This is going to be great."

Katherine swallowed hard. Great. How could it be great when the only man on Earth she shouldn't date was the same man who gave her butterflies every time he looked at her?

* * * *

Katherine ran through the door, dropped her bag at the top of the stairs and checked the answering machine. The light blinked with one message. She'd been playing phone tag with Jack since Monday. Now she was it. She looked at her watch. She had exactly thirty minutes to eat dinner and get back to school for parent-teacher conferences. If she wasn't so broke, she'd have gone to dinner with Pam and a couple of others. Monday evening, she'd called Jack to let him know the place was his, and he could pick up the keys and drop off a check for the first month's rent and the deposit after five. Tuesday morning he'd left a message saying he couldn't make it, but he'd come by Wednesday around five and did she want to go to dinner again? Nothing fancy, he knew a Lebanese deli by the mall that he liked but wasn't too expensive. Tuesday afternoon Pam had reminded Katherine about parent-teacher conferences Wednesday evening, so she left Jack a message saying she wouldn't be home Wednesday night, but someone would be there with the keys and the lease. She pressed the play button.

"Kate, it's Jack. I'll come by for the keys tonight. I'm on duty tomorrow, but if it's okay with you I'd like to start moving stuff in over the weekend if the weather's good. Sorry you can't do Lebanese tonight. Maybe some other time. See ya."

See ya. Katherine stood with her finger on the play button staring out the window, debating whether or not to play the message again just to hear his voice. And he called her Kate. She shivered. My God, she thought, I'm starting to sound like one of my students mooning over a cute boy. Spinning around, she hurried into the kitchen to open a can of soup for dinner.

The kitchen faucet was dripping again. Randy said he'd fixed it last time. Scowling, she fiddled with the knob until it stopped before getting her dinner ready. While she ate, she heard a vehicle in the driveway and absurdly hoped it was Jack picking up the keys earlier than expected. She peered out the window, smoothing her hair off her face.

Randy jumped out of his truck and grinned at the second floor. There was no way he could see her through the glare on the window. He did it because he was confident she would be waiting for him. She didn't like to encourage that confidence.

Groaning, she went down the stairs to open the door.

"Hey Kath. I told you I'd be here to fix that tarp."

"I need something else, too. The faucet in my kitchen is leaking again, and my tenant is coming by to pick up the keys."

Randy shrugged. "I'll hang around and wait for your tenant. Don't know why that faucet's leaking."

"Well, can you please look at it again?"

He shrugged again. "Yeah, I'll take care of it. Don't you worry about a thing. You just go to the parent-teacher conferences, and I'll take care of everything," he promised.

Katherine walked back up the stairs grumbling under her breath. By the time she headed out the door to go back to school, Randy was strolling around on the roof of the garage straightening the tarp as if it were the level and solid gym floor at school. "Randy!" she yelled. He continued to wander around as if she hadn't spoken, let alone yelled. She walked closer to the garage and cupped her hands around her mouth. "Randy!"

He spun around and started flailing his arms to catch his balance. Katherine held her breath as he struggled to keep his feet on the sloping, half rotten garage roof. He dropped to his knees with his hands outstretched for balance. "Jesus. Don't sneak up on a guy like that."

Katherine frowned. What was she supposed to do? Throw rocks at him? Men so rarely knew what they needed, though the idea of throwing rocks at Randy did have a certain appeal.

"You need to get your hearing tested," she snapped. "Listen, I left the keys and the lease in an envelope on the stairs right inside the door. He just needs to sign the lease and leave a check for first month's rent and the deposit. Okay? Everything's written on the envelope. And can you pull up the sign in the yard?"

"Whatever. I'll get it."

"And don't forget about the faucet. I've got it jerry rigged right now, but it's going to get worse."

"I'll get it!" Randy yelled down.

Katherine turned to get into her car. She really didn't want to get into another long argument with Randy right now. He treated her like a beleaguered husband one minute and tried to charm her the next. As she put the key into the door lock, she looked around. Randy had parked right behind her in the middle of the driveway, blocking her in. She stalked back to the garage. "Randy!"

"What!"

"You have to move your truck. I'm blocked in."

Randy sighed as if she'd asked him to pick up his truck and carry it to the street. He climbed down the ladder, muttering, and backed his truck out of the driveway.

Katherine drove to the school taking deep, even breaths.

* * * *

Jack parked in the driveway behind a rusted out yellow Ford pickup. The truck was almost centered in the driveway. It looked a little possessive.

He'd left Archer at his apartment because Katherine said she wasn't going to be home and a friend would be waiting, but who did she know who drove a junker like that? He had a suspicion in the pit of his stomach that the driver was male. He knocked at the door and waited impatiently. It shouldn't matter if another man had keys to her apartment. She hadn't declared undying love for him. Technically, she wasn't even his landlady yet. They weren't an item. He could barely call her a friend. Still, the fact that there might be another guy in her apartment burned him a little more than it should, and Jack couldn't stop himself from wondering what kind of man had keys to Katherine's place. He squared his shoulders and knocked at the door, aware he was preparing to size up the competition.

The guy who answered the door was good looking with shaggy blond hair and bright blue eyes. He had a smear of grease on his left cheek. "Yeah?" he said.

"I'm here to pick up the keys to the apartment."

"Oh!" The blond guy grinned. "So you're the tenant, huh? She left the stuff here someplace. Wait a minute." He jogged back up the stairs and Jack heard him rummaging around. Then he saw him walk across the hall and begin rummaging again. This guy was the competition? He was pretty good looking, but kind of scrawny. He didn't seem very bright, but she might like that. If she did, his opinion of her was about to take a plunge. He hated women who only liked dumb guys. It narrowed the pool of acceptable dates, since he didn't think he was Einstein, either. Still, after the conversation over dinner, he didn't think she had much patience for the truly slow witted. Which the blond guy seemed to be, based on how long it was taking him to find a piece of paper and a couple of keys that the efficient Katherine had to have left lying in plain sight.

"Do you need help?" Jack asked. He might get a look at her place this way. All he could see from this vantage point was a wall with a couple of framed photos he couldn't make out, and a sliver of hall.

"No. She said she left it out someplace."

Jack stepped inside the door and closed it behind him, telling himself he was keeping the heat in. The entrance way seemed cramped and narrow. It must feel confined to her after walking into that big bright foyer. He tried to imagine the foyer intact, with this dark stained, pine banister visible from the door. Could the blond guy be the other half of the 'we' she kept mentioning? He seemed familiar with the layout of her place. But if he was the other half of 'we,' why weren't they living here together? Why had she split her big house into two apartments? Jack glanced at the bottom step. A large manila envelope with printing on the outside sat on it, propped against the next step.

Jack cocked his head to the side to read the printing. Contains keys to front door and back door. Two copies of lease. Have him sign both copies of lease. Keep one, give him the other. Collect check for first month's rent and deposit. $1200 total.

Jack picked it up. That handwriting and the instructions could only belong to Katherine, so formal and elegant, clear and concise.

"I found it," Jack announced.

The blond guy stepped into the hall and paused as if he wanted to set off to another room. "You found it?"

Jack held up the envelope.

"Oh yeah. She said she left it on the stairs." The blond thumped down the steps, reaching for the envelope.

Jack opened it and dropped the two keys into his palm before the blond guy could get his hands on them and drop them through a crack in the floor. There were two copies of the lease so he skimmed the top one. Pretty standard. The text bent along one edge of each page as if it were photocopied right out of her book, or a book at any rate. Her signature already graced the bottom of both copies. He pulled a pen out of his jacket, glad he didn't have to rely on the blond guy for that, and signed both copies. Tucking one into his pocket, he folded the other around the check he had ready before putting it back in the envelope.

"All set." Jack held out the envelope wondering how well the blond guy would lose it before Katherine got home. "So you must be a friend of hers."

The blond guy grinned. "You could call me that."

Jack filed the comment for later consideration. "What's she up to tonight anyway?"

"Parent-teacher conferences. She forgot about it until yesterday. She forgets stuff all the time."

"I see." Jack smiled and held out his hand. "Well, good meeting you."

"Yeah, hey. Don't be a stranger." The blond guy pumped his hand.

Jack's mouth did not drop open through sheer force of will. Don't be a stranger? He was moving in downstairs. How could he be a stranger? "See ya."

He pulled the door open with numb fingers. Did it mean he would see a lot of that truck? Did the blond guy live here with her?

Couldn't be. She didn't have plans on Valentine's Day. If she was living with someone, wouldn't that imply automatic plans? Unless the guy worked long shifts. That would also explain why he hadn't been home all that day. But the garage fit two cars. If she had a car and the blond had the yellow junker, why would she tell him he could park in the garage? Unless they weren't living together, and he only came by occasionally. That thought unsettled Jack more.

Jack stopped before he opened his truck door. He considered going into his new apartment to eavesdrop. He might even want to stall long enough for Katherine to come home. He looked at the front yard and noticed the For Rent sign still there. He walked over and pulled it up. He turned it over in his hands. She never had put the phone number on it. That had helped his chances a lot. He propped the sign against the wall in the garage and took a minute to check it out. The two and a half car garage had a nice deep worktable along one side and a neat array of tools hanging from the peg board above it. Were those the dumb blond's tools? Jack shuddered and retreated to his truck after closing the garage door.

As he backed out of the driveway, he spared one last look at the battered truck. He hoped he wouldn't be seeing much of it. If Katherine liked him, Jack had misjudged her. He grinned at his refection in the side mirror. It also meant the competition wouldn't be able to out think him. Even if he wasn't supposed to date the landlady.

Chapter 3

Katherine smoothed her pink sweater over her hips, checking the clock for the third time in five minutes. She might have checked it more often than the students today. She had told Jack he could move in any time after he got the keys. He left a message on her machine saying he was moving in today. He had a couple of buddies who could help him and as long as the weather held, and if she didn't mind, he'd like to get settled in. That bit of news had upended her ability to teach. Her students had been too stunned by the reversal of their fortune to even be disruptive. Ms. Pelham, the meanest teacher in school, giving them class time on Friday to finish their homework so they wouldn't have anything to take home over the weekend? Who would have ever imagined? Katherine knew there was a rumor circulating among the students that she had a new boyfriend. The few seniors who could remember once, long ago in their carefree junior high days, when she had been happily engaged and had given easy days and light homework assignments were impressed. But less impressed than her sophomore honors class who didn't know she knew their nickname for her was 'Pelt Them With Homework.'

She looked over the class and every head was bent over a book or a paper. She didn't care what they worked on as long as they were quiet. The threat that she had a huge assignment prepared to hand out if they got wild had been enough. The fact that the folder she'd held up containing the dreaded assignment was full of blank paper didn't matter.

She turned back to the tenth grade essays she needed to finish grading. All her classwork needed to be done before she went home tonight. Yesterday, she had deposited Jack's check after school and spent last night prioritizing her bills. With that extra income, she could be back in the financial shallows soon. Maybe she would be able to afford a TV in time for summer reruns. Part of her wanted to believe it was that, and not Jack moving in today, that had her all atwitter.

She ran her marking pencil down the margin of the essay, toting up the number of infractions and weighing them against the number of positives, checked the name of the student and assigned a grade. C. This girl had started slacking off not too long ago. Katherine knew Melina could do better work. At parent-teacher conferences, Melina's mother had mentioned she thought her daughter had a new boyfriend, but she hadn't seen him yet. As Melina's mother had had to take off work for the conference, Katherine wasn't surprised she hadn't met the boy in question. He might explain the downward trend, though. Katherine knew there would be an argument Monday when she handed out the graded essays, because this one was superior to some others that had higher grades, and Melina was an accomplished debater despite what this essay showed. For a moment, she considered changing the grade to avoid the argument, but put away the paper before she was too tempted. She had experience fighting losing battles. Sometimes, she thought it was her real job.

Katherine turned to stare out the window. With no work to do this weekend, she would be free to…

To what?

Hang out with her tenant? Play with his dog? Pam had brought her a tube of tennis balls to celebrate renting out the apartment. She'd also commented on the sweater. Katherine looked down at it. She got compliments when she wore it, but she didn't know what had made her pick it out of the closet today.

Or rather, she did know, and she didn't want to admit it.

Pam had not pursued the subject.

She just didn't want to go home in the same baggy, drab stuff she'd been wearing for months. Not with Jack there. She wanted him to see her as pretty. Those golden eyes lit with pleasure at the way she looked. His big, capable hands closing around the soft sweater, stroking the knit. His soft lips covering hers…

She jerked when the bell rang and stood to cover the motion. "Have a good weekend everybody."

The hallway seemed more chaotic than usual. Katherine tried to keep thoughts of Jack out of her mind while she watched for trouble in the hall, but he kept slipping in. One of the junior boys joined his sophomore girlfriend at her locker, and he kissed her cheek. Katherine only realized she was staring when the boy looked up and blushed. Katherine tried to smile, but she could feel her own blush creeping up her neck. She turned the other way and found Pam staring at her.

Pam left her post beside her classroom door and waded across the thronging hall to Katherine's. "So, he's moving in today?"

"Yes. He had help today and he needs to get the old apartment cleaned before the end of the month."

Pam clucked.

Katherine looked up at her friend. Pam towered over her even when she wore heels, which she had today. Pam hadn't commented on those, although Randy had asked loudly if she had a hot date. Katherine crouched to pick up a discarded paper. Algebra homework due Monday. There would be panic on Sunday night somewhere in the neighborhood. She stood, folding the paper in half.

"You gave your kids a free day."

"I thought it might be nice. Let them have one weekend off." She shrugged.

Pam clucked again.

"Randy still hasn't fixed that faucet. I may have to break down and call a real plumber," Katherine said. "Honestly, I don't know why I had him even try."

"He's cheap."

"Yes, but I'm afraid he's making the situation worse. I could barely turn on the tap this morning." The hall emptied almost as rapidly as it had filled. Nobody hung out after school on Friday. A couple of students said goodnight as they darted past, but most made for the door as if they thought they might get extra homework if they made eye contact with the teachers.

Pam leaned against the wall and looked at Katherine. "So have you got a big weekend planned with your new tenant? You know, the one you can't date?"

Katherine rolled her eyes. "He's a tenant."

"But you got all dressed up for him." Pam's voice held a hint of sarcasm.

"It's business." Katherine smoothed her sweater over her hips.

Pam nodded. "Keep it that way."

"Yes, Mother." Katherine turned on her heel and walked back into her classroom for her book bag and coat.

"Going home already?" Pam asked from the doorway.

"Sure. It's Friday."

Pam groaned and walked away.

Katherine left the building, aware of how strange it was for her to be one of the first teachers to leave. Normally, she stayed until at least four-thirty grading papers and planning lessons. Today, there were no papers to grade or lessons to plan, because she'd had all day to get her work done. She should have found Randy to ask him about the faucet, but she had no desire to talk to him after that hot date comment. And besides, how difficult could it be to fix the faucet? The library had to have a book on it. She climbed in her car, prayed it would start, thanked it when it did, and then remembered she wasn't that close to disaster anymore. If the car didn't start, she could get it fixed. It would set her plans back by a month or so depending on the repair, but it wouldn't be the straw that broke the camel's back.

And she had Jack to thank for it. She drew a deep breath. After nearly two years of scraping, she was about to get some financial breathing room. He was her hero.

Dammit.

Resisting the impulse to close her eyes and remember what her hero looked like from the golden shade of his eyes to the way he filled out his blue fleece jacket, she put the car into gear. Couldn't start that. He was the worst person in the world for her to develop a relationship with. He was her tenant. And worse, he was a firefighter.

When she got home, three guys lounged on the front porch and Jack was nowhere to be found. They watched her pull into the driveway, and one jumped up to open the garage door. He met her at her car door, holding out a hand to help her out.

"Hi, there." He had a cute, crooked grin and a lounge singer's tone that made Katherine want to cringe back into her car.

"Hi."

"I'm Dan. Dan McWilliams. I work with Jack at the station." He drew her out of the car, but didn't step back.

She pulled her book bag between them. "It's a pleasure to meet you." Her face heated even though she recognized the conquistador gleam in his eyes. For an instant, she felt like a steak.

"Danny!"

Katherine's breath caught in her throat. There was the voice she longed to hear. She looked around for the source and wondered if she was leaping from frying pan to fire.

Jack strode up the driveway. "I think we're about ready to go back for another load. Hi, Kate. Have a good day at school?"

"Yes."

"I left Archer in the back yard." Jack gestured, and out of the corner of her eye Katherine could see Archer standing at the gate. "Come on up and meet the guys before we go." He reached around Dan and took her arm.

Every nerve in her body seemed to be located in her elbow where Jack's hand closed around it. She heard her car door close and then the garage door roll down. Archer whined and raced up and down the fence as they walked past. Jack wore a pair of jeans he must have had for a long time. They molded to his body in the way only familiar denim did. He had on a green sweatshirt. The weather had turned a little colder, but he didn't seem to notice. She noted that he seemed impervious to the cold, and told herself she should be glad he wouldn't notice if she kept the temperature low. But the thought seemed to come from another mind altogether because her mind was focused on his hand on her elbow.

"You met Dan." Jack said guiding her around the corner of the porch. "This is Kevin Marshall and Lew Draper."

"And they all work with you at the fire station," she muttered.

"Yeah."

Katherine licked her lips. Oh look, she thought, he asked his brothers to help him. Heroes to a man. Not that they seemed like bad guys. Kevin had a sweet face but wasn't as tall as Jack. Lew stood a hair taller, had a playful grin, red hair and green eyes. Dan with his lounge singer charm stood about as tall as Kevin. They all looked down at her pleasantly. Probably nice guys. All of them ready, willing, and eager to get killed in the line of duty. She drew her coat closed and folded her arms. "It's been nice meeting you, but I'm getting a little cold so I'm going to go inside. If you need anything, knock." She smiled and escaped their circle.

* * * *

Kevin waited until he heard the side door close before turning to Jack. "I see what you mean. Hot and cold running Katherine. What was that about?"

"What was what about?" Lew asked.

"Never mind. Let's go get another load. I think we can get the bedroom stuff this time." Jack shoved his hands in his pockets and walked back to his truck, all the while watching her closed door. He'd been waiting for her to get home all day. Every time they pulled in the driveway, he'd checked his watch to see if school had let out yet. He'd held them up on this last run shifting boxes around because he figured she might get home soon. He hadn't just wanted to see her, he'd been looking forward to it as a reward for a long hard day.

She'd seemed happy to see him when he got to her in the garage, but it might have been because he was rescuing her from Dan. She looked great in that pink sweater. So neat and professional, and at the same time utterly sexy and enticing. He wondered how her male students managed. If he'd had a teacher who looked like her, he'd have been inclined to get better grades. Or seek out tutoring.

But the moment he'd introduced the others, he could almost feel the sea change without having to see her face. 'And they all work with you at the station.' She said it like a curse. Like they shouldn't work with him. Or like they shouldn't be helping him move. He had to be missing something.

* * * *

Katherine retreated into her abbreviated home and stood at the top of the stairs scowling until she heard the trucks pull out of the driveway. They were all alike. They didn't work jobs, they married them. She looked down at herself. What was she thinking dressing to impress a guy who would be more impressed by a fire engine? If she even wanted to compete, she would have to wear red. It would add a little spice to her predominantly blue wardrobe. She bit her lip. An old picture hung at eye level. Gary wearing the uniform that never came off in his mind. It would be the same thing all over again.

But she wasn't supposed to be dating the tenant, anyway. She had to put him out of her mind. Stop acting like a moony kid. Be the landlord.

She hung her book bag on the back of her office door and stood looking out the window over the backyard. It always looked worse this time of year. The clean white snow melted, leaving behind the moss and weeds that grew in the deep shade of the two huge oak trees flanking the house. Another thing she'd always meant to get to with Gary, but had never had the time. The yard needed to be tilled to loosen the rock hard soil. Then fertilizer should be put down and tilled under, but it had to be the right kind and the dirt needed to be tested to find out what kind it needed. She had already done the research, but could never get Gary to till up the yard. Then later, she hadn't been able to get his buddies to do anything despite their promises at his funeral.

Something dark streaked around the garage and skidded to a stop at the bottom of the fence barking. Archer. He told her he left Archer in the backyard. Katherine grinned. This tenant she could be friends with. She hurried into her bedroom and pulled on a pair of jeans and a sweatshirt. Then she grabbed a tennis ball out of the tube in her book bag.

Christa Maurice

Archer met her at the gate, leaping up on his hind legs as if he knew what she had in mind.

"And what are you so excited about?" she asked him. She opened the gate and squeezed through the smallest opening she could, afraid the dog would make a run for it.

Archer yipped at her.

"Do you know how to play fetch? Do you?"

Archer leaped up on his hind legs so high his head came level with hers. Then he dropped back onto all fours and raced around the yard, ending up back in front of her.

Katherine pulled the tennis ball out of her pocket and held it up for him.

Archer barked, raced half way up the yard and back and barked again.

Katherine threw the ball as hard as she could. It bounced against the slope below the fence, ricocheted off a tree trunk and nearly sailed into the neighbor's yard, but snagged in a stumpy tree growing beside the fence and dropped to the ground.

Archer chased it from hillside to tree to fence, threw it up in the air, caught it, raced back and stood in front of her, the ball held in his salivating mouth. He wagged his stubby tail so energetically most of his hindquarters were in motion.

"Oh, so you want to play that way." She grabbed at the ball in his mouth, but he twisted away. She grabbed for the other side. He leaped away, yipping around the ball. She stalked him across the yard and leaped at him, but he slipped through her arms.

"I'll get you eventually." She laughed.

Archer snorted and watched her climb to her feet with the ball still clenched in his teeth.

* * * *

Saturday night, Jack knocked at Katherine's door. He heard her come down the steps before the door opened. She wore a yellow terry cloth bathrobe that she clutched closed with one hand while she used a towel to dry her hair with the other. As dirty as she'd gotten playing with Archer earlier, she'd needed a shower. But then she didn't know he knew she'd been playing with the dog. Kevin spotted her wrestling with him Friday, and today when Jack came back from cleaning his old apartment, he'd found her sitting on the back stairs trying to look innocent with leaves in her hair.

"Hi." She smiled. "Get everything set?"

"Yeah." He stopped for a moment because he couldn't remember why he'd come to her door. It wasn't so she could smile at him, was it? "Everything's here and the other place is cleaned up. I wanted to ask you a favor."

"What do you need?" She stopped drying her hair and stood with the towel in her hand leaning against the door still holding the neck of her robe closed.

Jack stuffed his hands in his pockets before they could get away from him and looked at her bare feet. The hem of a white nightgown hung below the robe. He didn't need to know she wore white nightgowns. It was one of those little facts that might keep him up all night, like the memory of the light tread of her feet overhead. Maybe he shouldn't have taken this apartment. Maybe he should have found some place else instead of tormenting himself being so close. He swallowed.

"I have duty tomorrow, and I don't have the dog door in for Archer yet. Could you make sure he gets out tomorrow afternoon? He needs to get a little exercise and do his business." Jack had never used the phrase 'do his business' before and it felt alien coming out of his mouth. But he couldn't imagine saying anything else to Katherine.

"Sure. I'll let him out for a little while."

"He likes to play fetch," Jack suggested. He'd found Archer chewing on a tennis ball this morning and had a pretty good guess where it came from.

She turned a becoming shade of pink. "Oh really? Well, maybe I'll play a little fetch with him. There are plenty of sticks in the back yard."

"You have to order him to drop it or he won't." Jack watched the blush spread across her round cheeks like a faint wine stain. "He likes to wrestle too."

She nodded, the pink deepening. "I'll keep that in mind. Don't worry, I'll let him out for a little while tomorrow afternoon. When do you get off duty?"

"Monday morning at eight."

"I'll miss you, then." Her eyes rounded with panic. "I mean, I leave for school about seven thirty. I won't see you."

"Oh. Then maybe I'll catch you after school." He lingered on the porch, knowing he should let her go back inside. It had turned cold, and she had wet hair tangled around her face. But he didn't want to let her go yet. He wanted to say something, but he wasn't sure what or if he would be able to say it at all. To be honest, he didn't want to say anything. He wanted to cup her blush-warmed cheek in his hand and kiss her pink lips.

"Thanks for letting me move in a little early. Most places would prorate for the extra week."

"No problem. I don't know how you could be expected to move and clean your old apartment between the last of the month and the first of the next month. That never made sense to me." She shifted her hand from the neck of the robe to the towel and her robe fell open enough that he could see her collar bones creating hollows below her shoulders. He wanted to trace the hollows with his thumbs to find out if the skin felt as soft and supple as it looked.

"Well, it's a neat trick. There's usually some magic involved." He shifted, trying to jar his gaze back to her eyes. With her throat exposed he was having a hard time focusing on her face. "So you'll let Archer out tomorrow."

"No problem." She beamed.

"Okay, thanks. See you Monday when you get home from school, then." He backed away from the door, not asking any of the questions he wanted to ask. Like who was that stupid blond man? And why don't you like me as much as you like my dog?

"Sleep tight. And be careful at work tomorrow."

He rolled his eyes. "I can't be careful. It's my job."

She laughed low in her throat and closed the door.

Jack stopped at the bottom of the stairs for a minute, remembering the laugh. If he didn't get it out of his mind, he wouldn't be getting much sleep tonight, and that would make tomorrow unpleasant. He walked back around to his own door and let himself in.

The place was a shamble of boxes. Archer had sacked out in the middle of the unmade bed. Jack opened a box and started pulling out linens. The little cabinet would be a perfect storage place for those. But he had to make the bed first or he'd end up sleeping in a nest of blankets again tonight.

"All right, dog. Off." He grabbed a pillow and pulled a case over it.

Archer groaned, but didn't move.

"Come on. Off." He put a case on the other pillow.

Archer shifted his head so he could give Jack a dirty look without having to stretch.

"My heart bleeds. Go lay on the couch." Jack shoved Archer until he jumped off the bed after giving Jack another annoyed glare.

Jack shook the fitted sheet out over the bed. As he worked, he strained to hear anything from her upstairs. Occasionally, he heard the light sound of her footsteps padding across the floor, but nothing else. No TV, no stereo. He didn't have any of his equipment hooked up yet, and he suspected once he did have something playing, even low, he wouldn't be able to hear her at all. That thought might make him learn to love the stillness.

The hair on his arms raised, remembering standing in the kitchen with the guys on Friday night watching her roll around on the ground, wrestling with Archer by the back fence. She had been dirty from head to toe and giggling. All three of his friends had stood in silence watching her for at least five minutes before they decided to get back to work. Kevin had dragged Jack away.

She had looked beautiful with her long hair spilling around her and her sweatshirt riding up to expose her bare midriff. They had been able to hear her laughing as they moved the last load into the house. Jack had even caught Lew peeking out the back windows. She must have realized they were back not too long after because it got quiet, and Dan noticed Archer sleeping in the last patch of sun. She'd worn him out.

Jack thought about his exhausted dog. He'd known Archer since puppyhood and he'd never seen him this tired. What would she do to him when she had him all day tomorrow? And more importantly, when would she be willing to wrestle like that with Archer's owner?

* * * *

Katherine threw the stick for Archer to chase down. She felt too tired to wrestle today. It had a lot to do with the fact that she'd been up before dawn listening for Jack. She had lain half awake in her bed listening to him walk around the dining room and the kitchen getting ready for work. He'd had a long conversation with Archer she couldn't quite make out. She'd tried to hear the words, but she knew in order to eavesdrop, she'd need to go into her office and crouch beside the heating vent. And that was no guarantee. Even if it wasn't despicable to spy in the first place. After a few minutes, she heard him walk out the front door. She waited for the sound of the garage door, but didn't hear it. That brought her awake. Why hadn't he opened the garage door? Was he standing outside? Was a friend picking him up?

She had slipped out of bed, cringing for a moment when her warm feet touched the cold floor. She had pulled on her robe and peeked out the window. From there she could see nothing but a small section of street. The northern neighbor's pine tree blocked the entire view that way and there wasn't a soul on the road to the south. Maybe he'd walked to work. He's said the station was close. Until now, the exact location of the local fire house hadn't been important, but things had changed.

After that, she hadn't considered going back to bed. She'd gotten up and eaten oatmeal, sending silent curses toward the once again dripping faucet until she thought up an excuse to go outside. The yard needed cleaning up. Over the winter, a lot of twigs and small branches had fallen, and they wouldn't go away by themselves. She dressed in long johns, paint spattered jeans, an old, out of shape turtleneck and a flannel shirt before heading outside to the garage for a rake she didn't need for this chore, just so she could check for his truck. The truck sat in the garage. But the only eyes peering out the breakfast nook window were Archer's. Might as well let him out now.

"You know, if I could teach you to pick up the sticks and take them to the trash barrel, I'd be all set," she told Archer, shaking the stick at him.

His eyes followed the stick.

She threw it as hard as she could and watched it sail end over end to the alley fence.

Archer raced after it. He seized something bigger than the stick and started dragging it toward her.

"If you think I'm throwing that, you've got another think coming." Katherine announced when she realized the dog had grabbed a medium sized tree branch. "How am I going to get it in the trash barrel?"

Archer dragged the branch to the porch and plopped down next to it, waiting for her approval.

"Very good." She patted his head. "Now do it thirty or forty more times."

He gnawed on the stick, watching her for signs of trying to take it away.

She picked up another stick and threw it. She needed to saw Archer's branch into manageable chunks. Inside the garage, she had Gary's tools stored. He'd never used them, and she didn't know why he bothered to keep them, but they were in perfect condition. She found a small saw and carried it out to the yard.

After twenty minutes, she'd reduced the branch to manageable chunks, worked up a sweat, and Archer had brought her another one. "Hey, what are you trying to do to me, animal? That whole clean up the backyard thing was just an excuse." She patted his head and picked up a smallish stick to throw. As he bounded to the back of the yard she heard a car pull into the driveway. Curious, she opened the gate and peered toward the street.

The car she couldn't identify, beyond knowing it was well out of her price range. The driver opened the door and stepped out. She was medium height, with shoulder length blond hair, exotically shaped eyes so blue Katherine could see them from the back of the house. She wore a cream colored suit with a pink blouse. Ignoring Katherine, she started toward the front door.

"Jack isn't home," Katherine called, and wished she'd kept her mouth shut. She didn't want this gorgeous woman paying any attention to her in her current sweaty, dirty state.

The woman turned toward Katherine, thrust out one hip and tapped one of her elegant, and no doubt expensive, shoes twice on the asphalt driveway. "Who are you?" she demanded.

"I'm—I own the house. I'm the landlord." Committed to a conversation now, Katherine stepped into the driveway, leaving the gate ajar behind her.

"Oh." She looked back at the house. "He isn't home. I suppose he's hanging out with that assortment of ruffians he calls friends."

"He's on duty," Katherine said.

The other woman pursed her perfect lips. "Exactly the same thing. If he isn't with that pack of rogues on duty, he's with them off duty." She pronounced the 't' in exactly.

Katherine bit her lip. She wouldn't have called any of the men who helped Jack move in ruffians or rogues. Of course, it fit the pattern of safety officers and their devotion to their jobs and buddies. She didn't have time to finish the consideration because Archer, having realized someone was in the driveway and the gate stood open, rushed around her, making straight for the other woman.

The woman screamed and threw her hands up, but Archer jumped on her, planting his big muddy feet on her suit jacket and swiping her cheek with his big pink tongue.

"You beast. You filthy, horrible beast!" she shrieked.

Archer dropped to the ground with his ears flattened to his head. He slunk back to Katherine and leaned against her legs, shuddering with misery.

"Oh no, your suit." Katherine covered her mouth with both hands. Right on the front of the other woman's jacket, on her shoulders, were two perfect dog footprints. Katherine knew it would be very bad to laugh, but she couldn't think of anything she wanted to do more. "Archer, that was bad. Bad dog."

Archer sunk lower and pressed himself against her legs nearly knocking her over.

"Now I'm going to have to go home and change. Tell Jack that Leia stopped by. Tell him I got the partnership. Maybe I'll call him." She threw herself back in her car and slammed the door.

Katherine grabbed Archer's collar and tugged him back into the yard. She couldn't explain why she was so pleased Archer had jumped on Leia, she knew she shouldn't be. "Good dog, Archer. You can jump on her anytime you like." She patted the dog's head. "Next time, try to knock her down."

That woman was beautiful. Stunning. Just the kind of woman Katherine expected to see buzzing around Jack. He claimed he wasn't dating anyone. Was Leia chasing him? Katherine wouldn't want to get in the way if she was. She looked predatory.

Not that Katherine meant to get involved with Jack anyway. He was her tenant and a firefighter. But that woman gave her another good reason to not have any interest. Katherine shook her head. She needed to leave a note for him before she forgot, or worse, had to tell him in person.

Sitting at her desk, she reflected on Leia. She seemed so confident, so sharp. Leia was a stunning woman with her perfect figure, flawlessly coifed blond hair and almond shaped eyes. Based on looks, she was perfect.

But she was also rude and arrogant. When she used the words 'rogues' and 'ruffians' it sounded contrived. And Jack seemed so down to earth. How would he be able to stand Leia once she opened her mouth?

Besides, she hated his dog.

Chapter 4

Jack opened the garage door so Katherine could pull in. In the three weeks since he'd moved in, Katherine had done everything in her power to avoid her tenant. Not that she didn't want to see him. No, she wanted to see him too much. She'd figured out his routine, one day on duty followed by two days off. On his days off, he took Archer for a long hike first thing in the morning. During the first week on the first of the two days off, he went out for the evening. She didn't know where, only that he was gone for the entire evening, and she hoped it was a pattern. She tried very hard not to speculate about where he might be going or who he might be seeing. Katherine molded her schedule around his so she was gone as much as possible when he was home, or at least inside when he came and went. She stayed late at school, went to the library, had dinner at Pam's. Anything to avoid crossing paths with him and turning into a babbling school girl again. Bad enough that she found herself staring at the wall, listening to him walk around downstairs.

Tonight, she'd been hoping his all-evening event was an every other week occurrence but since he was standing in the driveway waiting, she guessed not.

"Long time no see." He grinned, one hand resting on the garage door handle over his head, ready to pull it down the moment she stepped out. Katherine decided he looked like a male model posing for a picture.

"It's been really busy at school." she lied. He looked good in his long sleeved knit shirt. It left no mystery to the exact dimensions of his arms or chest. As her eyes skidded down to the floor in the hopes of not blushing or leering, she took in his jeans and work boots. Did he buy jeans that fit him so perfectly she could see more than she wanted to, or did he wear them until they fell off his body? Suddenly, she remembered what it had felt like that first day when she showed him the apartment and had stumbled into him when the back door flew open. The way his arms closed around her to keep her from falling and the solid muscle of his chest when he pulled her against him. And which now flexed as he pulled down the garage door.

"My poker game was canceled, so I'm gonna get that dog door in for Archer so you won't have to babysit him anymore." Jack gestured to the backyard where the back door was off its hinges and propped against the porch. She supposed she should have guessed the warm weather would bring him out, but it never entered her mind. "I'll fix it so it doesn't stick anymore, too."

"Good idea." She tried not to sound breathless, an act made difficult by the fact that she was breathless. She started for her door, intent on getting it between him and her as soon as possible. He had followed her down the driveway to her door, and he was entirely too close. She could smell the scent of his soap. It wrecked her ability to think straight. She stepped on the bottom step and reached into her mail box trying to act as normal as she wanted to feel by pretending he was just another student, hoping the act would sink in. So far, no success. Bills and junk mail. Nothing helpful in distracting her from Jack. Of course she didn't think a subpoena for a federal investigation would have been able to take her mind off Jack for long.

"I was looking at the garage roof. There's a pretty good hole developing there." He leaned on the railing, gesturing back at the garage.

"I know, I haven't been able to afford to get it fixed." She dropped the mail in her book bag, wanting to scurry inside her door and spy on him through her kitchen window.

"I can fix it. We can go Dutch on supplies." He smiled, but his expression faltered when she stared at him. He cleared his throat and looked at the garage. "The joists are still okay so far, but if it goes too long they might rot, and then we'll have a big mess on our hands."

Katherine blinked at him. 'We'll have a big mess on our hands.' The plural pronoun indicated a relationship. Her mind leaped over the idea that he might only mean two people sharing a garage to what she wanted to share. The way he was grinning at her made her think there had to be something more to the conversation, but her brain felt too fogged by his presence to figure it out. It seemed like a simple conversation. Was she missing something else?

"Did you hear me? Are you okay?" He stepped closer leaving her inches from testing out the texture of his shirt. His eyes, in the shadow of the house, looked dark with concern.

She couldn't take a breath without smelling his scent. Heat radiated off his body and seeped through her coat. It soaked into her body and brought her temperature to a nice simmer. "Randy put up a tarp to keep the water out until I can afford a roofer."

"There's still water getting in there. Not as much, but some. And you don't need a roofer. I used to work for my captain's brother-in-law on my off days. He's a roofer. I know my stuff. I'll get the supplies, and you can pay me back when you've got it, okay?"

She stared at him. "You're going to fix the roof?"

"Sure." He shrugged. "Get a couple of guys over here, and we'll be finished in a day."

"Well, I suppose." She shifted, moving her book bag between them. She had hoped the small barrier would help. It didn't. "If you know how to do it."

"I'll get the stuff tomorrow. If the weather's good, maybe we can get it done Monday." He peered at the sky. That meant he didn't notice she couldn't tear her eyes off him.

"That's fine." She started to turn to retreat into her apartment.

He grabbed her wrist. His grip was light, but he obviously had no intention of letting go. "Are you avoiding me?"

It took every thread of control to keep from collapsing into his arms when his hand closed around her. She met his eyes and swallowed hard. "Avoiding you?" she repeated.

"I haven't seen much of you since I moved in."

"Oh." She sighed, acutely aware of the pressure of his hand on her wrist. Her skin felt scorched. "It's just been really busy at school."

He stared at her a moment longer, as if he sensed the half truth. His mouth twitched. "Are you busy right now?"

"Now? I have some papers to grade. And lesson plans." Her body burned for him. She wanted that hand on her wrist to move up her arm. Around her shoulders. She wanted him to step closer. She felt herself beginning to lean forward, and pulled back.

"But you have all weekend to do that, right?"

"Grades are due Thursday." Katherine coughed. Her voice sounded hoarse, and her heartbeat pounded in her ears.

He frowned as if he knew what a flimsy excuse she had offered. "I could use a hand with this thing."

"You seem to already have it." She heard herself say. It seemed abnormally witty and intelligent for the fact that her mind didn't seem to be working. Must be lack of oxygen, she thought. I'm getting giddy. My face should be turning blue.

Jack released her hand, glancing at his own as if it had acted without his permission. "Sorry. Are you going to help me?"

She shouldn't go near him. Shouldn't chat with him. Shouldn't spend time with him. She should go inside and take a cold bath while thinking about income tax law. "I'll be back out as soon as I change."

He grinned. "Great. See you in a couple minutes. If you don't come out, I'm coming in after you."

She nodded. He'd let go of her arm, but it didn't matter, she could still feel his hand wrapped around her wrist. She fumbled the door open and hurried inside.

* * * *

Jack watched the door click closed behind her and wondered if she would come back. She was avoiding him. It was a hunch, but a strong one. He saw her on school mornings when he wasn't on duty and could watch her walk out to her car from the shadows of his kitchen. He didn't know any teachers, but it seemed a little strange that she would stay after school until six every night.

Unless she was meeting the idiotic blond guy.

Jack scowled at that thought. He was the type his sister favored in high school. She'd dated jocks because it made Mom and Dad happy, and because she could show off how smart she was. She'd kept the pattern in college, but in law school she'd quit dating. His parents believed she needed to apply herself to her coursework. Jack figured she couldn't find any more dumb guys to date. He doubted there were many football scholarships to law school.

His fingernails dug into his palms, and it hurt. A normal reaction to thinking about his sister. He flexed his fingers and walked back into the yard to figure out how to have Katherine help him. If he could keep her out here for a little while, she might realize he didn't bite. Unless asked. However, it didn't take two people to install a dog door unless one of them was spectacularly uncoordinated. The more time he spent around her, the more awkward he became. He felt more like a gawky high school boy now than he had in high school. If he got out of this little task without taking off his hand with the screwdriver, he'd be lucky.

"What do you want me to do?"

Jack looked up. She'd changed into jeans and a sweatshirt and pulled back her hair. A few tendrils had escaped and lay across her pinker than usual cheeks. She jammed her hands into her back pockets and stood with her shoulders drawn up and one knee bent. She looked beautiful. "Why don't you hold this up for me?" He shifted the door so he could plane off the troublesome corner. He could have braced it between his legs, but he'd insisted she help, so he had to give her something useful to do.

She knelt on the ground in front of the door. "Like this?" She pressed her palms against either side of the door and looked up at him.

Jack's breath caught in his throat. The sun shone across her face, bringing out the twinkle in her eyes and turning her hair red. She even had an eager smile touching the corners of her lips. Maybe she wasn't so frightened to be around him. "That's good. Hang on tight."

Archer walked over and started licking her face. She laughed and pushed him away with her shoulder. "Hey dog. You're getting me all icky." She wiped her cheek on the shoulder of her sweatshirt.

Jack picked up the plane and leaned forward to shave off a tiny bit of wood so the door would swing open without struggle. Katherine had taken her job seriously, focusing on the placement of her hands. Archer stood behind her with his head resting on her shoulder.

"He thinks he's a parrot," Jack said.

"He's my pal." Katherine leaned her cheek against Archer's, and the dog responded by giving her another sloppy kiss.

"He has taken a shine to you." Jack shaved off another sliver of wood, wishing she would let him get that close without freaking out. He would promise not to lick her cheek unless she wanted him to. He bit his lips to hide a smile.

"I throw a stick around for him sometimes. He seems to like it."

"Oh." Throw a stick? Yeah, and roll around on the ground wrestling with him and chase him around the yard like a little kid. No wonder Archer loved her. "Did you ever have a dog when you were a kid?"

"We couldn't afford it."

"Couldn't afford a dog?"

She smirked. "There were times Mom and I couldn't afford each other."

"What about your dad?"

"He died when I was ten. A bridge collapsed in a flood, and a family was trapped in their car. He was trying to get them out."

"I'm sorry."

She shrugged, keeping her eyes down. "It was a long time ago. With a few minor setbacks, I've recovered."

"What about when you started teaching? Couldn't you have afforded pets then?"

"No, I was busy paying off school loans, and my fiancé didn't like dogs. It didn't seem to be in the cards." She sighed, leaning against Archer.

"And you wanted to marry him anyway?" Jack put down the plane and stepped away grinning.

She looked up, and her desolate expression wiped the grin off his face. "I was in love, and it didn't matter. Haven't you ever been convinced you were in love and decided there were things you always wanted, but you were willing to give up for him? Well, her, in your case."

Jack lifted the door out of her hands. "I don't know. I guess so." He tried not to think about Maureen and the things he'd been willing to give up for her. Or the things he might be willing to give up for Katherine.

"I was happy, but I was lonely. I mean I was really happy. I don't want you to get the wrong idea. Gary was everything I could ask for. He had a lot of integrity. But then he was killed, and I was alone." She sat on the ground with her hands on her lap. Archer stepped in front of her, whining and pressing against her, his head leaning into her neck.

Her words had spilled out in a rush, as if it were important he understand. Or as if she were trying to convince herself? Jack's arms ached to hug her. He wanted to hold her and smooth away the pain of losing her father compounded by losing her fiancé. To kiss away her hurt and make everything better. Instead he stood clutching the door, watching his dog attempt to make her feel better and wondering what kind of a relationship she'd had when she described her fiancé as having integrity. Integrity was a great trait, but it wasn't what Jack wanted his future wife saying about him.

Katherine grabbed Archer's snout and started shaking his head until he pulled away and leaped at her, knocking her on her back laughing.

While they tussled on the grass, Jack installed the dog door in the hole he'd already cut. Father died at a young age. Poor childhood. Maybe not a perfect engagement that ended abruptly. What kind of guy wouldn't let his wife have a dog when she wanted one so much? What kind of guy wouldn't give Katherine anything she wanted in the first place? Integrity? At least it solved the mystery of 'we.' She'd had a fiancé who died. It didn't settle the question of the dumb blond.

"So what about you?"

Jack turned the door upright. At some point she'd stopped playing with Archer and turned back to him. He wanted another minute to recover from her pain, but he wasn't getting it. "Me?"

"Have you always had a dog?"

"Well, one dog. We got Cody when I was about four. My parents had her put to sleep right after I graduated high school. She was pretty old. My sister always said she hated Cody, but she sobbed when Mom and Dad had her put down."

Katherine stood up and dusted herself off. "Both of your parents are alive?"

"Two parents, three grandparents, one great grandmother and assorted aunts, uncles and cousins."

Katherine blinked. "Wow."

"They don't all live around here."

Katherine picked up a stick and taunted Archer with it before throwing it down the yard. "And you only have one sister?"

"Leia. She's a—What?"

Katherine's mouth dropped open. "Leia is your sister? The one who was here?"

Jack watched emotions flicker across Katherine's face. Shock. Horror. Guilt. Happiness? Why would she be happy about Leia? Nobody was happy to meet Leia. "She was here?"

"She stopped by shortly after you moved in. I left you a—Oh, God. I forgot to leave you the note. I never put it in your mailbox. It's probably still on the table. I'm so sorry. I meant to leave a note, but there was so much confusion after—" Katherine grimaced. "After Archer jumped on her."

"He jumped on her? Good dog." Jack wondered what she'd meant to say. So much confusion after what?

Archer started wagging his whole body.

"He left big muddy footprints on her shoulders."

Jack laughed. "Very good dog. You get extra treats."

Archer wagged harder, nearly knocking Katherine over.

"Why did she come over here?" Katherine's expression had settled on happy.

Jack sneered to cover for the thoughts working through his head. Her reaction to Leia was very odd in relation to reactions to his sister, and he usually got odd reactions to his sister. She seemed too pleased. "Probably rubbing in her partnership. She's the youngest person in her firm to be a partner, and so she'll be pretty puffed up about it."

"Firm?"

"She's a lawyer."

"A lawyer." Katherine smirked. "So. Are you going to do something with that door or did you want to stand around all day balancing it on your foot?"

He twisted the door to hide his red face. His toes were numb, but he'd forgotten it was in his hands. "Can you help me hang it? I need you to hold it in place while I put the screws back in." Another job he could do easier by himself, but if it brought her closer, why not?

She stepped forward. "What do you want me to do?"

Jack carried the door inside and held it up, trying to line it up to the old screw holes. "I need you to hold this steady right here while I screw it back in."

"I can do that." She reached across and held the door balanced on his foot.

Jack picked up the electric screwdriver and stepped next to her. Her arm brushed against his chest when he leaned in to hang the door. She was too close now, and he couldn't do anything about it.

Not that he minded. He wanted this. He'd planned on it when he asked her to help him hang the door. Her head came to the hollow of his shoulder. The perfect height. If he wanted, he could take her in his arms, and she would be leaning against his shoulder. And he wanted. He could smell the sweet, flowery fragrance of her shampoo and the dry scent of chalk dust. Her shoulder grazed against his chest close enough that he could feel her body heat. Her breath came in light shallow flutters, and he wondered if that was a good thing or if she was claustrophobic. Either way, the memory would make sleeping tonight almost impossible. "Nearly done with the top," he murmured.

"Mm." She adjusted her grip on the door.

Jack screwed in the last screw and lingered for a moment, breathing her scent. Then he knelt beside her to reattach the bottom hinge. From here, he had a great view of her curvy hips. She kept those covered with long baggy sweaters and loose dresses. He had a pretty good idea what her legs looked like, at least from the knee down. He wanted to lean his head against her hip, but that might make her jump away again, like she had when he'd closed the front door the day she showed him the apartment.

Archer came over to investigate and decided he needed to be in the same spot. He pressed against Katherine's legs, causing her to lean into Jack's cheek, so he got his wish. His body responded enthusiastically. How was he going to cover that?

"I had no idea this was going to be like playing Twister," Katherine commented.

"I'm almost done. Too bad we didn't give the dog something to do to keep him out of the way." Jack wondered if there was some way to stretch out the job. Drop a screw? Strip the hole? Would he look incompetent? Would that bother her?

"We'll have to remember that in the future."

Jack's heart skipped. 'In the future.' She would only say that if she thought they had one, wouldn't she? Or was she talking about the length of the lease? He put in the last screw and stood up. "All done, you can let go."

Katherine moved away so fast she stumbled over the dog. She looked flushed, but surveyed his workmanship as if it weren't unusual. "It looks good. What's that bar there?" She pointed, her face pinched with worry.

He looked at the dog door to see what might be alarming her. "It's a lock. Burglars sometimes use these to get into houses. I got this one so I could lock it when Archer wasn't shut up in here."

"Oh, good idea." She took a shallow breath. "Not such a difficult job."

"It gets better." He closed the door and opened it again. "Easy open, easy close."

"That's all it took?" She closed the door and opened it herself from the outside. "I thought it would have been more complicated than shaving a little wood off the side. Why did it stick before?"

"The house probably shifted a little so the doorway wasn't square any more, but the door still was." He shrugged. "It happens in old houses."

Katherine stared at the door. "The house shifts, and the door doesn't fit anymore. How symbolic."

Jack could see her headed into melancholy territory again. "Maybe next summer I'll repaint it. It looks as if it could use stripping and repainting. See where this is all rounded here?" He traced his finger along the edge of one of the door panels. "I think this was a sharp corner, but there's been so much paint put on it over the years it's rounded off."

"I didn't know you could do that. I guess it's easy if you know what you're doing. Is it very work intensive?"

"To take off paint? No. There's a chemical you use and..." He heard something. A siren.

"What is it?"

"It's the station. I didn't realize we were close enough to hear it. The engine is going out."

"The engine?"

Jack looked up the back yard as if he could see the station through the houses and the hill. "The fire engine. Listen, it's at the light on the corner." He turned. "Headed south."

Katherine turned and walked down the porch steps. Every movement rigid and controlled. She picked up a stick and threw it. Archer obliged by chasing after it and returning. She looked down at him with her hands on her hips. He dropped the stick at her feet and then turned and watched her over his shoulder, poised for her to throw again.

*   *   *   *

Closing the door, Jack walked down the steps to stand beside her. At some point, she'd taught Archer to drop the stick without a battle. He wondered how she'd done it, but didn't want to ask right now. Her gaze was fixed on the back fence as if she were afraid to glance right or left. His tools were scattered around the porch and yard, but she was concentrating on the dog as if he weren't there. Katherine runs cold again. Because he heard the engine going out? Or something else?

He wondered if her fiancé had been a firefighter. That would explain why she might have something against the department if they let her get into this mess, but he couldn't imagine any station abandoning one of their widows, even if she wasn't a widow in the strictest sense. Besides, he'd have remembered going to the funeral if he had been in the department. Everybody who wasn't on duty turned out for those funerals. There hadn't been so many funerals in his twelve years in the department that he'd forget. No, Gary hadn't been a firefighter.

This new knowledge didn't leave him any closer to figuring out why Katherine shut down when the engine went out. He scratched his head. "Is it okay with you if I strip and repaint the door?"

"If you want to. Let me see what colors you want to use. I'd rather you didn't paint the door hot pink with yellow and blue alternating stripes," she muttered.

"I won't do that." What just happened here? Up until a minute ago she'd been present for the conversation, now she might as well be in Alaska. "What's the matter?"

She turned to look at him, her eyes distant. "The matter?" Her tone had the effect of a cold shower. At least he didn't need to worry about her noticing his, ah, reaction.

He shook his head. How could he explain that for a minute he thought she might be interested and now? Now, she still stood close enough he could smell her shampoo and feel her body heat, but she was gone. As if something inside her had snapped shut. It was Maureen again. End of discussion. Closed for business.

"Never mind. It's not important." He started gathering up his tools.

She folded her arms. "Well, I need to get a lot of work done this evening. Good night." The gate closed with a snap behind her.

Jack listened to her door shut. She had to have something against the department. Every time it came up, she froze solid. He put the last of his tools in the case and as he latched it closed, he heard a car in the drive.

The blond guy's battered truck rolled to a stop in front of the garage behind her car. "Hey!" He waved as he jumped out. "How's it going?"

"Just fine," Jack said. What was he doing here? He heard Katherine's door open.

"Randy, you're here. Come on up."

Katherine's voice sounded warm and friendly. Jack ground his teeth. Why did she sound so inviting to this guy when she frosted him out?

"Hey." Randy headed for her door, grabbing a gym bag out of his truck. "What's up?"

"Oh, Randy." Katherine sighed.

Jack walked to the edge of the house. She must have been standing in the doorway because he couldn't see her. He watched Randy leap up the stairs two at a time before disappearing around the edge of the house. Jack scowled as the door slammed closed. Maybe it wasn't the department. Maybe she'd realized blondie was on his way, and she wanted to be ready for him. Jack felt his lip curl in disgust. The competition seemed to be winning. He wasn't sure he could take it if Randy's truck was still parked in the driveway in the morning.

* * * *

"Thanks pal. I didn't think I could stay there tonight."

"So was it worth skipping out on the poker game?"

Jack groaned.

Kevin handed him a pillow. "I knew it was a bad idea for you to get involved with her."

"We're not involved."

"Exactly." Kevin folded his arms. "You're not even involved with her, and you're torn up about it."

Jack sank down on the couch he'd just made up. "I don't get it. One minute she's happy to see me, and the next she's avoiding me for days. Then she's acting kinda weird and happy Leia is my sister, and then that idiot is getting a warm welcome. What does she see in him?"

Kevin sat down in his chair and got comfortable. "Maybe he's easy to handle."

"I'm easy to handle." Jack rubbed his fingers through his hair. "It's just—she seems so happy to see me sometimes. I get the feeling this is what real love is. You know, when you come home from work and there's a smiling face waiting for you. When you need somebody to understand, she's always there. When you need a good laugh, she knows it. When I'm with her, I feel as if it's where I belong. Like when I'm eighty years old waking up beside her, I'll be thinking, this is right. You know?"

Kevin laughed. "You are the last guy in the department I ever thought would be sitting around waxing poetic about being married. Well, maybe Danny's a little behind you, but you're right near the end of the line."

"She said her fiancé was killed."

"Sounds violent."

"That's what I thought. I didn't want to ask, but most people say someone died, they don't say that person was killed. And she didn't say he was murdered. She's an English teacher. You've gotta think she's using exactly the word she wants."

"I don't know her well enough to make that call. She probably is the type who uses exactly the word she means. Her fiancé didn't just die, and he wasn't murdered. He was killed." Kevin shrugged. "You'll have to ask her."

"Are you sure you don't remember a Gary in the department who died? Even a volunteer or a dispatcher or something. Somebody at a scene even."

"Positive. The only deaths in the department in the last fifteen years have been retirees and Tony Wells, five years ago. And if it was a civilian who died at a scene, and she still blamed the department, do you really think she would have rented to you in the first place?"

"I guess not."

"Maybe whatever happened to him was in the papers and I read about it. Ask your sister, maybe there was a court case involved."

Jack snorted. "I'll search back issues of the paper at the library first. I'm not desperate enough to ask Leia for help yet."

"You're getting there."

"You know," Jack said. "If it was in the paper it would have to be pretty violent. I wonder what happened and how long ago. It would take time to get over something like that."

"It would. The violent death of a spouse takes a little time to get over. He wasn't quite her spouse, but close enough." Kevin heaved himself out of the chair. "But it shouldn't be you anyway. You shouldn't be chasing your landlady. Widowed one year or ten. Good night, lover boy."

* * * *

Katherine hovered near her kitchen window listening to the faucet drip and watching for Jack's truck when he pulled in. She bit her lip. Where had he been all night? And why? He climbed out and started pulling large, awkward, plastic wrapped bundles out of the truck bed. She couldn't make out what the packages said, but she guessed they were roofing supplies. He also had a couple of sheets of thick plywood with him that he hauled around as if they weighed next to nothing.

He was so good looking. So nice. Handy around the house. He even smelled good. They had been having such a great conversation last night. It had been years since she talked to anyone about her dad. And the five seconds she'd spent with Archer leaning against her legs on one side, pressing her into Jack on the other side had woken her up three or four times last night.

Then, he had to go and spoil it all by pausing in mid-sentence because he heard a siren. Smacking her in the face with the fact that he was a hero for a living.

She watched him slide the pieces of plywood off the truck.

He was already acting like a husband. Fixing the back door Gary always told her couldn't be fixed. Fixing the garage roof. Having conversations with her. Gary hadn't been a bad guy, he was just always wrapped up in his work. The whole duty, honor, pride of being a police officer. It had never been quite what she expected, but she'd been more than prepared to settle into it. She could have been happy having more meaningful conversations with her friends than her husband and spending time at the bookstore because he was either on duty or hanging around with other off duty cops.

Then along came Jack who woke her up at night in a way Gary never had. Who raised her pulse by smiling. Who listened to her. Who made her feel more comfortable with herself than she ever had felt in her life. Who stayed home for the sole purpose of staying home.

But where had he gone last night?

She set down her coffee cup in the sink under the dripping faucet so it would fill up again. It didn't matter. He was the tenant, and she was the landlord. She pulled on her coat. He was also a hero for a living, and she couldn't do that to herself again. She hurried down the stairs. Never mind the fact that she'd spent most of the evening in the yard playing with Archer, waiting for him to come home, and never mind that she'd been awake most of the night listening for his returning footsteps. She threw open her door as he opened the back gate. The weather had turned cold again and in her hurry, she'd forgotten to put on shoes.

He stumbled back a step, startled, pulling the gate open.

She opened her mouth before she realized she was about to demand to know where he was all night. "You—got the stuff for the roof?"

He glanced back at the closed garage door. "I picked it up this morning. I talked to a couple of guys, unfortunately, I don't think we're going to get to work on it until the week after next. They've all got Easter stuff going on this week."

"Easter?" Katherine shivered as the wind blew through her wool socks. "Next Friday is Good Friday."

"I know." She stood on the landing, staring at him, willing him to tell her where he spent last night. Even if he was with another woman. It would be better to know than to guess.

"Is that okay?" he asked. Archer tried to push open the gate, getting his head and shoulders through before Jack penned it with his leg.

"That next Friday is Good Friday?" Katherine asked. *Where were you last night?*

He frowned. "That we'll start next week. It should only take a day, but you'll want to have your car out of the garage. In case something falls through."

"Falls through?" Katherine knew she should be alarmed, but all she could think of right now was that Jack had been gone all night and wasn't volunteering where he'd been.

"Tools. Drop a hammer, you don't want it going through the windshield." He paused watching her face. "Is it okay?"

"Sure. That's fine." She clenched her hands. "What do I owe you?"

"I'll figure it out when we're done. I like to overbuy and return what I don't use instead of having to make a supply run in the middle of the job."

"That makes sense." She pulled her coat tighter. "Well, I'm going to go back inside now."

"Okay." He smiled. "Anything else?"

"No." She heard herself whimper and hated it. *Where were you last night? Who were you with?*

"Well, you better get inside before you catch a cold."

"Do you have duty tomorrow?" She knew he did.

"Yeah."

"Be careful."

He chuckled. "I can't be careful. It's my job." He started maneuvering Archer back into the yard. "Come on, animal. Let's go inside. It's almost lunch time."

Katherine stood on the porch and listened to Jack herd his dog into the house and close the back door. When the sound faded, she went back inside her own apartment, cursing herself for acting like a teenager. What had she been thinking running outside like that? He had to think she was crazy. Asking him about Good Friday? And telling him to be careful? What did that mean? She hung up her coat and retreated to the living room and her book, which she didn't think she'd be able to concentrate on anyway.

* * * *

How often did she fall asleep after her alarm went off? How was it fair that she'd been awake since four-thirty only to drift off the moment she turned her alarm off? Katherine yanked a comb through her hair with one hand while gulping down a cup of coffee with the other. The combination of coffee and the toothpaste made her pucker, which seemed to be the perfect expression for the morning. She abandoned the cup in the bathroom and raced through the apartment trying to collect her book bag and lunch and get her arms through the correct sleeves of her coat. She ran out the door and had turned to lock it before she realized she didn't have her keys.

She dropped her book bag and lunch on the porch and ran back inside to the kitchen where her purse, keys inside, hung on a kitchen chair, very glad Jack was on duty this morning and not home to hear her thundering around like a herd of bulls.

She ran out the door and jerked it shut. Her keys seemed to have vanished. "Oh for heaven's sake. Where are they?"

Archer barked at her.

"Archer, hush." She found the key ring at the bottom of her purse and scooped it out. Locked the door. Grabbed her book bag. Ran to the garage.

Archer ran up and down the fence, whining with his ears pitched forward.

"You are not missing anything, you silly pooch. I'm late. I can't play with you this morning." She heaved up the garage door, jumped into the car, started it. Then, after she backed out, she hopped out again to pull the door down.

Archer had given up racing up and down the fence and plopped himself in front of the gate waiting for her. He'd come to expect a few rounds of fetch before she climbed in her car and drove away on the mornings Jack worked. He flattened his ears to his head.

Katherine hesitated in her car door. "I'm already late."

He stared at her.

"Oh, all right. Just one." She grabbed a stick lying in the driveway and threw it over the corner of the garage. Archer set off after it, and Katherine dove into her car.

She managed to get to her classroom before the first bell rang. The halls were already crowded with kids, making the trip to her classroom more of an obstacle course than she liked. She wished she had time to stop in the office and check her mailbox, but that would have to wait, along with the few other things she did in the morning, like photocopying and gossiping over coffee with Pam and Kitty.

Pam walked in as the first bell rang. "I thought you were starting Spring Break early."

Katherine frowned. Pam had been teasing her about all the late hours she'd been putting in to stay away from Jack. She'd speculated Katherine was working ahead so she could skip out to spend time with her firefighter. This wasn't going to help.

"I overslept." Katherine hung up her coat.

"I heard."

The vice principal poked his head through the door. The relief on his face would have been comical on any other day. "Oh good, you're here. We were beginning to worry about you."

"I'm here, just a little later than usual." She toted her book bag to her desk. "I shut off the alarm and fell asleep. I've never done that. I don't even have time to take my lunch to the refrigerator."

"I'll take it after homeroom," Pam offered.

Katherine sighed. "Good. Thanks. Now where is my lunch?" She opened her book bag and took out her grade book and the stack of homework papers she'd taken home to grade. "It's not here." She went back to her closet and opened the door, checking the pockets of her coat.

"Is it in your car?" Pam asked.

"No, I remember looking at the seat when I picked up my book bag."

"Did you leave it at home?"

Katherine searched her closet even though she knew it wasn't there. "I left it at home. And I don't have a dime on me for lunch." She rubbed her temples. "I don't believe this." The second bell rang and the classroom filled with students.

"Don't worry about it. If you can stomach the cafeteria food, I think I have a couple bucks you can have."

Katherine closed her closet door. "Thanks. Hey, you guys know the drill," she yelled over the noise of her homeroom class. "In your seats. Whose turn is it to take attendance?"

* * * *

Jack walked down the block toward the house. Katherine's Easter break should be starting tonight, so she'd be home for the next week. Kevin had talked him out of inviting her to Easter dinner on Sunday, but hadn't been able to talk him out of making sure he was home every off duty hour. Jack had been in such a hurry to get home he hadn't even bothered to change out of his uniform, even thought he knew she'd be in school until evening. Maybe with repeat exposure, her resistance would wear down and he'd be able to get some answers, like what happened to your fiancé? How long ago? And, when do you think you're going to start dating again? He'd decided during the last shift that he could wait. If she said five years, he could wait. And in five years, he could have found a house of his own and acquired a puppy she wouldn't be able to resist. He started up the driveway toward the front door.

After that conversation Saturday morning, he felt pretty sure something was up. After all, she'd run out of the house without shoes in the middle of March to talk to him about nothing. And she'd looked so worried and confused. He decided the blond hadn't stayed that night. He didn't know for sure how he figured in the picture yet, but it wasn't as her overnight guest.

Archer barked.

Jack changed course and headed for the back yard. As he passed Katherine's porch, he noticed an insulated bag sitting off to the side. He stopped and picked it up. It looked like one of those freebie lunch bags companies gave away, but he couldn't read the faded lettering on the bag through the cracked plastic. He'd seen it peeking out of her book bag every day when she came home from school. He opened it. It sure looked like a lunch. A small one anyway. Sandwich, apple, peanut butter crackers. He carried it to the fence. "So, dog, was Katherine in a big hurry this morning?"

Archer barked and then lolled his tongue out.

Jack looked at the garage door and noticed it was open about two inches, as if she'd pulled it down and not bothered to make sure it got all the way. Or pulled it so hard it bounced back up. "So she was running late and dropped her lunch. Is that what you're trying to tell me, Lassie?"

Christa Maurice

Archer barked.

"You wait here. I've got an errand to run." Jack went in the house for his keys. He knew which school she taught at, and thought he could find the classroom based on the way she described it last weekend when she'd stopped at the fence to chat on her way to the grocery store.

A sign on the door told him to go to the office for a visitor's pass, but he didn't think he needed one. He was only dropping something off. When he passed the office door, the kid monitoring the desk looked a little wide eyed, but didn't challenge him. It felt a little unnerving to be in a high school again. The whole building smelled like chalk and floor wax, and he would have sworn the floor was the same tile as his old school. In the stairwell he hesitated, trying to recall the bits she'd told him. Her room was upstairs so he walked up to the second floor. It faced west because he remembered her mentioning that she always looked forward to spring with mixed emotions—what with summer-crazy kids in a hot room at the end of the school year. The first west facing room at the top of the stairs was a disaster of paint splatters, long chipped tables and paper littering the floor. Then he noticed the door plaques on the walls. He sighed. It had seemed an impossible task once he got inside the building, but if they labeled all the rooms… *Ms. Pelham: English* was the third door on the west side of the hall. Inside, he could hear a burble of voices, but couldn't see anyone. He knocked.

* * * *

Katherine scowled at the door. She had the students working in pairs looking up terms for a vocabulary test next week, and so far they were on task, but any interruption might throw them. She hurried to the front of the room to answer it before the hyper kid up front took it upon himself to play doorman. But it was too late. Her student had pulled open the door and, instead of chattering with whoever was outside interrupting her class, he stood in the door with his mouth hanging open.

"Jason, what is it?" she asked, weaving through the desks. A hush started to swell around her. She knew from experience that classroom chaos was normally preceded by a hush, like tornadoes. She needed to get the intruder out before the kids got out of control. Whoever was out there had a good talking to coming.

"Ms. Pelham, there's a cop here," Jason blurted out.

Katherine lengthened her stride, hearing the noise level in the room rise as every one of her students decided they needed to know what was going on right now. For a dizzy instant, she thought there really was a police officer outside the door, and he'd come to tell her that her fiancé was dead. But no, when that happened they'd gotten her to the office before they told her. And her fiancé was already dead. He couldn't die again. She came around the corner and clasped Jason's shoulder too hard. Jack stood in the hall looking as if he wished he were anywhere but here.

"All right everybody, get back to work. Jason, I'm impressed that you don't know the difference between a police officer and a firefighter." She steered Jason back in the direction of his seat and clapped her hands over her head. "I'm going to be in the hall. I expect everyone's list to be done by the end of class. Remember, what you don't finish now you have to do at home." She stepped into the hall, propelling Jack in front of her.

He looked perplexed and a little embarrassed. "I'm sorry. I didn't think I was going to create a scene."

"A robin landing on the window sill creates a scene with that group. What are you doing here?" Katherine blinked, trying to drive away the dizziness that had set in earlier. Jack couldn't be here to tell her that her fiancé was dead. No one would ever come to her door with that news again. Why Jack was here didn't matter so much as long as it wasn't tragic.

He held up her lunch. "I found this at the house this morning. I thought you might want it."

Her throat closed, and for a minute she thought she might cry. It did matter why Jack was here. He thought to bring her lunch. "Thank you. Where did you find it?"

"On the porch. You must have dropped it."

She took the bag out of his hands and held it to her chest. "I overslept. I didn't realize I'd forgotten it until I got here."

"Sorry if I interrupted your class."

Katherine grinned. "Don't worry. Thank you." She resisted the impulse to kiss him.

"Well, I'll see you tonight." He took a couple of backward steps before he turned around and went down the hall to the stairs.

Pam stepped out of her room as he turned the corner. "Was that your fireman?" she whispered across the hall.

"Firefighter," Katherine said. He's not on fire, and he does his best to stay that way, she reminded herself, cursing herself for remembering what he'd said.

Kitty Reilly, the art teacher, came out of her room and stared down the steps until they heard the stairwell door clang closed. She hurried over to where Katherine and Pam peered down the hall. "Who was the hunka hunka burnin' man?"

"That was Katherine's fireman," Pam announced.

"Wow. He's hot. Look, he left little scorch marks on the floor where he walked." Kitty pointed to a tile. "Good job, Kath. My, my." She started fanning her face. A loud bang, followed by laughter, floated from her classroom. "Gotta go. When the cat's away, the mice wreck the place."

"That guy." Pam pointed down the hall where Jack had gone. "You can date him."

"He's still my tenant."

"Throw caution to the wind for once. What was he doing here anyway?"

"He brought my lunch." Katherine held up the bag, still choked up.

Pam looked at her face for a minute and sighed. "I'll watch your class while you run it to the lounge."

Katherine blinked and felt tears on her lashes. Pam was right. She needed a minute. "Thanks."

She hurried through the familiar halls to the windowless teacher's lounge. Why did that small gesture mean so much? It was so simple. It couldn't have taken him more than a few minutes. But it had been a very long time since any man had bothered to take time out of his day for her.

Why did he have to keep being such a great guy when she couldn't have him?

Chapter 5

"Jack, come help me with the leftovers."

Jack looked up, startled. His grandmother asking for help with leftovers? Usually she chased everyone out so she could make up care packages in peace. He glanced at his mother for confirmation that his grandmother had made an odd request. She looked stunned.

"Mom?" His mother stepped forward. "Are you sure you don't want me to help?"

"If I had wanted you to help, I would have asked you. I asked Jack to help. I want to hear all about his new puppy. Bring the ham," Grandmother ordered.

Jack picked up the platter and carried it into her tiny, hot kitchen. "Archer isn't a puppy, Grandma. He's almost two." He put the ham in the middle of the kitchen table and sat down to be out of the way. Most of the other dishes were already scattered across the table.

"That's nice." She set down the bowl of mashed potatoes that didn't appear to have been touched, but Jack had seen it when it came out of the kitchen and knew his family had done their best. "Tell me about the new girlfriend."

"New girlfriend? What new girlfriend? I don't have a new girlfriend."

"Jack. I'm your grandmother. I've been here for a long time, and I've learned a few things. Who's the new girlfriend?" She folded her arms and Jack recognized the gesture. If he didn't tell her the truth, he would never leave the kitchen. She'd keep him trapped here, plying him with questions until she got an answer she found acceptable. He could hear everyone moving into the living room to watch television and continue to talk about wonderful Leia's partnership. The only dinner where he'd managed to eclipse his sister was the one after he got his commendation. Leia had been miffed for weeks until his burns healed and the family's attention drifted back to her.

He wondered if getting married would one up her.

"Well?" His grandmother tapped her foot.

"She isn't my girlfriend, Grandma."

"But you want her to be. Here, you reach down some plastic containers and tell me the trouble."

Jack went to the cupboard over the stove and wondered if his grandmother owned stock in Tupperware. She seemed to have an endless supply. Every piece he owned he'd gotten from her, and it had come full of leftovers. "She's my landlady."

"Oh, that's right. Your mother said you rented a new apartment." She arranged her containers into battle formation and set to work on the green bean casserole.

"It's the first floor of a house. She lives upstairs."

"That's good. She's close. You'll grow on her."

"I'm not sure if I haven't already. She acts funny sometimes." Jack slouched into a chair.

"How?" She started heaping mashed potatoes into containers, sending the most with him.

Jack watched her, knowing he'd be trading bags with Leia in the driveway. It wasn't that he didn't like his grandmother's cooking or that he didn't appreciate it, but he could cook for himself and Leia couldn't boil water in a microwave without causing a minor kitchen fire.

"Well, sometimes she's really glad to see me and sometimes not. The other day I took her lunch to school for her, and I thought she was gonna start crying she was so happy, but the week before that she avoided me."

"Why did you take her lunch to school? Is she a teacher?" His grandmother moved onto the ham, wrapping the bone and placing it in his bag. He'd have to remember to get it before Leia left with it. The guys at the station loved his split pea soup, and Archer would love the bone.

"She teaches high school English, and she forgot it. She said she overslept."

"Then she was probably having a bad day, and you made it better. If she's emotional that might be why she teared up."

"You're not making me feel better, Grandma." He reached around her and pinched off a piece of ham.

She swatted his hand away. "I should be. You did what any good friend should do, and you need to be her friend first."

"I'd gladly be her friend if she'll let me." Jack thought back to the day she'd helped him hang the door and then curled up in her shell until

Randy showed up. He still didn't know how Randy fit into this, but he couldn't talk that over with his grandmother.

"Why is she renting? Other than the fact that teachers have never been paid enough."

"Her fiancé died, and she was falling behind in her bills."

His grandmother turned around, putting down her carving knife and pinning him with her sharp, wise eyes. "Her fiancé died? How long ago?"

"I don't know."

"That's very important." She shook her finger in his face. "If it was recent, she's going to be very vulnerable. You better be gentle."

"Grandma!"

She sighed and folded her arms. "I forget who I'm talking to. You will be. Your cousin Gregory wouldn't."

Jack glanced at the kitchen door as if Gregory would choose that moment to need a glass of water.

"What else do you know?" his grandmother asked, picking up her knife again.

"I don't think she was happy with her fiancé. She described him as having integrity."

"Nothing wrong with a man having integrity." She sorted the containers into stacks. "Your grandfather had integrity."

"Grandma, if someone asked you about Grandpa would you say he had integrity first?"

She paused for a minute. "No. I suppose you're right. I'd say he had a good sense of humor and a nice smile. You get your smile from your grandfather, Jack. Now, what else?"

"I know her father died when she was ten, and her mother is her only family."

"Poor dear. Next time you should invite them both to dinner. There's always plenty. " His grandmother started wrapping deviled eggs in plastic sandwich bags. "Does she like your dog?"

"She likes my dog better than she likes me." Jack stared out the back window. He hated being jealous of his dog.

"That's a good thing. Isn't it?"

"I guess. It gets her to hang around with me."

"Hand me down some grocery bags, would you?" His grandmother waved her hand at another high shelf.

She had nearly finished packing up the leftovers from the entire dinner and was ferrying hers to the refrigerator. How had he missed her doing all that work? When had she divided the bread, the broccoli and the ham gravy? When he got to be her age he could only aspire to be that quick and efficient. He tried to imagine Katherine at eighty-two and couldn't. Every time he tried, he remembered her answering the door in her bathrobe the day after he moved in. Or rolling around in last fall's leaves with Archer. Or waiting while he hung the back door. He was going to have to wait and see.

"So what does this girl look like? Is she pretty?" His grandmother asked arranging containers in bags.

"Grandma, she's beautiful. She's got long brown hair that turns red in the sun. And the most gorgeous brown eyes. And she's smart and she's funny. And she's sweet and nice. She sounds like a really good teacher, and she loves her job."

"Tell me, do her feet touch the ground when she walks or does she float?" His grandmother fluttered her hand over the empty dishes.

"Grandma!"

"Here, help out an old woman and put these in the Frigidaire." She gestured to the bags on the table and carried the dishes to the sink. "I think it's wonderful that you like her so much. A husband should always love his wife the same as he did the first moment he saw her, and he should always love her a little bit more every day too."

Jack loaded the bags in the refrigerator. "How am I supposed to do that?"

"You'll know when the time comes." She wiped the counter down. "I think she'll be better for you than that Maureen."

"You never met Maureen."

"I know, but I'm listening to the way you talk about her. I was afraid you were going to end up married to that Maureen, and you weren't going to be happy. She wasn't for you." His grandmother sat down at the kitchen table. "Now, come sit and tell me all about her all over again, starting with why you didn't ask her to dinner today."

Jack sat down across the table. "First, I want to know how you knew."

"Jack, you've been nice to your sister all day. You were hardly here for dinner. You walked in with a silly smile on your face." She patted his hand. "I would ask if you like your new place, but I think I know the answer. Now, what's her name, and why isn't she here?"

* * * *

When Jack pulled in, the sun had set. Katherine stood in the back yard playing fetch with Archer. Or rather, Archer was playing. Katherine threw the sticks hard enough that he could hear them whistling and smacking the back fence. She didn't seem to have changed from where ever she had gone to celebrate the holiday. She wore gray wool slacks, a red sweater and black pumps whose heels sunk into the thawing yard. She had her hair pulled into such a tight bun that her ivory skin stretched. Or it could be the grimace on her face pulling her skin. He closed the garage door and walked over to the fence.

"Hello."

"Hi," she growled. She whipped another stick at the fence so hard her entire body shook.

Jack opened the gate and noted that Archer didn't even break in his game to greet him. Some loyalty. But the more Jack watched his dog, the more he realized Archer wasn't playing either. He seemed to be approaching this session of fetch like a job. Running after the stick, finding it, bringing it back, dropping it at Katherine's feet so she could pick it up and throw it again. As if he were trying to provide comfort in the only way he knew. After the long conversation he'd had with his grandmother, he'd been feeling pretty good. Even Leia's digs hadn't gotten to him.

But it looked as if Katherine hadn't had such a relaxing day.

Jack swallowed. "So did you have dinner with your mother today?"

"Yes," she growled.

He closed the gate. "When did you get home?"

"About an hour ago."

Jack rubbed his nose. If she'd been playing fetch like this for an hour, she was going to be sore. "Did you have a good time?"

"My mother is of the opinion that my life should stop because the man I would have married has died. She feels that I should remain loyal to his memory by not dating and not marrying ever. Like she did. She's sorry Gary and I didn't marry and have children before he died."

Jack filed the information about marriage. This wasn't a good time for that conversation. Archer carried the stick back and dropped it at her feet, but she didn't move to pick it up.

Katherine started rubbing her shoulder. She patted Archer on the head. "Sorry, boy. My arm hurts."

"You should put ice on that before it gets bad."

"I suppose I should." She started to walk past him, but he stopped her.

"Hey, I can't let you stew all night like this. Come on inside. I'm pretty familiar with sore muscles, and I'll be happy to listen." He put his arm around her shoulders, careful to not put any weight on the sore one, and guided her inside. "You want some coffee?"

"Sure." She sank down at the table and looked around the kitchen. "It looks nice in here."

"Oh, thanks." Jack got an ice pack out of the freezer and wrapped it in a towel before laying it over her shoulder. She put her hand next to his to hold the ice pack in place. Jack left his hand beside hers for a moment, wishing he had the courage to take it in his. She seemed so alone. Archer had already gone under the table and curled up around her feet. Jack couldn't do that, so he moved away from her before he tried.

"So what happened with your mother?" He busied himself making room for his grandmother's care package in the refrigerator.

"My mother is the Grand Master of guilt. All I had to do was mention I was thinking about dating again, and she started in with what would Gary's family think?"

"What would they think?" Jack got the coffee maker going. If she was only thinking about dating, then she wasn't dating the blond with the rusted out truck. Good, very good. But her late fiancé's family made for more and worse competition. He couldn't compete with a dead man.

Katherine snorted. "They wrote me off the minute they cashed Gary's life insurance check."

She rotated her shoulder under the ice pack. "My mother knows what buttons to push. It's not as if he died a hero's death, and I should live the rest of my life as a monument to him. It's nothing like what happened to Dad." She paused, studying the table top tracing the wood grain with her fingertip. Jack wished he were as observant as his grandmother. His grandmother would be able to read Katherine's mind by the way she sat at the table.

Katherine looked up and tried to smile. "The other day when you came to school with my lunch, Jason, the kid who answered the door thought you were the police. Before I saw it was you, I thought I was living that day all over again. Funny how the mind works isn't it?"

"How so?" He sat down across the table from her. So the police had come to tell her Gary was dead. Was that normal? Pretty soon, he'd need a notebook soon for all the little pieces of this mystery. Her face looked a little less pinched and tired now. For a sore shoulder, she needed aspirin. He got up to get her some.

Staring at her hand spread out on the table, she sighed. "When Gary was killed, I was at school. We had a couple of city cops roaming the halls at the time because there had been some trouble, and one of them came to my door. He said I was needed in the office. They didn't tell me until I got downstairs." She shook her head. "I don't know why that came to mind. We haven't had police monitoring the halls for years. And they can't exactly come and tell me my fiancé is dead again, now can they?"

The coffee maker gurgled to a finish, and Jack got out two cups, glad to be able to keep his back to her. If he had known that, he would have taken her lunch to the office and dropped it off there. At least they had been sensitive enough to get her out of class before they told her. "Cream and sugar?"

"Please." She sighed. "I'm sorry to dump this on you. Holidays suck for me. But you look like you had a good day. You had dinner with your family, didn't you?"

"At my grandmother's house. She's pretty with it for eighty-two. She always does all the cooking herself. Bread from scratch and everything."

"Eighty-two? Wow. I don't know what bread looks like before it gets to the grocery store wrapped in a plastic bag. Thank you." She lifted one of the coffee cups out of his hand. "Was your whole family there?"

"Just Grandma, my parents, my sister, and a couple of local cousins." Like Gregory who wouldn't treat her so gently.

"Oh, your sister." Katherine smiled.

"Here, take these. It'll help you stop hurting." He dropped two aspirin in her hand. "My grandmother asked why I didn't bring you."

"Me?" Katherine put one of the pills on her tongue and chased it with a swallow of coffee. "Why?"

Jack wanted to kick himself but decided she would notice that. He needed a convincing white lie quick. "She knew I had moved, and she asked about my new neighbors. You're about it."

She dropped the other aspirin in her mouth. "We do have neighbors on either side, you know. Across the street too."

Jack shrugged. "I haven't met them yet." He wanted to know more about her late fiancé, but he couldn't think of a good way to steer the conversation back that way and he wasn't sure he wanted to. She looked so much more relaxed and almost happy.

She giggled. "To tell the truth, I don't know them very well either. I know their names to say hello to, but I don't know anything about them. I'd only moved into the house a few months before Gary died, and I guess I've been kind of a loner."

"We'll work on that."

She laughed. "Are you going to teach me to be outgoing?"

"If you like."

She looked at him with an odd exasperation. As if she was pleased and sorry at the same time, but she was still smiling.

I would, he thought. I'll help you with whatever you want as long as you keep smiling at me like that, or smiling at me at all. "So, what do you plan to do with your week off?" he asked before he said something stupid.

"I thought I might do some laundry, if you don't mind. And I need to change the furnace filter. I need to get into the basement for both of those."

"Sounds like fun. You can do it today it you want. I don't have any plans."

"I thought I would do it when you're on duty Tuesday. I don't want to be underfoot." She sipped her coffee, holding his gaze over the rim of the cup.

"I don't mind. Go on." He'd picked up his coffee cup and started to take a drink before he realized she knew his schedule. It took some skill to not cough.

"Thanks." Finishing off her coffee, she stood. "I'll go upstairs and get my hamper. The day is getting better already." She left the ice pack on the table.

Jack put the ice pack back in the freezer, feeling pretty pleased. He'd managed to finagle her into hanging around all evening, and she admitted it improved her day. He liked being an improvement. Walking through the living room, he made sure it was tidy. Then, he turned on the television, so she wouldn't feel as if he had prepared the place for a date, and lit a candle, so maybe she would feel as if he had.

She knew his schedule. Why had she paid enough attention to his comings and goings to figure it out? He couldn't keep track of trash day, and she knew his work schedule three days in advance. That had to be a good thing.

She knocked at the front door. When he answered, she stepped inside with a blue laundry basket in her arms. While she was upstairs, she'd changed into white sweats and a long green sweater and taken her hair down. "I'm back. Pretend I'm not even here."

"It's no trouble. I'm glad to have the company. You need some help?"

"I know the way." She hurried through the foyer with her head down as if she didn't want to spy and slipped around the basement door. Her feet pattered down the stairs. He already knew the sound of her footsteps from listening to them over his head for the last month. Jack went into the kitchen and looked around for something to snack on. The cupboards didn't seem to contain the perfect food that would look impressive and not look as if he was trying to butter her up. Popcorn seemed too easy. Baking too showy.

Archer watched him open and close cupboards. Then, the dog walked to the basement stairs and looked down. He sat down at the edge of the hall where he could hear her and watch Jack.

Katherine banged around in the basement for a few minutes and then the washer started to fill. The washer lid closed with a bong, and Jack heard scraping.

Jack wandered back into the living room still pondering appropriate snack food and dropped onto the couch. He'd ended up with a political talk show on. Archer jumped up next to him and settled in for a nap. Jack started channel surfing to pass time while he waited for her to come upstairs. He'd gone through the entire lineup before it occurred to him that he hadn't heard anything in a while.

"Katherine? What are you doing? Hanging out with the spiders?"

"My laundry," she answered.

"Well, yeah, but what are you doing right now? It sounded like you got a load in."

"I did."

"You're allowed to come upstairs."

There was a long pause, and Jack considered going down after her.

"I didn't want to be underfoot."

He rubbed his hand through his hair. Hanging out in the basement would improve her day? Maybe appropriate snack food wasn't as big a question as he thought. "You don't have to sit in the basement while you wait. Come on upstairs and watch some TV."

She appeared at the bottom of the steps. "Are you sure it's not a problem?"

"I'm sure. Come on up. I was thinking about making some popcorn."

She smiled.

Jack went toward the kitchen, listening for the sound of her footfalls in the stairs. He got out the air popper and the popcorn before he turned around to check that she had made it upstairs.

She stood at the edge of the hall, poised as if to flee.

"Popcorn?" He tried to sound light, but he couldn't tell if he'd succeeded. She leaned against the edge of the stove with one hip, reminding him of how curvy she was under her sweater.

"Sure." She smiled again and hugged herself.

Jack dumped a little more popcorn in the popper and switched it on. He stepped back and leaned against the counter with his hands behind him. It seemed like the safest option. The green sweater she wore seemed to draw out the color in her eyes. Her lips shone. She was the only woman he'd ever seen who looked great in Chapstick, and he felt pretty sure he'd never look at lip balm the same way again.

Archer stationed himself between them and in front of the popcorn popper.

Her eyes swept down to the dog when he moved and then up Jack's body to his eyes.

Jack froze for a moment. He'd been staring, and she'd caught him. He took a deep breath. "Doesn't look like there's much on TV. I've got a couple of movies around. Unless you have something in mind to watch."

"No." She drew a deep breath. "Whatever's on is fine. I haven't watched TV in months."

"Why not?"

"I had to trade it for some maintenance. The DVD player broke months ago, and the TV was the only thing I had to trade."

"So you don't have a TV at all? Do you read all the time?"

The popcorn popper blew a kernel out of the bowl. It skidded across the counter and Archer snapped it up as it dropped off the edge.

"Yes. The librarians all know my name." She rolled her eyes. "I walk in and they all whisper 'Katherine!' Kind of like Cheers, only quieter."

"Well, feel free to come down here to watch." Jack peered into the popper. When she'd first said she didn't have a TV, he'd worried she was one of those intellectuals who disdained television. That would have been very uncomfortable. He'd have to reassess his entire view of her. But if she'd had to trade it away in lieu of cash for work on her house that made his heart ache more. "Do you want something to drink? I've got beer, soda, water, milk and iced tea."

"Just water. I can get it. Where are your glasses?"

"Second cupboard next to the fridge." He pointed.

She opened the cupboard and took out two glasses. "What did you want?"

"Get me a soda. Thanks."

Leaning into the refrigerator, she took out a can of pop and the water jug. He thought she was watching the glasses too intently, but wasn't sure why. Did she feel as nervous to be with him as he did being with her? Replacing the water jug, she said, "All set. How's the popcorn coming?"

"Fine. Why don't you take the drinks and surf around on the TV until you find something. I'll only be a minute." He busied himself getting butter out of the refrigerator and melting it in the microwave. He heard her switching channels looking for something to watch. So far so good.

He drizzled the butter over the popcorn and carried the bowl out to the living room.

Katherine sat in the chair inside the archway with her feet curled under her, balancing a box in her hands. She looked up. "Your assessment of the options was correct. Nothing on worth watching."

He glanced at the TV. A nature documentary about sharks. At least it wasn't politics. "What's that?"

She held up the box. "A game. I noticed it under the table."

"Oh, I stuck it under there when I moved in and never put it away."

"I've never played this one."

Jack looked at the box. Jenga. Leia had given it to him for Christmas a couple of years ago. It had looked like one of those 'I didn't know what to get so I grabbed this' gifts, but after he'd played it a couple of times, he'd decided he liked it and decided maybe she had put some thought into it. It also took time. Time that might keep Katherine hanging around. "It's fun. You want to play? You've got time while you're waiting on your laundry."

She shrugged. "Sure. If you like."

Jack put the popcorn bowl on the magazine stack and dumped the box out on the table. Archer positioned himself next to the popcorn bowl. Jack scooped up a handful of fluffy white kernels and tossed one to the dog who snapped it out of the air, unfortunately he nearly crashed into the table in the process. Katherine knelt next to the table and watched Jack set up the game. "My mother and I used to play Yahtzee a lot."

"My family went through a Monopoly phase when I was in high school." Jack leaned back from the table when he placed the last block in place. "We must have played Monopoly every weekend for six months."

"All the way through?"

"All the way through."

"Monopoly isn't a game, it's a commitment." She leaned forward and scooped out a handful of popcorn, which she ate one piece at a time.

"I've got that too. Monopoly," Jack added when she turned to look at him.

"I don't think the laundry is going to take that long." She leaned on the table. "So how does one play this game?"

"You have to move the blocks from the bottom to the top without knocking over the tower. Like so." He nudged one block out of the bottom level and set it on the top at a right angle to the level below. "You're only allowed to use one hand at a time, and you can take blocks from any level below the top completed level."

She nodded. "So it's my turn."

"Go ahead."

She studied the tower, and Jack used the opportunity to study her. Her shoulders weren't drawn up to her ears and her face wasn't set with helpless pained lines. She didn't have her jaw clenched, wrecking the elegant shape of her mouth. Even her eyes seemed brighter. A few strands of hair slid over her shoulder and lay against her sweater.

"What?" She touched her cheek as if she thought there might be something on it.

"Did you take your turn?" Jack looked at the tower. There was a block missing from one of the middle levels and placed beside his at the top.

"Did I do it wrong?" she asked, frowning at the tower.

"No. I wasn't paying attention." *Or I was, but not to the game.*

She climbed to her feet, careful to not bump into the table.

"Where are you going?" he asked.

"The washer's done."

"It is? You need any help?" He started to stand.

"I'm just switching things from the washer to the dryer." She raised one eyebrow. "I'll be right back." Jack could only stare after her as she left the room. Standing, he carried his drink to the kitchen. Archer followed him. The glass was over half full, but he needed to move around and clear his head. Pacing would feel good about now, but he was pretty sure she would be able to hear him through the floor. He had to get a grip on himself before he said or did something stupid. Surprisingly, he hadn't done anything yet. This might be a record, the longest time they'd spent together without him making her freeze up. If he could keep not doing whatever it was he did until she finished her laundry, next time would be easier. But since he didn't know what not to do, he didn't know when to stop himself. Returning to the living room with the dog on his heels, Jack took his seat by the coffee table.

By the time she came back upstairs, he'd pulled himself together, but he fell apart again the moment she sat down. Wafting around her was the scent of laundry soap which, for some reason, smelled heavenly.

"Did you take your turn?" she asked, settling into her seat.

"No." He knelt next to her.

"Why?"

"Why?" He had deteriorated from not being able to pay attention to not being able to think at all. With her so close, he wanted to touch her, hold her. Confirm she was here. He still hadn't recovered from the desire to hug her earlier.

She selected one kernel of popcorn from the bowl and tossed it in her mouth. "Why didn't you take your turn?"

Did she know how dumbfounded he felt to have her sitting next to him, playing a game like an old married couple? "I didn't want you to think I was cheating." He picked a block at random and moved it to the top of the stack.

When she nudged a block with her finger, the whole tower shifted. "Oh. Now I see the challenge. This is going to get worse, isn't it?"

"Only until it collapses."

"This isn't for people with unsteady hands." She tested another block. It started to slip free and then snagged. Growling, she leaned across his lap to get a better angle on the piece. A lock of her hair curled across her shoulder. The light from the candle caught in it bringing out tiny sparks of red. For an instant he considered wrapping it around his finger to see if it was as soft as it looked. She wiggled and tugged the block free, barely avoiding bringing the entire tower down, and placed it on top.

Jack looked over the tower, picked a block, pulled it out and put it on top.

"How did you do that?" she wailed.

"I looked for the one that would slide out easiest."

"So did I."

He shrugged. "I guess I've had more practice than you."

"You fink. You tricked me into playing a game you're good at so you could trounce me. Well, we'll see." She leaned her chin on her hands and studied the tower. She was quiet for so long, Jack started to wonder if he should tell her about the time limit when she spoke softly.

"So you're a firefighter."

"Yeah." His heart squeezed at the tone of her voice. She sounded so sad. Almost as sad as when she'd been talking about her husband. He'd never questioned his profession before. Not when his parents were horrified and frightened. Not when his sister graduated law school with honors and started making twice as much money. Not even when the victims screamed at him because he didn't get there fast enough. But the tone of her voice made him do it now.

"Why?"

He looked over the tower and tried to think of an acceptable answer. Any other time dozens of answers would have come to mind. Now, nothing. "It's where I belong."

She glanced up at him. "Of course."

He tested her tone for anything. Was she disappointed with that answer? With him? Was she proud? She sounded resigned. Like she knew all too well why he did what he did. "Why did you ask?"

"I don't know." She chose a block and slid it free. "Your turn."

He reached out and tugged on the first block his hand found. The entire tower shifted and gracefully tipped over.

"Oops." She pursed her lips. "So I guess that's how the game is played, huh? What do I get for winning?"

Jack turned toward her. Her bright eyes rested on him and her hand lay on the coffee table between them. He moved his hand so his fingers covered hers and studied the way his hand looked, lying across hers. Her thin delicate fingers were hidden by his. He looked up and met her eyes. Now they seemed unguarded for the first time since he'd known her.

Licking her lips, she left them parted.

He wanted to lean down and taste them. To see if they were as delicious as they looked. Gathering his courage, he brushed her hair off her shoulder. It felt as soft as he had hoped. Like silk sliding across his fingers.

"Katherine," he whispered.

"Dryer," she said.

"What?"

"I have to check the dryer." She jumped up and all but ran for the basement.

Jack leaned on the table and dropped his face into his hands. "I am so stupid." He could still feel the texture of her small hand under his. It made him wish he either hadn't touched her at all or had closed his hand around hers so he'd have the memory of holding her hand the way he wanted to. "I blew it," he told Archer.

Archer, still guarding the popcorn bowl, looked at him.

He knew what he had to do, but backing away to give her more breathing space was the last thing he wanted to do. In fact, he'd prefer to jump right in and save her. She might be more newly single than he thought, and she might not have recovered. If she was involved with that blond guy somehow, that was another wrinkle. He knew she wasn't dating him, but they might be dating in a sense she didn't admit to herself was dating. Hanging out was dating in some circles, and casual sex was not dating in others. If she didn't want to upset her mother, she might be not-dating Randy while seeing a lot of him.

His grandmother would never forgive him if he didn't move gently. He collected the Jenga blocks and put them away before he climbed up on the couch. Her shark show had ended. It hadn't seemed important a minute ago, but now he needed something to do so he started flipping channels, searching and promising himself he'd be good. He picked up the popcorn bowl and balanced it on his lap.

* * * *

Katherine leaned against the dryer. It was nowhere near finished, but she'd had to move away before she did something stupid like kiss him. He was her tenant and a firefighter. She shouldn't be kissing him. She shouldn't be sitting next to him trying to play a game and having trouble concentrating. Now she had wet clothes and couldn't leave. This was a mistake, and it had been the moment she agreed to it.

But she wanted more than anything to be near him.

Sighing, she folded her arms. She'd let herself in for it by asking why he was a firefighter. He gave the answer she expected, and the last one she wanted to hear. She looked around her hideous basement. The low ceiling. The plentiful spiders. The uneven floor. At least she'd fixed the leaky walls. It felt as if she'd been living the last couple of years in this basement, maybe not literally, but in her mind. Stooped, jumping at shadows, stumbling over her own feet. And Jack was upstairs. Upstairs where the kitchen, the heart of the house, was.

I read too much into things.

Still, if the analogy wasn't perfect, it was close enough. She walked to the foot of the stairs. What was she going to do when she got upstairs? Tell him what was going on in her mind? That would be too awful. Try to pretend nothing happened? Would he allow that? He was one of those hero types who liked to face things head on. Wait and see what he did?

There's a thought.

Katherine took a deep breath and walked up the stairs.

Jack had sprawled on the couch flipping channels. "Your shark show was over."

"Oh." She sunk down in the chair and looked at him. He lounged back with the popcorn bowl resting on his lap. "Tired of games already?" she asked and then she cringed inwardly, wondering how he would take that question.

He glanced at the game and back to the TV. "Maybe later. It'll still be there."

Katherine bit her lip before she could say, 'but will you be?' Of course he would be. He wasn't on duty until Tuesday.

"Dryer not finished?"

"No. I was mistaken."

He nodded. "Popcorn?"

Christa Maurice

"No, thanks." She stared at the box on the table. Maybe for some reason he was waiting for her to make the first move. Or maybe her first assessment had been right, and he didn't have a care in the world. Just because she had a rather startling surge of hormones did not mean he had. Just because she thought his voice had deepened with emotion when he said her name a moment ago, didn't mean it had. She'd been living alone somewhat longer than the four years since Gary died, and couldn't judge.

He settled on a documentary about the Civil War.

Archer started to snore. Jack nudged him, and the dog shifted.

A siren went past the block, and Katherine turned to look in the direction it had gone.

"Police," Jack said without taking his eyes off the television.

"I know." She leaned back in the chair. How many years had that sound instilled fear in her? How many nights had she sat bolt upright in her empty bed because she heard a siren? She couldn't go through that again. No matter what she thought she felt for Jack, she couldn't.

And why did the thought make her want to cry?

After what seemed like an eternity, the dryer buzzed in the basement and she went back downstairs to deal with her laundry.

Chapter 6

Jack looked down the driveway. A police cruiser rolled to a stop at the bottom, blocking it. An enormous black officer got out and started toward the garage, scowling. His round face looked as if it would be more comfortable smiling, but Jack had no illusions about his mood changing soon.

"What's going on?" Lew asked, crouching back on his heels.

"I don't know. I'll take care of it." Jack made his way to the ladder. Kevin and Dan had started ripping off the old shingles on the other side while he and Lew patched the hole. After that incident on Sunday, he;d been trying to keep a low profile. Katherine had been quiet and melancholy while she finished her laundry. He hadn't seen much of her Monday, and he'd been on duty all day yesterday. He'd been hoping a little time would smooth over the awkwardness. She hadn't frozen up, but it still hadn't been a good evening. The cops showing up wasn't a good sign.

"Hi. Can I help you with something, Officer…" Jack gleaned his name off his tag. "Howard?"

"What are you fellas doing up there?" Officer Howard stood with his hands hanging at his sides as if he wanted to be able to draw quickly.

"Fixing the roof."

The officer glanced down the driveway and across the street at the collection of cars his friends had arrived in. "What's your name?"

"Jack Conley."

"Are you a professional roofer, Mr. Conley?" The officer's voice held a distinct ring of doubt.

"No, I'm a firefighter. I just need to fix the hole in my garage roof. Do I need a permit or something?" Jack wanted to stick his hands in his back pockets to do something with them, but he also didn't want to make any sudden moves.

Christa Maurice

The cop rested one hand on his gun and moved one foot back. His scowled deepened. "Okay, pal, what's the story?"

"I told you. I'm fixing my garage roof." Jack stepped back. He didn't know many cops, but he recognized a firing position when he saw one. Was this guy going to pull his gun because they were fixing the garage roof? Over the officer's shoulder, Jack noticed a police van glide to a stop across the street.

"It's not your garage roof. This house is owned by Katherine Pelham," the officer growled, snapping Jack's attention back to the big man in front of him.

"Well, yeah, she's—"

"Vince!" Katherine's door banged against the railing. Her voice rang so sharp Jack nearly flinched. The cop did. His expression lost all confidence. Jack heard a hammer clatter behind him. He glanced back and saw Kevin and Dan scrambling for the tool as it slid off the roof into the weeds at the property line. Katherine noticed none of this because her eyes were fixed on Officer Howard. "What are you doing here?"

"I thought something fishy was going on." The officer seemed to shrink. His voice developed a minor whine.

Katherine walked down the steps and planted herself between Jack and the officer. "Your response time is slipping. I called you over a year ago." Jack thought he heard ice shattering in her voice.

"Yeah, about that." The officer pulled his feet together and shifting his hands away from the gun. His shoulders slumped. He looked more like a kid in trouble with every passing moment. "I meant to get back to you."

"I'm sure you did." Katherine folded her arms. "But as you can see, I've got it handled now."

"Listen, I'm sorry I didn't get back to you." The officer fidgeted. "I kept meaning to call and things kept getting in the way. I didn't hear you got engaged again. He's a fireman?"

"I didn't." Jack heard a crackle in her tone. "And it's firefighter."

"You—ah…" He glanced over her shoulder at Jack. "So he's not…?"

"He's my tenant, if it's any of your business. I had to rent out the bottom half of the house."

The officer scratched his head. "I'm sorry about that, Kathy."

"I'm sure you are. You seem to be sorry about a lot of things." She shifted, and Jack read contempt in every muscle in her body. "Maybe it would be easier if you kept the promises you made. Or is this how this brotherhood thing works? The promise is to the brother, and once he's gone, it doesn't count anymore?"

"Kathy, that's not fair. I miss Gary as much as you do."

"That isn't the issue. When Gary was alive, I never said anything about the amount of time he spent with his buddies. I never complained about the weekends I spent alone because he was at a gun show or the shooting range. I didn't even complain when you sainted Gary after he was killed. I will complain about promises not kept. You got your war hero, and I was left with a house I couldn't afford, a pile of bills taller than me, a leaky garage roof," she gestured toward the garage.

Jack had to hop back a step to avoid being backhanded.

"And nobody to turn to. You said you would help me, and you didn't."

Vince's eyes went from Katherine to Jack to the garage and back to Katherine. His expression set and hardened. "Well, I'm glad you feel so martyred, Ms. Pelham. And if you think the Fire Department is going to be any better, you're wrong."

He turned and walked down the driveway to his patrol car gesturing to the other officer who had stepped out of her van.

Katherine stood watching. Jack wanted to reach out to her, but he didn't know what kind of reception he'd get. She looked as if she might explode if jostled. When both vehicles disappeared behind the neighbor's pine tree, she turned, keeping her back to Jack, and bolted into her apartment.

Jack turned back to the garage open mouthed. Dan and Lew stared. Kevin waved him toward the house. Swallowing hard, Jack walked up to Katherine's door and knocked.

"It's open!" she shouted.

He moved through the door as if he expected the floor to collapse and looked up the narrow staircase. She stepped out of a doorway at the top of the stairs.

"Do you need something?" she asked.

"I wanted to know if you were okay."

"Okay?" She smiled, but he saw a trace of bitterness. She folded her arms. "As okay as I am ever meant to be."

Jack walked up the first four steps. "Are you sure? I thought you might want to talk. That seemed like kind of an ugly scene out there." He sensed a little coldness but wasn't sure if it was directed at him or left over from Officer Howard.

She shrugged. "It was coming. I knew he'd call or come over eventually. It's not like he didn't know where I lived. He was here three or four times a week before."

Jack climbed two more steps. She seemed far away, and he didn't know if he could close the distance between them. But this wasn't like when she withdrew from him. It felt more as if she were lost and he had to find her if he could. "So. Your fiancé was a cop?"

"Yes. We got engaged right after he joined the force." She glanced over her shoulder at the pictures on the wall.

Jack climbed the last three stairs. "Is this your engagement picture?" Now she stood only an arm's length away, and he still didn't think he could reach her. He focused on the picture on the wall. She looked very young and happy in her burgundy dress displaying her ring for the camera. Next to her stood a muscular guy wearing a police dress uniform. Jack couldn't quite make out his face because the bill of his hat shaded what it didn't cover. "You look beautiful."

She folded her arms. "It was a long time ago."

"Some things don't change."

She bit her lip.

Jack made a pretense of studying the other pictures. There was a snapshot of Katherine with a woman who could only be her mother at Katherine's college graduation. Another of Katherine on a beach in bikini. And one of Gary beside a car. Jack could see the other man's face there. He had a strong jaw and dark eyes. He could understand how a woman would be attracted to a guy like him, but Jack still couldn't understand why he hated dogs.

"Are you guys going to finish today?" She stepped backward into the room behind her.

"Sure." He looked over her head into her kitchen. "Shingling won't take any time at all." Her kitchen was carpeted in a tan Berber carpeting and seemed crowded, but he supposed it had been a bedroom before the remodeling. The faucet dripped into a coffee cup.

"I'm sure your friends are waiting for you out there. You shouldn't keep them waiting."

There was more dismissal in her tone than he was used to, and it made him want to hang around. He studied her face. Fury, like an impending thunderstorm, gleamed in her eyes. But her jaw, though clenched tight, shivered with tears.

"Kate," he said.

"I'd like to be alone, if you don't mind." She spoke through clenched teeth.

He nodded. "You know where to find me." He walked down the steps, hoping she would change her mind, but she didn't.

They had all gotten back to work, but stopped when he climbed on the roof.

"Did he say her fiancé was Gary Ringer?" Lew blurted out.

Jack nodded. "His name was Gary. Why, do you know who he was?"

"Oh man, yeah. You don't remember?"

Jack leaned forward. "What?"

"When her fiancé died."

"What do you know, Lew?" Kevin settled on the peak of the roof.

"A couple of years ago, Gary Ringer was shot by another cop. My cousin's a 911 dispatcher, she saved all the articles." Lew looked at the house and shook his head. "Man, that was awful."

"I remember that," Dan said. "It was all over the papers for weeks. There was an inquest and everything. She was that guy's fiancé?"

"She's gotta be. I'll get the articles from my cousin."

Jack looked at his hands. He remembered reading about Officer Gary Ringer being shot, but it had been years ago. He recalled some kind of scandal, but not the details or the pictures in the paper. It didn't seem important at the time. Tragic and difficult, but he hadn't matched up the name until now. If she had been engaged to Gary Ringer, it explained a lot.

* * * *

Katherine sank down on the top step. Fat tears slid down her cheeks. She heard the pounding resume on the garage roof. At the rate they were going, it would be finished before long, and Jack would be waiting around for her to open up. It would be so easy. She'd already found herself telling him things she never told anyone. He cared enough to make sure she was all right. It had taken all her will power not to sink into his arms and let him kiss it all away. From the look in his eyes, he would be more than willing. Gary had never been this much of a true companion.

'If you think the Fire Department is going to be any better, you're wrong.'

Vince was right, of course. She couldn't leave herself open for that again. No matter how much she cared for Jack. No matter how much she wanted him. No matter how her heart ached for him, she couldn't have him. He was off limits. She pressed her forehead against her knees and sobbed.

* * * *

Jack walked to the station on Friday in a black mood. He'd stayed home all of this week just to see Katherine, but on Sunday had been the awkward laundry thing and then Wednesday the cops showed up. She hadn't left her apartment all day yesterday. Once, while he was in the backyard with Archer, he saw the curtains twitch in the room beside her

kitchen, but other than that—nothing. He'd even kept the stereo off to
hear the sound of her footsteps. He'd spent an hour yesterday lying on the
couch staring at the ceiling, willing her to come talk to him. He hadn't left
the house in case she came down.

But she hadn't. She'd stayed sequestered in her apartment.

"Hey, I got that stuff from my cousin." Lew leaped up as soon as Jack
walked into the locker room. He reached into his locker and pulled out a
scrap book. "I can't believe I didn't recognize her. She was all over the
papers."

Jack opened the first page of the scrapbook and found a newspaper
clipping about a robbery at a convenience store. He looked up at Lew.

"Beth is kind of a police groupie. It's back here further." Lew flipped
through several pages before he stopped. "Here."

Jack looked at the picture before the headline. She wore a navy blue
dress he recognized, and her hair was pulled up. The picture had been
taken from above, but she had her head cocked back as if she were staring
at some high point on the church wall, and he could see her face. She
looked serene. To an outsider she seemed calm, but Jack could see how
tightly she held her jaw and the tension around her eyes. An officer in
dress uniform sat next to her, but he had his head tilted forward and all
Jack could see was the top of his head and his large black hands clasping
hers. Vince Howard. Surrounding them on all sides were police officers in
dress uniforms leaving her pale face floating in a sea of blue. He wanted
to go home and hug her.

"Officer Ringer's fiancée at yesterday's service," Kevin read the
caption. "Officer Ringer, photo supplied by Arden Police Department,"
he read under the picture beside it.

Jack didn't even look at the picture of Gary. He couldn't tear his eyes
from Katherine. She looked so strong and steady and calm. He turned the
page and immediately wanted to punch the photographer who took this
picture. In this one, Katherine was being carried down the church steps by
Howard and another officer, her face crumpled with grief.

"That one is from the *Cambridge Sun*. Beth hates it, but my grandmother
gave it to her." Lew commented. "*The Journal* only printed nice pictures.
They let her have her dignity. Beth says *The Sun* goes for the throat."

"*The Sun* is only a half step above a tabloid," Kevin added.

Jack didn't say anything. All he could see was Katherine surrounded
on all sides by police. In every picture, she had someone in a blue uniform
at her elbow or with an arm around her shoulders. According to the
articles Jack skimmed when he could tear his eyes from the pictures, an

investigation cleared the officer whose gun discharged during a struggle with a suspect, killing Gary. They described her fiancé as a paragon of police virtue, listing his exemplary record and mentioned Katherine having won an award for teaching the previous year.

And three years later, they hadn't even been able to call her back when her garage roof started leaking.

"What a bunch of jerks," he snarled.

"Excuse me?" Kevin asked rearing back.

"Look at them, all circling around her trying to get some of her fiancé's glory to rub off on them. Trying to cover up the fact that one of their guys screwed up and killed one of their own. And then they dumped her." Jack snapped the scrapbook closed.

"Gentlemen, can we get the day going?" The captain stood in the doorway with a clipboard under his elbow.

"How could they?" Jack shoved the scrapbook at Lew. "They left her high and dry."

"Left who high and dry?" the captain asked.

"His landlady. She's Officer Ringer's widow. Sort of." Lew placed the scrapbook in his locker.

"I remember that incident. He was shot in some kind of messy business, wasn't he? She's your landlady?"

"How could they forget about her?" Jack asked the captain. "How could they promise to help her, and then not even return her calls?"

The captain shrugged. "It's hard to look at a widow and not want to promise her anything. Lots of times you end up making promises you can't keep. And when she's not a legal widow..."

"But Cap, we keep our promises," Dan pointed out. He stood by the door to the showers with his arms folded, looking almost as angry as Jack. "I'm still on Daisy Wells' speed dial. And that was five years ago."

Cap shrugged. "Some of us take our promises more seriously than others. And sometimes sticky business gets in the way. Ringer was shot by another cop. They had to protect their own."

"That's not how you protect your own," Dan grumbled.

"We never accidentally shoot anyone," Cap pointed out.

"But she thinks we're like them," Jack said.

"Well, you'll have to change her mind. Now, can we have lineup, or would you rather discuss your new girlfriend a little more?"

"She's not my girlfriend."

"Not yet," Kevin said, walking past him out of the locker room.

* * * *

Katherine knew she would have to face him eventually. She lay on her bed watching the sun creep across the ceiling. Yesterday, she'd avoided him the same way she'd avoided him Thursday. She stayed in. She'd even gone to the library to stock up on books and she'd already finished two of them. The third was not going to last the day. At least there was school to look forward to tomorrow. It would give her a good excuse to be away. She had lesson plans ready to be disrupted by assemblies for the rest of the school year. Her stomach had dropped when she realized school would be out in two months, and she had all summer to spend with her new tenant.

She couldn't avoid him all that time, even if she got another job again. And she couldn't be near him without wanting him.

Sticking her foot out from under the covers, she tested the air. Cool but not cold. She slid out of bed. The floor felt a little colder than she liked, but she couldn't do anything about it if she wanted to afford the heating bill. She padded to the kitchen to make a cup of tea without a robe or slippers. Maybe the cold would shock some sense into her, but she couldn't help wondering how warm it must be in Jack's bed, curled up between him and Archer, languid and sated and... Katherine shook her head to drive out the image. Maybe she should get her own dog to warm her bed. Significantly less trouble than worrying about Jack every time he went on duty.

In the kitchen, she noticed the faucet had stopped dripping, leaving her with only a half cup of water for tea. She grimaced. Now she'd have to fight the knob to get water. She grabbed the knob with both hands because, since the last time Randy 'fixed' it, it refused to budge otherwise, and twisted.

The knob snapped off in her hand. Cold water sprayed up, fountaining against the ceiling.

Katherine stumbled backward, dropping the knob. "Oh my God!" She stared at the water showering off the ceiling for a moment before diving under the sink and pulling out the pots and pans. She leaned back to check which side was spraying, banging her head on the cupboard. Then she ducked under again and grabbed the right shut off valve, which promptly fell off in her hand. She opened her hand and looked at the knob. It was cracked clear across.

Randy. That idiot Randy. He broke the valve and put it on anyway.

She scrambled to her feet, gaping at the disaster. Cold water splashed against the ceiling, ran down the walls, and soaked into the carpet, making it squish under her feet. In minutes it would be raining in Jack's kitchen.

Jack.

"Jack!" She screamed. She thundered down the stairs and outside, clutching the shut off valve. She slipped at the corner of the house and almost went down in the oregano, but caught herself on the edge of the porch.

"Jack!" She almost managed to stop before slamming bodily into Jack's door and began beating on it. Inside, Archer barked like a wild thing.

* * * *

Jack rolled out of bed when the alarm sounded and couldn't understand why he couldn't get his turnout pants pulled up. His feet wouldn't go into the boots and the suspenders were missing altogether. He also couldn't understand why Archer was at the station. The alarm sounded funny, more like a woman screaming. He staggered across the floor and about the time he tripped into the door jam, he realized Archer wasn't at the station. He wasn't at the station either. And these weren't his turnouts, they were jeans. The screaming woman alarm wasn't the alarm, it was Katherine screaming his name.

And it was raining in the kitchen.

He yanked open the front door.

"The faucet—it broke—" Katherine thrust a small silver object at him. "Water everywhere!"

Jack looked at the object. It kind of looked like a knob, but it had cracked clear across. Katherine was wet and barefoot in a night gown. Water rained through the ceiling. The pieces came together as Archer charged past him out the door.

"Wait a minute." He ran to the back door and flung it open. He grabbed the entire toolbox. He ran around the side of the house with Katherine on his heels and took the stairs two at a time.

Water shot out of the knob stem straight to the ceiling, splashing down in all directions and soaking into the carpet, which explained the rain.

Jack grabbed a heavy glass pot off the floor and put it over the knob stem redirecting most of the water into the sink. He ducked under the sink, snapping open his toolbox at the same time. He located his small wrench by feel. A moment later he had shut off the water. Then he leaned back on his heels and listened to the dripping from the ceiling for a minute. When he turned around Katherine had come to a stop in the doorway with one fist pressed against her mouth and the other gripping the door frame.

"Oh no." She moaned. "Look at the ceiling. Look at the floor. Oh God, it's soaked everything in your kitchen."

"I can fix it." He stood and found the knob in the sink. The screw was stripped. "I'll replace this piece, and you're good as new."

"New is what led to this." She wrapped her arms around herself and started shivering.

Then Jack noticed she was wearing only a white nightgown. A wet, white nightgown. He tried to focus on her face, but it was hard not to stare. She was sexier than he'd imagined. Especially with her arms wrapped around her, mounding her breasts together. Through the wet cotton, he could make out her dusky pink nipples, erect from the cold. The nightgown also plastered across her hips, giving him a perfect view of her narrow waist and generous hips. He knew he was too cold and too groggy to be this aroused, but couldn't convince his body of it.

"Then I'll make it better than new." He walked across the room and put his hand on her shoulder. Her skin felt icy. "You're freezing."

"It doesn't matter. I'm so stupid. I should have known better than to hire the school janitor to put in plumbing. God only knows what else he screwed up." She hung her head. Some of her hair slithered forward and started dripping on the floor.

"School janitor?" Jack paused remembering the blond guy answering her door when he came to sign the lease and saying 'you could call me that' when Jack asked if he was a friend. He'd assumed they were more than friends, not less.

"Oh, Randy's fine building things, but he doesn't know the first thing about plumbing, no matter what he says."

"Randy put this in?" Blondie was the school janitor? Nothing more than a hired hand? And when he came over that night, he was coming to fix the sink?

"Yes. Oh, he is dumb as a box of rocks, and I'm dumber for hiring him in the first place."

Jack put his arms around her shoulders trying to tell himself he just wanted to offer comfort and not believing a word of it."I can fix it. It'll be all right."

She leaned against him sighing.

His heart pounded. Her breath whispered across his bare chest. She shifted so her body pressed against his, warm and wet. Her damp, wild hair clung to his shoulder. He let his hand slide down the slope of her back, catching on the fabric of her nightgown, melding her tighter to his body. Her breath caught.

She turned her face up, locking his eyes to hers. Her parted lips trembled. Then she rose up on her toes, wrapped her arms around his neck, and pressed her lips against his.

* * * *

Though she may have initiated the kiss, she lost control of it immediately. Jack pulled her against his hard body as he tasted her lips in a leisurely pace. She warmed under his expert touch. Her blood temperature rose to a rolling boil. His hands slid up her back, leaving scorched skin behind and dragging her nightgown up to the top of her thighs. Her whole body smoldered.

She moaned, incapable of coherent thought. Somewhere in her mind she knew she shouldn't be doing this.

But she couldn't remember why. She tried to follow the thought. It seemed important to someone, but that someone wasn't her at this moment. Her feet no longer touched the floor. The only solid thing in her universe was Jack. He had one arm secure around her back keeping her body tight against his while his other hand caressed her cheek. Trailing down her body, he brushed the side of her breast, making it ache to be caressed more. His heart beat against her ribs.

Breathing quickening, he lifted his soft mouth from hers and started working his way down her throat, murmuring her name. She buried her fingers in his wet hair. Her head bent forward. She brushed her lips along his collar bone, tasting his skin.

Her hands slipped across his powerful shoulders, pulling her body against his. Skin burned under her fingers. One of his hands trailed around her waist. It dipped down, cupping her buttocks. Something in her belly knotted and opened at the same time and a liquid heat spilled out. His hands slipped under her nightgown and over her hip. She gasped as his hands closed around her naked waist. He could almost encircle her with his fingers and they burned into her like molten steel.

Archer's bark jerked her back to reality and out of Jack's arms.

She stumbled into the door frame across the hall and put one hand over her mouth. It felt bruised and swollen. The cold room and the wet carpet under her feet shocked her. She looked down at herself and realized her cotton nightgown had become transparent when it got wet.

"Nothing like making a bad situation worse," she whispered. Her throat threatened to close on a sob. Her entire body wanted to fall forward into his arms. Back where she felt warm and safe and beautiful.

Jack looked stunned. "What? What bad situation?" He reached for her.

Christa Maurice

"I can't do this." She whirled around and sprinted for her bedroom, all the while trying to shake her nightgown back down to cover her.

Jack followed close behind. "Why can't you do this? You just did."

She grabbed her robe and held it in front of her.

"What are you doing in my bedroom?" she demanded. She wanted to stop shivering, to present some kind of composed exterior, but at the moment she was hot, cold and shattered. The world had flattened and shifted. Not square any more, that's what he'd said about the door. She didn't feel at all square either.

Jack took one more step inside her bedroom. "I'm trying to get a simple answer."

Archer walked between them and jumped on her bed. Jack's eyes followed him enviously. Glancing over her shoulder, she saw Archer had made himself comfortable in the exact center of the bed. She took another step back and bumped into the mattress. He might never forgive her for this.

It didn't matter. No more heroes.

"I can't. Are you going to fix the faucet or not?"

Jack threw his hands up. "Of course I'm going to fix the faucet. I said I would. Katherine, what is going on?"

"Nothing." She yanked her robe on and tied the belt so tightly it threatened to cut her in half. Her mattress pressed against the backs of her thighs, and Jack loomed in the doorway, not even an arm's length away. It would be so easy to reach out to him. To pull him closer. Everything seemed less square with each passing moment. The sooner she got him out of her bedroom, out of her apartment, the better. Before she did something else she'd regret.

"Nothing is going on."

"Is there another guy? I know it's not Randy."

"What do you know about Randy?"

"Damn little, but I know you're not seeing him." Jack's voice verged on a shout, but she refused to flinch under his anger.

Katherine pursed her lips. "I don't think that's any of your business."

"Oh really? Is that before or after what just happened? Because I think it might change a few things between us." He gestured toward her kitchen, smacking his hand against the wall. She flinched. Then she noticed a long thin bruise on his shoulder that looked very new. It was right about where she'd kissed him.

"Well," Katherine's mind went blank. She wanted it to change things. Wanted more. Before she knew what it was, she'd wanted it. And now—

now she didn't know how she'd survive the day knowing his hands would never touch again. "Well, it doesn't. Do you want to move? I'll let you break your lease." Her knees almost gave out. She had not planned on saying that. She hadn't planned any of this. The landlord book didn't have any text on dealing with overwhelming attraction to your tenant.

What if he did move out? Out of sight would not be out of mind with Jack Conley. Especially with him working three blocks away. She had visions of herself deciding to take long walks around the neighborhood just to walk past the station on the off chance she would see him.

"Move," he repeated, taking an uneven step backward out of her bedroom. "Move? No. I don't want to move." Opening his mouth to speak, he stopped and shook his head. "I'm going to need a part to fix that sink. I'll have to get it when the hardware store opens. Archer, come."

Archer leaped off the bed behind her and followed Jack down the stairs. Katherine managed to keep her feet until she heard the door close. Then she let go and sank down on the bed. Her whole body ached with wanting him and her cheeks were scraped raw by his rough face. Everything scraped raw. She pulled her knees up to her chin and rolled sideways on the bed.

What if he changed his mind? What if he decided to break the lease? What if she lost him? And if she didn't lose him, how would she be able to face him now that he knew she slept without panties?

* * * *

Jack managed to get as far as the foyer, but had to collapse on the two odd steps sticking out of the wall. They would have been the beginning of the staircase. Then, he'd be able to walk upstairs and shake some sense into her. He'd be able to bend her back on that bed and finish what they'd started. Slouching against the wall, he listened for her. Whatever she was doing, she was being quiet about it.

He'd thought everything would be all right when she told him Randy was the school janitor.

He'd thought when she kissed him it would work out.

He'd thought when she responded so eagerly all the uncertainty was over.

Break his lease?

Treat her gently, his grandmother said. Well, what had happened could hardly be considered gentle.

But well worth it. Closing his eyes, he recalled her expression. He could go to his grave happy with the memory of her sweet face turning up toward his. Those soft, dark eyes focusing on him with desire. He'd been too stunned to react. She'd dropped her defenses before he'd had to breach them and been so pliable and soft in his arms. A little hesitant, but with very little direction, eager. The light touch of her hands on his shoulders. The texture of her hot mouth brushing his skin. The breathy gasp when he wrapped his hands around her waist. He could still feel her body pressed against his.

He stood up. It was time for a cold shower. Even wet and cold, she had the ability to arouse him more than he liked. Stopping in the bathroom door, he savored the memory of standing in her bedroom door. Even furious and yelling at him, he'd wanted her. He'd wanted to step forward, take her in his arms and lay her back on her bed. But his grandmother told him to treat her gently.

That wouldn't be treating her gently. And he would never be happy with once. He wanted always. Kevin said he wasn't the type to settle down, but Kevin hadn't gotten a good look at Katherine. Hadn't listened to her laugh or seen the well of despair in her eyes. With a little persistence and a little patience he could heal her hurt and hear her laugh for the rest of his life.

That meant a cold shower and a long talk. He turned on the cold water full blast and stepped under it without taking off his jeans.

Chapter 7

When she opened her door at his knock four hours later, she looked hunted and afraid. He had mopped up his kitchen and bathroom and taken Archer for a long run waiting for the hardware store to open. That pretty much burned out most of the frustration, but upon seeing her again, he realized it hadn't come near to reducing his desire.

"You came back," she said. She dressed in worn jeans and a holey sweater. Her eyes looked a little puffy and her face seemed pale as if she had been crying, and he wondered who for. Him? Herself? Gary?

"I told you I would." Trying not to touch her on the cramped landing, he stepped through the door holding up a plastic hardware store bag. "I got what I need to fix the faucet."

She stumbled up a step bringing her eye level with him. She held one arm across her chest. "You don't have to do this. I can get Randy—"

"No." Brushing against her sort of accidentally, he walked past her up the steps. He wanted to gather her to him again. She looked as if she needed to be held, but he didn't want a repeat of this morning. After what happened this morning, he was pretty sure he'd end up shouting at her. They had to talk, and they couldn't do that at top volume. "He wouldn't fix it right this time, either. I promised I would fix it, and I will."

She followed him up the stairs to the kitchen where she'd carpeted the floor with pastel bath towels in an attempt to clean up. All her pots and pans stacked in front of the stove except the one he'd used to redirect the fountain earlier. For some reason she hadn't moved it. His tool box sat where he'd dropped it as did the wrench under the sink. Did she not even want to touch his tools? Was she that angry? Or was this fear? He hated the idea she might be afraid of him.

"How bad is the damage downstairs?" she asked. She stopped in the doorway and stood with her arms wrapped around herself. The pose brought to mind the image of her in her wet white nightgown. No, the long run that had worn out Archer had not cooled the tiniest portion of his passion.

He crawled under the sink to attach the shut off knob and get her out of his line of vision. "It wasn't bad. A lot of the water went down the walls and into the basement. I have to wash a few dishes, but otherwise I'm all cleaned up."

"Nothing was damaged?"

"No. Most of what came through the ceiling went into the bathroom anyway." He had to work to keep his voice light. Tension crackling under the surface of her words. Ducking out from under the sink, he looked around the room. "It looks like you need to do some laundry."

"Yes, I will. I can do it while you're on duty tomorrow night if you don't want me underfoot." Her voice sounded soft with hopelessness.

"You won't be underfoot." Then he stood up and moved the pot covering the knob stem.

"I can wash your dishes for you. You know, to make up for getting them dirty in the first place."

He looked at her, trying for once to see her as a person and not as someone he wanted to hold. She seemed very small and unnerved. As he watched, her cheeks turned pink, blending into the scratches he left there this morning. Her shoulders tensed, and he wondered if he would find her in the back yard playing fetch with Archer again. Between him taking Archer for runs and her playing fetch, the dog would be in great shape. They would still be wound up like tin toys, but the dog would sleep soundly. "It's up to you. If you want you can get a load started now."

"I suppose I could." She started gathering damp towels off the floor. "Hopefully we'll get a warm spell soon so the carpet will dry out."

He turned away, hoping she would feel comfortable enough to come closer if he wasn't facing her. This was like coaxing wild deer to eat out of his hand. He dropped the washer in place and then looked back at it. There should have been another washer there. He picked his washer off and double checked. No washer. "I think I found the problem."

She stopped next to him with a pile of towels draped over her arm. "What is it?"

"Randy installed this?"

She nodded, looking from his eyes to his hands.

"He forgot the washer. He must have kept tightening until the screw stripped and the stem snapped."

She leaned forward and looked at the knob stem. He could smell her hair and feel her hip and arm brushing against his. Maybe Archer would like to go for another long run this afternoon.

"I am so stupid. I should have known better than to hire him."

Her sour comment brought him back to the subject at hand. "It's not your fault. He told you he could do it." From this position, he could put his arm around her shoulders. He could pull her against him in a comforting way. Just comforting, not attacking. Wait, hadn't he been trying to comfort her this morning?

"He said he could, but obviously he couldn't."

Jack shifted away before the urge to draw her back into his arms overwhelmed him. "Well, he lied." He dropped the washer in place. "I think we should talk about what happened this morning."

Tension flickered through her. She stepped away leaving one towel on the floor. The one under his feet. "I don't think there's anything to talk about."

"Katherine, something happened here. Something really…good. I think we need to talk." He turned, crouching to get out a screwdriver, and realized she had left. He heard the door at the bottom of the stairs close. Well, she wasn't talking, but she was doing her laundry. That had to count for something.

* * * *

Katherine opened the washer lid and stuffed her towels into it. This was not a good decision. Now, in an effort to get out of a conversation she didn't want to have, she had locked herself into being around him all day.

She hadn't been sure he would come back after this morning, regardless of what he said. Promises were made to be broken, weren't they?

But he had come back. She had listened to him moving around in his apartment this morning, as she tried to sop up the water in the carpet before it filtered through and made his mess bigger. He'd taken a shower first, which seemed like an odd decision since they were both soaked already, unless that kiss had affected him as much as it had her.

The thought of his kiss brought all the sensations of it rushing back to her. The dizzying, aching, hunger of it. She had never felt so overwhelmed. The touch of his lips on hers, his hands pulling her against him, the sweet, salty taste of his skin. Her entire body burned with the contact. That one kiss held more passion than her entire relationship with Gary.

Sucking in a sharp breath, she shivered. She needed to get her wits about her before she saw him, otherwise she might end up deeper in this mess. She'd said she would wash his dishes. Maybe elbow deep in soapy water she'd be able to keep her mind off his body and his lips and his…

The washer waited for her to add detergent and close the lid. She looked around for her detergent and realized she'd forgotten it. Left on autopilot, her brain obviously didn't work very well. Running back upstairs would put her back in his company before she was ready. If she was ever going to be ready. She borrowed a cup of his laundry soap and started upstairs.

Leaning in the bathroom before venturing to the kitchen, she checked the ceiling. The water hadn't stained the bathroom paint at all, but the kitchen ceiling tiles had a couple of wet spots that would become ugly brown stains. He'd heaped all of his dishes on the counter. She started filling one bowl of the sink and found dish soap in the cupboard in exactly the spot she'd kept it when this had been her kitchen. When she had the wash sink filled, she lifted out the light blue dish drainer and started filling the other bowl with rinse water. She picked up the first plate and looked at it. His dishes were real ceramic. White with black stripes around the rims. Eight each of plates, dessert plates, saucers, dainty teacups, and soup bowls. Why did he have such a nice dishes? When she met Gary, he had been eating off paper plates so he wouldn't have to wash. But Gary had been twenty and only on his own for two years. Maybe if he'd gotten to be Jack's age as a bachelor, he would have gotten some real dishes.

Why was Jack still a bachelor? Was every woman in the city blind? If he weren't a firefighter, Katherine would have been overjoyed to have him look at her. To be honest, she was overjoyed anyway. What had she thought before he moved in? Polite, handy and heroic? He'd saved the day this morning. She didn't know what she would have done without him. Called Randy? She shuddered, imagining the scene this morning played out with Randy. No, she'd never let him touch her. She'd have shouted at him, skipping the kisses. And she'd have managed to put on some clothes before he showed up.

Polite, handy, and heroic. If only it weren't for that last part.

She picked up a dainty teacup and dipped it into the water.

"You are washing the dishes. Here, I'll dry." He opened a drawer and took out a dish towel covered with butterflies.

She wanted to tell him no, but with him so close she doubted she could form a coherent sentence. Dipping the teacup in the rinse water she held it out to him. "Nice dishes."

"They used to be my mom's. She got a new set when I moved out on my own and gave the old ones to me. I think she got a new set so she could give me the old ones. I never use these teacups." He held one up and it looked tiny in his hand. "I keep them to keep the set together. Did you get your towels going?"

"Yes." She cleared her throat because her voice seemed to be stuck in it. "Yes. I had to appropriate some of your laundry detergent."

"You what?"

She glanced up at him and realized her mistake. Looking at him was bad. It made thinking more difficult than necessary. Thinking was already nearly impossible. "Borrowed. I forgot mine upstairs."

"I thought you took off pretty fast." He picked up a stack of saucers and put them in the cupboard. "You know I still think we should talk about this."

"I'd rather not. I'm trying to forget it happened." She blinked back tears. That wasn't true. She would never forget. She didn't want to. No matter how much she wished it hadn't happened, she would never want to forget.

"Why?"

How could he sound so reasonable? So calm? Did he feel that detached after their little encounter this morning? "Because I just—I can't—Will you stop pushing me?"

He stepped back from the sink. "I'm not pushing. As I remember, I wasn't the one who started things this morning."

"Yes, well, I'm humiliated and would rather let it go." She dipped her hands in the hot water feeling for another plate.

"I was delighted."

She turned on him. Delighted. He had the nerve to say delighted? He—he looked hurt. Her fury drained away. "Oh, Jack. Can't you see it's not you I don't want, but what you represent?"

"What do I represent?"

"You're Pandora's Box. You're the worst thing in the world for me."

Jack folded his arms across his chest. "I'm not very good at debates, so why don't you spell it out?"

Dish water dripped off her fingers and splashed on the floor. "Do you know the story of Pandora's Box?"

"Don't use your education on me. My sister does that, and I hate it." His jaw tightened.

Katherine looked at him. "I think no matter how nice the box is to look at or how much I want to open it, I shouldn't. There's bad things in there. Do you follow me?"

"No. That doesn't make any sense at all. First of all, I'm not a box." He tried to smile, but it wilted into a smirk

"I was making an allusion to Pandora's Box. Pandora was given a beautiful box by the gods. They told her to never open it. Once they told her she couldn't look in the box, it was all she could think about. So she opened it and out flew all the plagues of the world. Don't you see? All I have to do is know that I can't have you to want you." It sounded plausible, even if she didn't believe it.

"So you're trying to say it's not me you want."

"It's not you. It's that I can't have you."

"Why can't you?"

Katherine held her breath. How was she supposed to explain to him about her vow to never fall in love with another hero when she couldn't justify it to herself? Telling him she couldn't date her tenant would be too easily fixed. He'd move out and start sending flowers. Jack seemed like the sending flowers sort. The rest of his life he'd be trying to woo her, and she would spend the rest of her life resisting. They were a shipwreck. "We're wrong for each other, Jack. I would end up hurting you as much, or more, than you would hurt me. Trust me, I've been there. This bed of roses has too many thorns."

He stared at her, but sagged back against the counter as if he'd lost the will to stand up.

"I think this is going to be bad for both of us. I don't know if I'm ready to start another relationship." It would be best for both of them, she told herself. She had to be an adult. Clasping her wet hands together controlled some of their shaking. One stride would take her into his arms. One stride and everything would be all right, for now. But the first time she heard the siren might undo her. "I'm afraid." That was as close to the truth as she could manage.

He surveyed her for a long minute. She watched his eyes move across her body, not lingering anywhere. Then he sighed and shrugged. "If that's how you feel. We can still be friends, right?"

She nodded.

"Are we going to finish the dishes?"

She turned back to the sink. The water had gotten cold and her hands were shaking so hard she could barely pick up the plates. How was she supposed to be friends with him when standing next to him sent her into a slow burn? She handed him the last plate. "I'm going to check my towels."

Katherine fled to the basement. She pulled the heavy wet towels out of the washer and stuffed them in the dryer, trying not to focus on Jack. Not think about his smile. Not think of his eyes. Not think about him at all. By the time she went back upstairs, he'd moved into the living room and was sitting at the coffee table with a box in his hands.

"What's that?"

"Trivial Pursuit."

"I haven't played that since college."

"You have time while your towels dry," he suggested. "I thought we could play a round."

"Is this one of those games you're good at?" she asked, settling on the floor, keeping eighteen inches of carpet between them as a buffer. With that and the game between them, she might be able to maintain some sanity.

"You won the last game I was good at." He opened the box.

"Touché." She picked up a box of question cards. "Do you play the long version or the short version?"

"Usually short. If we're going to play the long version, I can get out Monopoly. Besides, I don't think your laundry will last that long. What color do you want?"

"Brown. Art and literature is my specialty." She smiled. It felt nice. They could be friends. They could play board games and watch TV. It would be enough.

Handing her the brown game piece, he said, "I wonder why." He took the yellow game piece out and set it in the middle of the board before handing her a die. "Roll to see who goes first."

"Where's Archer?" She looked around realizing she hadn't seen the dog since she came in.

Waving in the direction of his bedroom, Jack coughed. "Sacked out. We went for a long run this morning so he's pretty tired."

"I got you two up awfully early."

"Gotten up at worse times."

Suppressing a shudder, she tossed the die across the board. It stopped on three. "Anybody's game there."

His roll came up a six. "My lucky day," he grumbled. Rolling again, he got a four. "A history question please."

"What do the fighting ships Arizona, Oklahoma and Utah have in common?" she read. Then she flipped the card over and looked at the answer.

"They were all sunk at Pearl Harbor."

"Do you sit around night memorizing the answers? You get a wedge."

He took out his wedge while she rolled and moved her piece onto Entertainment. "You could take Art and Literature."

"I like to get the difficult ones out of the way first."

Jack pulled a card. "What film's climax takes place on the face of Mount Rushmore?"

"Wait. I know this one. It's a Hitchcock movie." Katherine rested her fingertips on the table. "It's not *Rear Window*. It's not *Strangers on a Train*. Is it *Vertigo*?"

"*North by Northwest*. Also known as *The Man in Lincoln's Nose*." He intoned the answer like a game show host as he slid the card into the back of the box.

"It is not. *The Man in Lincoln's Nose*?"

"I told you, I have a friend who's a movie junkie. My turn." Picking up the die, he rolled. A four moved him onto Entertainment.

Katherine groaned. "What film featured Bogey as Dobbsy?"

Jack smiled. "You're not going to get mad are you?"

"Don't tell me you know the answer to this too?" She put the card in the back of the box. "I knew it. You memorized all the answers. You're a…a ringer."

"*The Treasure of Sierra Madre*." His long fingers flicked the die in her direction as he got out his wedge. "And I'm not a ringer, I just happen to know a lot of useless trivia."

She rolled a five and landed on Arts and Literature. "Finally. Maybe I can catch up."

"Maybe." Pulling a card he grinned. "Who was Time's Man of the Year for 1938?"

"That isn't the Art and Literature question," Katherine protested, leaning over his shoulder. The scent of his soap enveloped her. Irish Spring. She should have stuck with her eighteen inches of buffer.

"No cheating."

"I want to see the card."

He held up the card so she could see he had indeed read the Art and Literature question.

"Oh good lord. I don't know. 1938? Teddy Roosevelt?"

"Hitler."

Katherine flopped on the floor. "You're killing me."

"And for the record, I have not stacked the cards against you either." He rolled a two and moved onto Science and Nature. "Question please."

Sitting up, she pulled a card and laughed. "I should have gotten this one. I can quote Shakespeare in my sleep."

"But what's my question?"

"What venomous snake is known as the gentleman among snakes?"

"Boa constrictor?"

Katherine grinned. Finally, he got one wrong. "Rattlesnake."

"I should have known that." Jack raised one eyebrow.

"I know. I did." Katherine landed on roll again twice before settling on Geography. She couldn't believe she was losing so badly. It reminded her of girls in school who lost to boys they liked so the male in question could feel superior. *The way she had with Gary.*

"You have an even chance of getting this one right. Which is colder, the North or South Pole?"

"There's a difference? Gee, I'm doing so well. Got a coin I can flip?"

"Are you always such a sore loser?" Jack asked.

Katherine paused and looked at him. He had slouched against the couch, watching her with half serious eyes. Sore loser? Maybe a little. More than a little. Why? Was it her lack of one-on-one people skills again? Or couldn't she concentrate with him sitting beside her as if they hadn't nearly had sex this morning? "I'm sorry. I guess I'm a little too competitive. But you are killing me."

"I am." He grinned. "But I'm being a sore winner."

She growled, smiling. "All right. Which is colder, the North Pole or the South Pole? I guess I'll say the South Pole. It's bigger."

"You're right."

"I am?"

"That's what is says. It docsn't say the South Pole is bigger, but I'll take your word for it."

"So I get a wedge?"

"If I agree to give it to you."

The blue wedge balanced temptingly in his palm. What was he trying to do? "If you agree? Now you are being a sore winner." She reached for it.

As she stretched, he pulled it away until she found herself with her arm across his chest and her hand planted on the floor too close to his thigh. The heat of his body tangled around her like a net.

"What are you doing?" she demanded. The awkward pose brought her uncomfortably close. Another couple of inches and she'd have her lips pressed against his. She was too close to remember why that would be bad.

"I used to drive my sister crazy doing this."

"Are you going to give it to me or not?"

Raising one eyebrow in challenge, he smirked

Her breathing wanted to run rampant and there were a few other body parts that were up for the race. "Jack, please give me the wedge?" If she waited long enough, he might come to his senses before she lost hers, but how long was going to be long enough? He didn't move. "No wonder your sister hates you."

"Oh, this has nothing to do with why she hates me." His smirk broke into a full grin. "Aren't you going to try and get it?"

Katherine put her hand on his thigh this time and leaned across his lap reaching for his hand which he had drawn further away. Soon she'd be lying across his lap. What was he doing? He came up with the friends idea. Her pulse throbbed through her brain again, disrupting any useful thought patterns. "Please give me the wedge."

"Pretty please?"

She turned her head to look him in the eye. Now he really was too close. "Pretty please?"

"Of course I will give you the wedge." He didn't move to hand over the game piece. For a moment it looked as if he would lean in and kiss her again. She locked eyes with him, willing him to either kiss her or end it. Her chest constricted with anticipation, not sure which she wanted.

"Buddy." He put the piece in her hand and helped her up. He stood. "Isn't it about lunch time?"

"Lunch?" Katherine repeated. She shook her head. For some reason she couldn't remember the purpose of lunch. "I don't know."

He walked into the kitchen. "We can finish the game later. You staying for lunch?"

Katherine looked down at the blue wedge in her hand. It was the piece she wanted. However, it didn't seem to be the ending she'd hoped for. "I guess so. Do you need help?"

"No." His voice sounded a little sharp. She froze and thought she heard him draw a deep breath. "I've got everything under control. Spaghetti okay with you? Meat sauce?"

"Sure. Maybe I should check the towels." She stood up and hobbled toward the cellar stairs. Her body ached in ways she couldn't explain. It wasn't as though they'd been wrestling on the floor.

Jack met her in the short, dim hall at the top of the stairs. He reached for her and then jammed his hands in his back pockets instead. "Listen, I'm not mad. This friends thing is going to take a little getting used to. It was easier when I thought you were dating somebody else." Swallowing hard, he started to reach for her again, but dropped his hand to his side.

The friends thing had to go. It wouldn't work. It couldn't work, not with her feeling the way she did about him. "Who did you think I was dating?"

Jack scuffed the tile with his toe. "Randy."

Inappropriate laughter bubbled up and overflowed. He looked so embarrassed. So incredibly, adorably embarrassed.

"Randy! Are you kidding? What would I be doing dating Randy?"

Jack flushed. "I didn't know. I couldn't figure it out either, but he was around all the time."

"Because he was constantly fixing the faucet." Katherine sagged against the wall, chuckling. "Me and Randy, that's rich."

"It's a natural assumption. He had keys to your place."

"He doesn't have keys to my apartment," she said, a chill sweeping over her. Did Randy have keys? Had he somehow made a set while he was working on the house? Had he made a set from Jack's keys? If he had keys, he could do anything and with his ego he would think she invited him. Katherine had a sudden, horrible vision of herself trying to give a statement to one of Gary's friends. Would they even believe her? Her stomach knotted.

"I thought he had keys. Kate, relax. He probably doesn't."

"You haven't seen him around when I'm not at home, have you?" Her voice sounded too shrill to her ears.

"Kate." Jack put his hands on her shoulders. His grip felt strong and sure. His calm flowed into her. "I *thought* he had keys. I haven't seen him around. Don't get freaked out. He was inside when I came to sign the lease, and I made an assumption. And then that one day he showed up and went inside with a gym bag."

"That's what he carries his tools in." She narrowed her eyes. "You thought he was sleeping with me? What did he say?"

"Don't get mad." Jack put his hands up. "I didn't have much to go on, and I read into things a little bit. Or more than a little."

Katherine swallowed. Randy didn't have keys to her place and probably hadn't said anything to Jack that he hadn't said to her. Jack assumed something was going on, Randy fed it. She had to stop assuming the worst. Randy was harmless, and Jack had been jealous. That thought warmed her. Jack jealous. He was still watching her with concern. She raised one eyebrow. "More than a little bit?"

"A lot, then. A whole lot." He spun around and headed back to the kitchen. "I feel like I'm in high school again. I should be passing you notes in biology asking if you want to go to the dance."

"There is a dance at school in a month. I'm supposed to chaperone." She put her hands behind her back and crossed her fingers but she wasn't sure if she hoped he would accept or think she was joking. A high school dance? Why in heaven's name would he want to go to a high school dance? She didn't even want to go, she'd just drawn the wrong piece of paper out of the hat at the last teacher's meeting.

He stopped at the end of the hall and studied her. "Are you really asking me to a dance?"

"Yes." She swallowed hard.

"Do I have to rent a tux?"

"It's not the prom, a suit will do." The image of Jack wearing a suit came to mind, and she was glad they had never bothered to put a light in the hall because she could feel heat rising on her face which he wouldn't see in the dark.

"I'm not on duty, am I?"

"No." She wanted to pinch her lips closed. Wouldn't it have been easier to announce that she had worked out his schedule until summer? She had it coded into her lesson plan book, his duty days and his semi-weekly night out.

"Okay." He shrugged. "Sounds like fun. Are you going to check your laundry?" He walked around the corner into the kitchen.

"My laundry?" How had he missed that?

He leaned back into the hall. "That was why you were in the hall, wasn't it?" The kitchen light lit his face, and she could see his amused grin.

Jerking open the door she ran down the stairs.

* * * *

Jack put a pot of water on the stove to boil and started hauling vegetables out of the crisper to add to the sauce, grinning. A high school dance. She had asked him to a high school dance. There was no way she'd planned it, based on the rosy blush on her cheeks, but that didn't matter. Now that she'd asked he wasn't letting her out of it.

Even better, she knew his schedule a month in advance. Poker had been very good training for keeping that realization off his face when she let it slip. This being friends wouldn't last forever with her paying that kind of attention to detail. She'd cave and tell him what the real problem was so he could fix it and spend the rest of his life with her. Until then, there were high school dances.

From the basement, he heard her yelp so he went to the top of the stairs. "What's the matter?"

"How did this happen?" Katherine howled, which didn't answer the question at all.

Hurrying down the stairs, scanning the floor for giant furry spiders to rescue her from, he found her holding a tie dyed towel. "What's the matter?"

"Look at this." She shook out the towel and held it up for him to see.

Pink bath towel with odd blue blotches on it. Maybe not the most beautiful pattern he'd ever seen, but if she liked it... "What's wrong with it?"

"It's got blue marks all over it." Reaching in the dryer she pulled out a yellow towel with the same odd markings and draped it over the pink one on her arm before reaching in for another pink and blue towel. "I don't understand how this happened."

"My jeans." Jack cringed. "I threw a pair of jeans in there this morning and forgot all about them. They were, ah, wet." He coughed. Of course they were wet. He took a shower while wearing them.

She started pulling towels into his laundry basket. His jeans tumbled out mixed in a wad of pastel and blue towels. "I don't believe it. One pair of dark blue jeans and all my towels now come in a pretty new design."

"Except for the one you left on the upstairs floor." He stopped, realizing he shouldn't have been paying that much attention to her towels. But she shouldn't be paying that much attention to his schedule either.

She raised one eyebrow at him. "Yes, except for that one towel."

"I'm sorry, I forgot all about those jeans. I threw them in there when I left with Archer and didn't think about them again. I can buy you new towels." He stepped forward, ducking under the low hanging pipes.

"It's okay. They're still absorbent, even if they look funny. Nobody sees them but me. Especially now that Randy isn't using my bathroom." She winked.

"Hey, it was an obvious assumption."

"Oh sure, whatever you say. I thought you were making lunch." Sneering playfully, she picked up the basket.

"Well, you were yelling. I came to the rescue. I thought you were being attacked by those big black spiders you claim live down here."

"They do." She walked past him with the basket perched on her hip.

"I've never seen one."

"I told you they were fast."

At the bottom of the stairs he decided to wait until she was halfway up. Being right behind her at hip level was too much temptation, and he didn't want to screw this up again right away. Make lunch, play nice and try to figure out what she needed. And get ready to escort her to a dance. He grinned to himself. That, he decided, could be a really fun evening.

* * * *

Katherine sprinted into school Monday morning. Even though she'd stayed up late with Jack finishing a second round of Trivial Pursuit, she didn't feel the least bit tired. They were even now. He'd won one, and she'd won one. Next time, maybe she'd talk him into Monopoly. A huge stack of fliers sat in her mailbox, but she didn't want to waste time sorting through them all now, so she shoved them in her bag on the way upstairs. All the rooms were closed and dark. She flicked on the lights in her own classroom and hung up her coat. Then she looked out the door to see if Pam had shown up yet. Nope, not yet. Katherine fussed with the attendance sheets and sorted through other memos. A reminder about the dance with a hand written note about her chaperoning. A memo about the next teacher's meeting when they would be looking for suckers for prom. Depending on how this dance went, Katherine might not dread that. Someone selling a used car. A collection for a wedding gift for one of the science teachers. Katherine looked at Pam's door again. Still dark and closed. The memos she trashed before starting laying out worksheets for her classes on the side counter.

Pam's lights flickered on.

Katherine ran across the hall, sliding the last two feet to Pam's desk. "Guess what?"

"Jack asked you to marry him, and you gave in."

Katherine put her hands on her hips.

Pam turned away to hang up her coat. "What?"

"Jack is going to come with me to chaperon the dance." Katherine put her hands behind her back. "He's off duty that night, and he said it sounded like fun."

"He's never chaperoned a high school dance, has he?"

"Pam!"

Pam turned around with her book bag in her hands. "You're very excited about this for someone who wasn't going to get mixed up with any more heroes. Did you change your mind?"

"No. We have an understanding now."

"An understanding." Pam nodded. "And how did this come about?"

"My faucet broke." Katherine perched on the edge of Pam's desk. She knew she was grinning like a school girl, but she hadn't been able to stop since last night.

"What does your faucet have to do with this?"

"Well, my faucet broke yesterday morning. Jack fixed it for me, and then he kissed me, and we had a long talk and decided to be friends."

"Whoa. Back up." Pam closed her closet door and turned to Katherine. "Kissed you?"

"Who kissed who?" Kitty asked, walking through the door with a cup of coffee cradled in her hands.

"Jack kissed Katherine," Pam explained. "What do you mean he kissed you?"

"The fireman?" Kitty leaned on one of the student desks.

"Pam, he kissed me, and it was like nothing I experienced in six years with Gary."

"Wow." Kitty sighed. "Does he have any brothers?"

"A couple hundred, I'll venture. Thousands if you go national." Pam sat down behind her desk. "He's a firefighter, the definition of brother is a little different for them. And I thought you didn't want to get involved with that again? Kitty, did you make coffee or what?"

"I'll go get the pot." Kitty set down her cup and darted out of the room.

"I'm not. I told you, we have an understanding."

"Why don't I believe this is going to hold?" Pam folded her arms. "I seem to remember you complaining about how Gary never did anything with you because he was always out with the guys and how they mattered more than you did. Is the fire department different?"

"It doesn't matter." Katherine could hear herself, but not believe it. She wanted it to not matter. She and Jack could just be friends, but she could remember what his lips felt like on hers, and how he had teased her with the Trivial Pursuit wedge. "I'm free and independent. We're friends," she said firmly, as much to remind herself as to tell them.

Kitty hustled through the door with the coffee pot and two mugs. "What did I miss?"

"Katherine and Jack are going to the dance a week from Friday. She thinks they can be friends," Pam said.

"I thought men hated that," Kitty said pouring two cups. "The whole 'let's be friends' thing."

"He suggested it." Katherine picked up a coffee cup. Kitty made the worst coffee on Earth, and for some reason everybody on this wing still let her make it.

"It doesn't sound kosher to me." Pam picked up the other cup, sipped from it, made a face and set it down.

"Why don't you want to date this guy anyway?" Kitty asked. "This has never made sense to me."

Christa Maurice

"He's a firefighter. He risks his life by vocation. I don't know if—" Katherine's voice choked off.

"You don't know if you can do that again," Pam finished.

"Is it better to have long dull memories or short happy ones?" Kitty asked. "Look at Darlene McConikee. She's been married to Frank for twenty-five years. Twenty-five boring years of cleaning the garage every spring and going to Atlantic City for two weeks every summer. Their major form of entertainment is chaperoning school dances. I saw her lesson plans once, she's been using the same lesson plans for the last fifteen years."

"Everybody reuses lesson plans," Katherine protested.

"She stopped crossing out the old dates in 2002."

Pam folded her arms. "Kitty, I fail to see what this has to do with Kathy and her fireman."

"Everything." Kitty set down her coffee cup. "If you had to choose between a few exciting years with the hero or twenty-five boring ones, which would you want?"

"I'd hardly describe my years with Gary as exciting." Katherine took another sip of coffee and regretted it.

"Yes, but you said that one kiss was like nothing in your entire relationship. Imagine what the rest would be like," Kitty said smugly.

Katherine peered into her coffee cup to hide her blush. It was too easy to imagine. Her subconscious showed little movies to her every night. And the images had gotten a lot more vivid now that she had something to base them on. So what was better? Twenty-five boring years ending with her sitting next to a casket or a few happy years ending the same way?

Twenty-five boring years of sleeping through the night or six happy years waking up every time a siren went off? Did Darlene kiss her husband goodbye every morning wondering if he would come home that night?

"I don't know, Kitty. Darlene is probably never going to have the police show up at her classroom door and tell her they need to speak to her in the principal's office." She set down her cup and walked out of the room.

Chapter 8

Katherine sat in bed with the blankets nested around her hips, staring at her closet. She didn't want to look as if she'd been trying to impress him, but here it was two weeks before the dance and she was already worrying about what to wear. This rated as lovesick and pathetic for a woman who had sworn to herself, and to him, that their relationship would never go beyond friendship.

The phone rang.

Katherine threw off the covers and ran to get it. Who would call at eight on a Sunday morning? Visions of her mother lying in a twisted heap, just able to reach the phone were crowded out by visions of her mother's doctor looking sorrowful at the prospect of delivering dire news. Then she imagined Pam with the phone pressed against her cheek, sobbing with the children clinging to her. That in turn was replaced by the fire chief calling to tell her Jack had been killed in an early morning blaze, very sorry. As her fingers touched the phone she remembered Jack left for work a few minutes ago. She heard him put Archer out and set off up the street, whistling. Now that the weather was nice enough to have windows open, she could hear everything. Jack in the backyard. Archer barking at squirrels. The odd car backfiring. Each and every siren within five blocks. Not having a television or stereo to drown out ambient noise didn't help her nerves at all.

But there hadn't been any sirens this morning. She'd have heard the engine. She knew its distinct tone now. Besides, he hadn't had time to get the run if there had been one, let alone get to a fire and be killed. And why would the fire chief call his landlord anyway?

"Hello?" She couldn't keep the panic out of her voice. It still had to be bad news. No one called this early for no reason.

"Hey Kate, it's Jack." He paused. "Are you okay?"

"Sure." Katherine's heart clattered around in her chest as if it had come loose from its moorings. "I'm fine. Why?"

"You sounded a little wound up. Are you sure you're okay?"

"I'm fine. What did you call for?" Katherine shifted the phone away from her mouth and took a deep breath. She had to stop imagining worst case scenarios every time the phone rang.

"I left something at home. I wondered if you could bring it to me." He paused again. "I didn't wake you, did I?"

"No, you didn't wake me." *I was lying in bed like a school girl thinking about what I'm going to wear to a dance in two weeks.* She twisted and untwisted the phone cord around her finger. "What did you need?"

"I left my St. Florian medal at home. It's kind of a lucky charm." He chuckled. "I was hoping you could bring it up here."

Katherine combed her fingers through her hair. A medal? A lucky charm? He was calling at daybreak on a Sunday to ask her to bring his lucky charm to the station? He wanted her to go into his apartment unattended for a trinket? Her mother was fine. Pam was fine. Not an emergency at all. "A medal?"

"I always have it with me on duty and I forgot it this morning. I guess I don't need it if you're busy."

He did want her to go unattended into his apartment. "It's not that. I don't know if it's a good idea."

"Why?"

"Well, my book said I had to give tenants twenty-four hours notice." She wondered if she would be able to go in and not rifle through his medicine chest. Her heart was still pounding, but for a different reason now. She could only hope if he heard it, he would assume it was interference.

"Kate, I'm giving you permission to go into my apartment. I won't call the landlord police or anything."

"The Fair Housing Bureau."

"Them, then. I won't tell a soul. Can you bring the medal?"

"I guess so." Katherine licked her lips. Permission to check out his apartment and a chance to pay him back for bringing her lunch to school. Almost too perfect. "Where is it?"

"That's the thing. If it was where it was supposed to be I would have it. It's supposed to be on my dresser in my bedroom."

Katherine felt her body get warm. His bedroom. Not just his apartment, he wanted her to go into his bedroom.

"But it might have fallen on the floor. Or it might be on the nightstand beside the bed. Or I could have put it in the cabinet. You know the top part where the windows are? I was in there yesterday, and I might have put it there, but I don't think so. It might have fallen out of my pocket on the bed."

Not only did he want her to wander around his bedroom, he had practically invited her to lounge on his bed. Katherine squeezed her eyes closed. "So you want me to search the place?" she said when she could manage to speak without squeaking.

"I guess so." A voice spoke behind him. "Dan has volunteered to be your witness that I gave you permission to inspect the place."

"Tell him thank you. What is this thing I'm looking for anyway?"

"It looks like a dog tag. You'll know it when you see it."

"I hope so." Katherine licked her lips.

"Thanks, Kate. I really appreciate this."

"I'm sure. I'll be over as soon as I find it."

"Good. See ya."

"Good-bye." Katherine hung up the phone. He wanted her to go into his apartment, into his bedroom, to find a lucky charm. Rubbing her face, she looked around the room to confirm she had had the conversation she remembered having. She must have. Which meant she did have permission to go into his apartment alone and look around his bedroom.

But first she had to get dressed.

Five minutes later, Katherine stood outside Jack's front door with her copy of the front door key. She took a deep breath. This is a favor for a friend, she told herself. It's as if Pam had asked her to stop by her house to pick up lesson plans. There would be no spying. She unlocked the door.

Though she'd been inside a dozen times, she hadn't looked around because she didn't want to be nosy. But without an audience, it seemed less nosy.

The foyer was still an empty room. He had a prefab bookcase in the corner and an easy chair with a reading lamp beside it in front of the window. He'd hung a couple of family pictures on the wall. She'd never had a chance to look at them before. His parents looked more or less as she'd expected. In one picture, an old woman smirked at the camera. The eighty-two year old grandmother, she decided. He also had a picture of his sister at one of her graduations, judging by the robe. And there was one picture of a yellow Labrador panting at the camera. Cody.

She glanced in the living room, but it held no real surprises other than general neatness. Until now she'd assumed he tidied up for her, but it didn't seem any messier now when he hadn't expected her to see it. Other than the sloppy magazine stack on the coffee table and the half-chewed rawhide bone in the middle of the floor, his living room could have been in a Better Homes and Gardens photo shoot. The kitchen wasn't a surprise either. Neat, functional, one coffee mug in the sink.

She stopped at the bedroom door. There never used to be a door here, just an open doorway, but she had decided it would have to be the bedroom and would need a door, so Randy hung a door, complaining the whole time. Nudging the door open with the tips of her fingers, she expected it to be snagged on a pile of dirty clothes any second. She'd never seen a man's room that didn't have a pile of dirty clothes on the floor somewhere.

The door swung open. Bed made. Drawers closed. Floor clear. The bedroom was as neat as the rest of the apartment.

The curtains hung open, flooding the room with light which gleamed off the glass of the built in cabinet. He had a queen-sized bed with a heavy, dark wood headboard. The dark blue bedspread had an Archer-sized depression in the middle of it. She walked over to the dresser, built of the same dark heavy wood, and scanned the top. Nothing that could be the medal lay there. In fact, almost nothing littered the top of his dresser. He had a dish with a few coins and his truck keys in it, a plastic comb, a full bottle of aftershave she'd never noticed him wearing, and a pair of sunglasses. She glanced under the dresser, but it didn't seem to have so much as a dust bunny, let alone a medal.

Next, she tried the nightstand. The medal wasn't under the lamp or the alarm clock and there was nowhere else for it to hide. Pulling open the drawer, she found a package of cough drops, a box of Kleenex, and a paperback mystery novel. No medal. He probably had it in his pocket sandwiched between an expired fast food coupon and his pen knife. He seemed to keep more in his pockets than in his apartment.

Shading the glass with her hand she looked in the cabinet. On the top shelf he had more framed photographs. She stood on her toes, but couldn't see anything else. On the second shelf along the back wall was a framed certificate she couldn't read for the shadow of the shelf above it so she opened the case and took it out. The commendation. Why did he have it sitting on the back of a shelf in his bedroom, instead of hanging in the foyer with his pictures? Her teaching award from the newspaper looked very similar, and she had it in a file folder. Maybe he viewed his award the same way she viewed hers. Nice, but it was her job, it was expected she would do it well. Of course her job didn't carry as much inherent risk. She cradled the frame in her hands reading it. It didn't tell what he'd done either. All it said was "for bravery above and beyond the call of duty" in fancy script, which left a lot up to the imagination.

She put the frame back as she found it and examined the rest of the shelf for the medal. He probably did have it in his pocket and didn't know it, because he had everything in his pockets. Leaning down she looked at the bottom shelf. The medal lay half under another paperback novel toward the back.

And behind the novel, shoved all the way back in the corner, was an unopened box of condoms.

Katherine reared back sputtering. Condoms. "What are you doing with a box of condoms?" she demanded. "Are you hoping one of these days I'll be down here doing laundry and watching a movie and one thing will lead to another? Do you think I'm going to change my mind? Or I'll give in to your overwhelming masculinity?"

Archer started barking in the back room.

Katherine stormed into the kitchen and yanked open the door. Archer bounded in and jumped on her, knocking her back into the door frame. Her head bounced against the wood. "Hey! Get down!"

Archer dropped to the floor and cringed.

Katherine touched the back of her head. "I've got to train you out of that habit," she grumbled. She had a tender spot on the back of her skull that would make brushing her hair fun for the next couple of days, and rule out barrettes.

Archer half perked up when she didn't yell again, but kept his ears down.

Katherine watched Jack's dog. Enthusiastic and hopeful, but never cruel. Just like his owner. Jack probably had condoms around for any dates he might have. She quelled a flash of jealousy thinking he might have dates that would go that far. Some other woman would enjoy feeling those hands against her flesh and taste his mouth over hers.

Some woman who would never be her. Katherine couldn't get mixed up with a man so willing to get killed in the line of duty he got a commendation for it. But she could hardly tell him 'you can't have me, but you can't have anyone else.' That wouldn't be fair. She had no right to pry either. He'd probably forgotten the condoms were there. They were friends, nothing more. Someday she would have to go to his wedding and watch him marry some other unlucky woman who didn't yet know the joys of lying awake at night listening for sirens and waiting for the police to knock on the door.

But the idea he had them, they were ready, sparked the desire she'd been trying to smother. He would be ready any time. Her skin burned remembering the way his hands had caressed her. She wanted to fall into his bed and bury her face in his pillow. Her belly warmed at the idea. It was all too easy to see herself in his bed. To see him beside her. To feel the way his hands would stroke her and the way his lips would taste her. To know the weight of his body on top of hers.

She squeezed her eyes shut and opened them, blinking. The fact that she assumed he had them for her said more about her than him. Archer stood watching her. She patted him on the head.

"It's okay, boy. We'll work on your jumping problem later. You want to walk up to the station?"

* * * *

Jack stood at the top of Worchester staring down the road. Where was she? How long did it take to find a small object in a neat apartment? He'd narrowed it down to one room. Parts of one room even.

"Still no sign?" Kevin asked, peering down the street beside him.

"No."

"Takes a long time to search a whole apartment." Kevin started back to the station.

"She isn't searching the whole apartment."

"That's what you think." Kevin disappeared into the apparatus bay before Jack could shout something smart at him.

Jack looked at his watch.

Archer turned the corner first, followed by Katherine. Archer stopped when he spotted Jack, barked and started pulling Katherine forward. She stopped, and twitched the leash. Archer stopped dragging her and heeled. Jack smiled. She'd had to have taught him that trick. Half the time Archer about pulled his arm off. He started down the block and met her halfway. "You found it?"

"Of course." She held up the medal. "It was in the cabinet."

He took it and dropped it in his pocket. "You want to come up to the station?" he asked. She looked great this morning. Her long hair blew across her face, glinting in the sun. She brushed it back with her free hand, watching him. Her jacket hung open showing a pink cotton knit v-neck shirt. If he stepped a little closer he'd have a great view down her cleavage.

"Why?'"

He met her eyes wondering if she'd read his mind. "I thought you'd like to meet everybody."

She frowned at him. "I've already met them. When you moved in, remember?"

He couldn't tell her he wanted them to meet her when she wasn't likely to start running cold, could he? She hadn't done that since the morning of the faucet disaster.

"I know, but you only met them once. Besides, I think they want a report on the inspection."

"What inspection?" she asked, turning pink.

"Of my apartment." Jack watched the glow gathering on her cheeks. Kevin had been right. She'd taken the opportunity to look around his place. At least there wasn't anything to find. Or he hoped there wasn't.

"Hmm. I guess so," she said looking at the pavement to cover her blush.

Jack resisted the temptation to drape his arm across her shoulders as he led her to the station. It had to be enough that she fell into step beside him. She did look great this morning. He wondered if he thought so because he was about to show her off to the guys or if he was starved for the sight of her.

"Are you allowed to wander this far from the station?" She switched the leash to her other hand so Archer wouldn't walk between them.

"I could hear it if we got a call." Jack clasped his hands behind his back. She didn't want the dog between them. Definitely a good sign. "Did you have any trouble finding the medal?"

Archer stopped to sniff something interesting.

"A little. Then your dog attacked me." Katherine paused until Archer finished his investigation.

"Attacked you?"

"He noticed me inside, and when I opened the door he jumped on me and knocked me into the wall." Katherine rubbed the back of her head.

Jack stopped. "Did you get hurt?" They had reached the end of Worchester across from the station. He'd stepped off the curb before he stopped, but she hadn't, giving her a few extra inches. She stood almost eye to eye with him. Perfect kissing angle.

"No, he knocked some sense into me." She grimaced.

"Are you sure?" Jack reached toward her intending to check the back of her head, but she stiffened. He dropped his hand. While she might not want Archer between them, she also didn't want him touching her. Fair enough, for now.

"It was nothing." She walked around him and stepped off the curb.

Kevin and Lew leaned on the engine watching them cross the street.

"Hey Conley, did your mom bring you your lunch?" Lew called.

"Aw come on Lew, she's not old enough to be his mom," Kevin pointed out. "She's his girlfriend."

"She's not my girlfriend," Jack said. He glanced at her, worried how she would take that comment and caught her eyes skimming over the engine. Something else to file away for later consideration. Then she smiled as if she hadn't a care.

"I'm his dog walker," Katherine announced.

Lew crouched and started rough housing with Archer. "Conley, maybe you should train your dog to bring stuff to you when you forget it."

"Yeah, very funny. I didn't train that dog to fetch. Kate did." Jack gestured toward Kevin first. "You met Kevin and Lew."

"Nice to see you both again."

"Indeed, madam." Kevin raised her hand to his lips and kissed it.

"Show off." Jack lifted Katherine's hand out of Kevin's, but didn't let go.

"Dingbat." Kevin shot back, looking at Jack and Katherine's hands.

"Kevin is my best friend in the entire world," Jack explained, ignoring Kevin's questioning eyes. "I do not know where I would be without his kind encouragement."

"A true boon companion, I can tell," Katherine said, but with a twinkle in her eye that gave away her real meaning. Jack watched her face, enjoying her brightness this morning. Something about it felt strange, but she looked so great he decided to wonder what might be wrong later. Besides, right now she was letting him hold her hand.

"Do I detect the dulcet tones of a lovely woman?" Dan wandered around the front of the engine from the direction of the day room.

"Dulcet?" Lew asked.

"Word a day calendar." Dan caught Katherine's free hand and kissed her palm after nudging the leash strap out of the way with his thumb.

"I already tried that." Kevin pointed out.

"Didn't work, huh?" Dan asked, still bent over her hand.

Katherine pulled her hands away from Dan and Jack and folded her arms. "I'm a high school teacher. I'm not so easily charmed."

"What if I quote Shakespeare?" Dan assumed a heroic pose. "'But soft, what light through yonder window breaks. It is the dawn and Juliet, the sun.'"

Katherine looked up at Jack as if she were unsure how to take Dan's goofiness, so he rolled his eyes at her. She smiled, and it took his breath away. It nearly made up for the loss of her hand. "Nope, that doesn't do it either," she said.

"Wow, she's tough. I give up." Dan stuck his hands in his pockets and rocked back on his heels.

"Quitter," Jack coughed.

"So did Jack pass muster?" Lew asked, standing up. "Can you bounce a quarter on his bed?"

"Oh sure. A whole roll of quarters."

Dan brightened, but Jack put up one hand before he could comment. "Don't start."

Katherine looked at each of their faces and nodded. "I see. On that note, the dog and I are going to the grocery store to pick up some milk and then home." She took a step backward, got tangled in the leash and stumbled. Jack caught her before she fell. "Thank you. Nice chatting with you all. Don't you have kittens to save from trees or something?"

"That's Jack's department," Kevin said.

Jack grumbled over his shoulder as he walked Katherine down the driveway. "Thanks for bringing my medal."

"No problem." Katherine kept her eyes fixed on the sidewalk.

"What are you doing for the rest of the day?" Jack studied the tilt of her head, trying to read her mind.

"Getting milk, reading a book, playing with your dog, grading some essays. Nothing exciting or life threatening." She started twisting the leash around her wrist.

Before Lew started talking about his bed, she hadn't been at all nervous or upset. Even after she'd checked out the engine she'd seemed fine. At least she hadn't gone cold.

"Well, I better get going. I've got a whole day of excitement waiting for me. Be careful." She started down the sidewalk so abruptly she took Archer by surprise.

"I can't be careful. It's my job," he called after her, pretty sure she couldn't hear at the pace she was going.

"You're right."

Jack turned at the sound of Kevin's voice. His friend was watching Katherine walk down the street. "About what?"

"She's cute. She's fun. I can see why you've skipped so many poker games lately to stay home." Kevin stared down the road after her. "That wouldn't be hard to stay home with. Definitely more interesting than a bunch of guys playing poker."

"And Bobbie." Jack reminded him. Bobbie was a firefighter from eleven who joined them most weeks. A tall, brawny woman who many of the guys forgot was female, until the annual Christmas party when she pulled out her dresses and make-up.

"Yeah, and Bobbie."

Jack frowned. "Something's bothering her. She seemed a little tense." Jack pulled his medal out of his pocket and looked at it. "She's usually a little better than that."

"Usually?"

"Ideally." Jack turned the medal over and dropped it back in his pocket. "She's getting better all the time though."

"She thinks you're going to die today."

"No, I don't think that's it." Jack tapped his foot. "I don't know what to think sometimes."

"Well, from out here it looks like you might have picked a winner for once." Kevin shrugged. "Come on. Any minute now Cap's gonna start yelling. We've got a white board session this morning."

Jack took one look up the road at Katherine, who had turned the corner and disappeared. Something had been odd about her this morning. She looked radiant and happy, but somehow it seemed forced, as if she had something to hide. Shaking his head he started back to the station before he could get more harassment about being love sick.

Chapter 9

Jack knocked at Katherine's door precisely at six. He'd have had a hard time explaining lateness tonight, since picking her up required walking around the side of the house. Still, he'd nearly been late because he changed clothes…twice. He tugged the jacket of his charcoal gray suit and hoped it would meet with her approval.

Since the day she'd brought him his medal at the station, she'd been quiet and thoughtful, but he didn't know why. She'd spent the normal amount of time hanging out and playing with Archer, but her heart wasn't in it. Her sophomore class was studying *To Kill a Mockingbird* and would be watching the movie in two weeks so she should have been pretty happy. Last weekend over popcorn, she had given him a guided tour of the film, telling him where the movie differed from the book. But she still seemed withdrawn and unhappy. If he could just take her into his arms and make her tell him what was wrong, he could fix it. Because taking her into his arms had worked so well last time, he resisted the urge and struggled to wait her out.

The door opened. She stood inside with her coat and purse draped over one arm. "Maybe I should change." She had on a black dress with a mock turtle neck, a narrow-waisted violet blazer and simple black pumps. She wore her hair swept up in a French twist and looked as elegant as Audrey Hepburn in *Breakfast at Tiffanys*. She took a step backward, frowning. "I have a red jacket that would look fine."

"What's wrong with the one you have on?" He put his hands behind his back before he reached out and brushed his hand down her sleeve to see what her jacket felt like.

She tugged his purple tie. "Don't you think it's a little too cute that we match?"

"No. Come on. You don't want to miss our reservations, do you?"

She pulled back, her face tense. "You made reservations? Where?"

Christa Maurice

He slipped his hand around her elbow. He could smell perfume, which he'd never noticed her wear before. Was she wearing perfume for him? The scent was light and flowery. He wanted to take her in his arms and kiss her now, forget about fixing anything. "Come on, we're going to a school dance, aren't we? I'm supposed to take you to dinner first. It's a rule."

She locked her door. "Where's Archer?"

"Where he always is." Jack guided her down the stairs. "Stop being so nervous. Haven't you ever been on a date before?"

"I'm out of practice."

Jack opened the truck door and helped her in. "You look lovely." This close he could tell she had on make-up too. Not much, but on normal days she wore nothing more than Chapstick. Tonight her lips seemed redder, and he noticed a golden glow to her eyes. How likely was it that she'd dressed up, put on perfume and worn make-up to chaperon a high school dance? A knot formed in his throat. "You really do look lovely tonight."

She looked at him and then dropped her eyes to her lap.

When he climbed in the other side she started rooting through her purse. That was one of her little habits. He wanted to reach across the seat, pull her into his arms and kiss off her lipstick. Then she would have something to do because she'd have to put on more. He started the engine and backed out of the driveway.

* * * *

Katherine walked through the echoing halls with Jack following behind her. She knew she was sending mixed signals, and she hated herself for it. Telling him she wanted to be friends and then she dressed up for him. Saying she needed to keep her distance, but leaning across the table to touch his arm over dinner. At least he'd been joking about reservations. He'd taken her to the Lebanese deli he'd suggested going to before he moved in. The guy behind the counter knew Jack's name and brought him special dishes, but it was cheap. She'd have felt guilty if he spent a lot of money. As it was, she felt pretty sure she would have to pay for her mixed signals. She didn't want to price of dinner added to the tab.

"We can hang our coats in the teacher's lounge. Well, I can hang my coat. It's down here." Walking down the steps to the teacher's lounge she could hear her own yammering ringing off the cement block walls. As usual it felt like descending into a crypt.

"Lovely. This isn't where you banish the bad kids? I keep expecting to run into the boiler." Jack ducked under the lintel and turned a sharp corner into the lounge.

Katherine's nervous giggle died in her throat. Darlene and Frank McConikee relaxed on the threadbare couch waiting for the dance to start. Frank was a paunchy late-middle-aged mid-level manager at one of the big corporations downtown. He always looked smug and bored. Darlene was a thickening late-middle-aged algebra teacher. Katherine stopped at the sight of them, and Jack bumped into her. He put his hands on her arms, and didn't bother to move back. She almost shivered at the reassuring weight of him. Lively, exciting Jack behind her. And Darlene and Frank McConikee in front of her. Kitty had captured the question perfectly. She'd rather be dead herself than survive as Darlene McConikee. "Hi Darlene, Frank."

"Hello Katherine." Darlene stood, towing Frank to his feet behind her. Her voice, Katherine noticed, was colorless. She wondered how Darlene's students stayed awake in class. Maybe she didn't notice they were all sleeping.

"I didn't know you were chaperoning tonight, too." Katherine wanted to lean back against Jack. She couldn't have explained why she felt so unnerved to be confronted by McConikees right now, but the thought of their lives made her want to burst into tears.

"We like to chaperon," Frank said. "We do most of the dances." At least she thought it was Frank. Their voices sounded alike.

"I didn't know that." She turned, pressing her shoulder against Jack. "This is my tenant, Jack Conley."

"Pleasure to meet you," Darlene said. "Katherine, I still miss having your fiancé here."

Katherine's mouth went dry. Gary always liked chaperoning dances. Now she did sag back. Jack's hands tightened around her shoulders. She hadn't remembered how life-sapping being around the McConikees could be.

"Katherine used to bring her fiancé to the dances. It was always very effective to have a police officer here in dress uniform," Darlene informed Jack. "Well, we'll see you in the cafeteria. The kids should be arriving soon."

They walked out past Katherine and Jack.

"What was that?" Jack whispered, still holding her upright.

Katherine shivered as his breath crossed her cheek. "I have no idea." Pulling away from him, she went to hang up her coat and purse. She kept her back to him as she crossed the room trying to control her emotions. Coming face to face with Darlene had reminded her of what an awful thing it would be to have to live like that.

But if she couldn't stand complete safety, and she couldn't stand risk, what could she do? "You realize that woman is teaching a generation to hate algebra?"

"Maybe that's why I didn't like it." He hovered near the door. "So your fiancé used to come to these things in dress uniform?"

"Nothing scares a high school kid like a cop in dress blues." Katherine turned back to Jack. He seemed to take over the room. He stood tall enough to reach up and touch the low ceiling without straightening his arm. Gary never could have reached it. Why did she insist on comparing them when she knew Gary would come up short? "It was a power trip."

"So what are our duties for tonight?"

"Keep the kids from having sex, getting stoned or drunk, or fighting on school property." She smiled. "I warned you it was work."

"Do we get to dance?"

She walked back toward him. He'd been so gentle and solicitous. He'd even said she was lovely. How long had it been since anyone said she was lovely? How long had it been since anyone made her feel lovely? Wasn't there a happy medium between Darlene McConikee and being alone at twenty-five?

"We get to dance, but stick to other chaperons. The girls will be fawning all over you, but don't dance with them, don't touch them, and don't let them get you alone. It's an awful thing to have to say, but they're all underage, and they know it. You can't trust them, or you could find yourself on the sharp end of a lawsuit."

He picked up her hand when she got close enough and pressed her knuckles against his lips.

"I only want to dance with you," he murmured.

Katherine heard a whimper and realized too late it had come from her. She had spent the last month trying to figure out why she'd invited him to this dance, but the answer seemed to be getting further away, not closer. "I thought we were just friends."

He straightened up, the seductive gleam in his eyes replaced with the usual bright grin. "We are friends. Good friends."

"Who do you think you are, Harrison Ford?" she asked, recalling the evening they'd rented *Clear and Present Danger* and watched it with a bowl of popcorn and the dog between them.

"Sure, if that's what you want. Now how do we get to the cafeteria from here?" He peered out the doorway. "I hope this place never burns. It's a maze."

* * * *

The cafeteria was loud, dim, and decorated with paper streamers. Not much had changed in high school dances since he graduated. They seemed a lot more fun then. To fill the time, Jack pondered how dull this was and waited for the DJ to play a slow song so he could ask Katherine to dance. It felt as if hours had passed since their last circuit of the cafeteria, but it couldn't have been more than forty-five minutes. He didn't want to check his watch to find out, fearing serious disappointment.

Katherine was deep in conversation with the football coach who, over his scarlet and gray striped tie, wore a whistle. Jack doubted it could be heard over the pounding bass. The coach wandered away, and Katherine turned to him with a strange smile. She gestured for him to lean down, so he did and could, for the first time since stepping into the cafeteria, smell her perfume over the scent of too many teenagers and floor wax.

"I now know more about the Ohio State Football program than I ever wanted to know," she said through her teeth.

"Lucky you." He chanced kissing her temple because he saw a girl headed their way. He'd been mobbed by girls all evening. At least it provided the opportunity to be affectionate with Katherine, and she couldn't object. Especially after one of her students told her how lucky she was. He wondered if she was starting to crumble by the way she blushed. Then music wound to a stop and the DJ started talking about an upcoming band candy sale.

She smiled at him. "More defense?"

"Incoming." He nodded in the direction of the girl walking toward them. She looked a little formal to be a student, but she seemed to be about the right age, and she hadn't been deterred at all by his display so Jack pressed the advantage and draped his arm over Katherine's shoulders. How could she not see how perfectly she fit against him?

"Kitty," Katherine grumbled under her breath. "Hello, Miss Reilly. What are you doing here?"

The girl stopped in front of Katherine grinning. She touched her curly brown hair, batting her eyelashes. "Hello Ms. Pelham. This must be your friendly neighborhood fireman."

Katherine's smile seemed brittle and sarcastic. "Let me introduce you. Jack Conley, this is Kitty Reilly. She teaches art."

Jack shook her hand and decided her occupation explained her folkie looking skirt.

"I've heard so much about you. That was so nice the day you brought Ms. Pelham her lunch." Kitty grinned.

"You've heard so much about me?" Jack asked. He looked from Kitty to Katherine and back again. He couldn't tell for sure, but it looked as if Katherine were blushing.

"What are you doing here, Miss Reilly?" Katherine asked again. She shifted so Jack's arm slipped off her shoulders. "I know you're not one of tonight's chaperons."

"I came to see what was going on. Doesn't the cafeteria look nice, Mr. Conley?"

Jack felt more than heard Katherine's groan. He shrugged. "I don't have anything to compare it to." He wasn't sure why Katherine would be angry, or even if she was angry. She turned, giving him a view of her elegant profile, and studied a group of kids in the corner.

"That's a lovely tie, Mr. Conley. And it even matches Ms. Pelham's jacket. You don't wear that jacket very often any more, Ms. Pelham. You used to wear it all the time." Kitty stood with her back to the dance, focusing on Katherine and Jack.

"No, I don't. It drifted to the back of my closet, and I only remembered I had it the other day." Katherine thwarted Kitty's efforts to monopolize them by staring across the room.

"Isn't it funny how those things work out? And you just found it in time to match Mr. Conley's tie." Kitty grinned at Katherine, who ignored her, and then at Jack. He tried to smile noncommittally. Had Kitty Reilly heard a lot about him, or was she pulling Katherine's strings? And if she was pulling Katherine's strings, would she stop? He was on shaky enough ground without her help.

"I smell smoke," Katherine announced.

"Smoke?" Jack scanned the room for an ignition site.

"One of those kids is smoking." She started across the room.

Jack trailed after her, relieved when Miss Kitty Reilly didn't follow. Katherine waded into the middle of a large group and plucked a cigarette out of the lips of a kid near the wall. He froze, and his friends backed away.

"It's against school rules. It's against the law. And it makes you stinky, sickly and wrinkled." Katherine used the lit cigarette like a pointer, shaking ashes on the floor between them. "I advise you to quit now before you get kicked out of the dance, and we call your parents."

The boy who had been smoking paled. "I'm sorry. I just—"

"No. Don't let me see it again." Katherine turned and had to stop short before she ran into Jack. She stepped around him holding the cigarette out like a dead rodent.

Jack followed her to a table where she dropped the cigarette in an abandoned drink and threw both in the trash. They ended up on the opposite side of the cafeteria from Kitty Reilly. Very clever, he thought. It looked unintentional.

"I thought the place was on fire," he said. At least it was quieter here. He might be able to talk to her.

"No." Katherine leaned against the wall. "Kids think they can be cool and get away with smoking on school property. I strive to embarrass them as much as possible."

Jack leaned his shoulder against the wall and looked down at her. She seemed to have regained her composure, so it might be a good time to shake her up again. "So, they've heard all about me."

Katherine stood up, not stiff, but no longer relaxed. Her eyes swept the room. "Kitty is a little strange. She was very interested after you brought my lunch to school. She's asked a lot of questions."

"So what did you tell her?" Jack reached over and brushed a lock of her hair back. His fingers caressed her neck. She didn't move. How would she react if he leaned over and kissed her neck? He wondered if the DJ had any slow songs to play. He hadn't played any yet, and at the moment nothing would make him happier than to take Katherine for a whirl on the dance floor.

"I told her you were my tenant and you worked for the city fire department." Katherine kept looking around the room. Jack could see her searching for a good reason to set off after another student.

"Is that all?"

"I told her you have a dog, too." She zeroed in on a dark corner.

"Is that because you like Archer more than me?"

Katherine met his eyes, startled. "Jack! I—Melina!" She hurried around Jack.

Jack turned to follow her in time to see her wrap her hand around a girl's upper arm and yank her backward. It took him a minute to realize the girl's shirt hadn't started out half unbuttoned. The boy she'd jerked the girl away from wore baggy jeans slouched to his hips and a sleeveless undershirt despite the chilly spring air, and he looked angry. She had focused on the girl, obviously not seeing the threat on her left. Jack crossed the floor before the boy leaped at Katherine. He straight-armed the boy, stopping his momentum.

"What!" Katherine looked up at Jack and then at the boy, startled. She collected herself. "Melina, I don't care what school your boyfriend is from, but he isn't welcome here."

"He didn't mean it, Ms. Pelham. We'll behave. I promise," Melina wailed, fumbling to button her shirt. "I love him so much."

"If he loved you, he wouldn't be groping you in public and humiliating you."

"Or attacking a teacher," Jack added. He'd released the boy, but stood tensed to grab him again if necessary. Now he knew why Gary Ringer came to these things in his dress uniform.

"What's going on here?" Coach thundered, appearing out of nowhere and alarming several nearby groups of students.

"Melina's guest was just leaving." Katherine glared at the boy.

The coach blew his whistle, which actually *could* be heard over the music, and two large boys appeared. Jack guessed they were football players. Possibly tackles, judging by their shoulders. "We'll escort him to the phone where he can call his ride."

"Melina, what are you thinking? Your mother wants you to go to college." Katherine put her hands on the girl's shoulders, guiding her away from the trouble.

"You don't know what it's like," Melina groused, not looking back as her beau was led out of the school cafeteria.

Katherine snorted. "No, I was never a teenager."

"But Ms. Pelham it's different now. It's not like it was when you were in school."

"Some things never change, and it's always easier to slide down than it is to work up. Trust me, I waited tables for years before I met my fiancé, and he encouraged me to go to college."

She led the girl toward a lighted table by the punch table, and Jack had to stay close behind to hear them. "If you hang out with losers, you're going to end up losing. Why did you quit the debate team?"

"I hate it. It's stupid."

"That's not how we work. 'It's stupid' is not a reason, it's an excuse. What are your reasons? With supporting arguments." Katherine sat down at a table with Melina beside her.

Jack sat across the table from them and watched her work. He couldn't catch all of the conversation, but he could see Katherine guiding her student to a reasoned conclusion. Keeping a steady calm and good humor throughout, she stayed a jump or two ahead of Melina's reasons without letting her know it. From Leia's stories, he decided Katherine would have made a good lawyer. But she wasn't using her skill with words to confuse or beat down her student. She was teaching. Jack could almost see the girl stretching to meet her. Learning not just why she should work hard in school, but also how to reason. Melina, he realized, wanted to impress Katherine.

The exchange left Katherine animated, her eyes shining with passion. Jack couldn't remember ever seeing a teacher enjoy her work like this. Her bright eyes followed Melina's, and her quick fingers gestured, picking up points for further consideration and moving back through the logic path to clarify. Jack wished he could watch her teach. He found himself wondering again how the boys in her classes resisted her. What male in his right mind would not be attracted to that enthusiasm, that joy? How could he get her to look at him that way?

After what seemed like a long time, Katherine pointed toward the cafeteria doors. Melina stood up and a middle-aged woman crossed toward them smiling. The three of them stood for a few minutes talking, but Jack couldn't hear a word of it. He wouldn't have been able to follow the conversation anyway, he was too busy admiring Katherine.

She looked so beautiful and confident. Her hair had started to come loose and dark locks trailed down her cheeks and neck. Laughing, she waved as Melina and her mother walked away. Then she turned to look at him.

"Are you okay?" She laced her fingers together.

He stood up. "Sure, why?"

"You looked a little dazed. The music getting to you?"

"No." He took a deep breath and tried to act calm. He looked around the room and realized the dance was winding down. The crowd had thinned out. "What was that all about?"

"Melina is one of my honors students, but she's been headed downhill fast for a couple of months. Her mother told me she's been hanging around with a bad crowd. Her mother was a teen mom, and she doesn't want that for her daughter." Katherine smiled and Jack's heart squeezed. "I hoped I'd get to talk to her tonight. I didn't think I'd have to humiliate her to do it. Don't you sometimes wish you had someone older and wiser around to tell you when you were running with the wrong crowd?"

"Gary talked you into becoming a teacher," Jack stated. He hadn't been able to figure out what Katherine saw in her late fiancé, but he thought he might have found it.

"Oh, that." Katherine looked at the floor. "Gary was studying for the police academy when I met him. He would sit in my section for hours studying. He told me I was wasting myself waiting tables and encouraged me to go to college. We had planned to get married after I settled into my job, but his family kept getting in the way." She shrugged. "It was a long time ago."

A slow pulsing ballad came on.

"You owe me a dance, don't you?" Jack asked, hoping she wasn't too upset thinking about Gary and the people who apparently didn't want to be her in-laws. They were idiots.

"I don't remember that being in the bargain, pal."

Reaching for her hand, he said, "You can't drag me to a dance, and then not dance with me." He pulled her to the floor and slipped his arm around her waist.

With her hand in the middle of his chest she pushed him back an inch. "Remember where we are."

"I remember." Repositioning his hand to her hip where it belonged he looked down at her. She was still on duty, scanning the dance floor for infractions and mayhem. In his arms, she seemed so small. Most of the time he'd spent with her had been sitting on the floor at his coffee table or playing with the dog in the backyard, and neither activity gave him a good reference point for her size. Now with her in his arms, he remembered her head came exactly to the hollow of his shoulder, and he barely had to bend his arm to rest his hand in the curve of her waist. If he pulled her against him, he be able to feel her molded against him, but knew he'd never get away with that, not here in the school cafeteria with her students and coworkers looking on. Would he feel uncomfortable kissing her at the station? It was a different situation to be sure. Here she had students who had to see her as a teacher, not a woman.

Still, what would it be like to pull her into his arms in the middle of the apparatus bay and kiss her like he wanted to with the guys roaming around and no doubt stopping to stare and critique? Of course, he had yet to kiss her like he wanted to anyway. That Sunday after Easter had been too much of a surprise for him to enjoy touching her. And later, she'd been so determined they remain friends that she'd kept plenty of space between them at all times. But her determination seemed to be slipping. He hoped he could hold out long enough to not rush her.

"What are you thinking about?" she asked.

She almost startled him into admitting the truth. "Nothing. Why?"

"You've got a very odd expression on your face. I get the feeling you're cooking up something new to harass me with." Her lips curved into a devilish smile.

He wanted to lean down and kiss her, but thought that would be a great way to get evicted. Right now, the lure of her lips almost made it worth the risk. Almost, but not quite. "No. Just thinking about not stepping on your feet." Instead he dipped her and felt her grab him.

"Liar," she said when he set her back on her feet.

"Can't blame me."

She pushed her jacket sleeve down using Jack's shoulder. "It's almost time to go. After this song, we can make a break for it. Can we stop in my room and get my grade book? I forgot it this afternoon. Do you mind?"

"No." The song was ending and Jack wondered what had happened to long slow ballads. It didn't feel as if they had been dancing for more than two minutes. He'd been hoping for at least fifteen.

Stepping backward, she slipped out of his grasp. "Shall we say our *adieus*, grab my grade book, and hie off for west Arden?"

"Ready when you are," he lied and followed her around the cafeteria. Most of the kids had left. The McConikees were picking up trash. Mrs. McConikee said goodnight, taking another opportunity to mention Gary. Jack hoped Katherine didn't hear. Who in their right mind would keep reminding a woman of her dead fiancé? Before going back to the teacher's lounge for her coat and purse she spoke with the vice principal and then the football coach. Then she led him through halls he didn't recognize.

"This should only take a minute." Katherine hurried up the hall ahead of him. Her shoes made a loud, authoritative tapping in the empty halls. "Did I hear Darlene McConikee say something about Gary?"

"I didn't think you noticed," he mumbled. The silence in the halls was deafening after the music in the cafeteria. Her hips swayed as she lengthened her stride. He tried to focus elsewhere, but the bake sale and pep rally signs didn't hold the same appeal.

"That woman must live in a time warp. Kitty said she's been using the same lesson plans for fifteen years. She doesn't even change the dates." Katherine started up a narrow flight of stairs two at a time. She seemed to be in flight from him.

He picked up his pace to catch up. "Is that unusual?"

"Well, everybody uses old plans to a certain extent, but not the exact same ones. Things change from year to year." She glanced over her shoulder as she exited the doorway at the top of the stairs into a dark hallway. "Assemblies, snow days, broken copiers. It's almost impossible to predict what's going to happen two months in advance, let alone all year." Swerving toward a door she pulled it open. It took him a moment to realize this was the same hall where he brought her lunch, but they'd approached it from the opposite direction. "This will only take a minute."

The lights in her classroom flickered and buzzed when she switched them on. Jack paused in the doorway to let his eyes adjust.

Going directly to her desk, she opened a drawer. With one hand she sifted through it, while pulling out her hair clip with the other. Jack watched her hair uncoil over her shoulders. So strong and confident on steady ground. He wanted to be her steady ground and he didn't want to wait for her to make up her mind, he wanted to convince her.

Jack didn't remember moving forward, only realizing he had when she turned as he put his hand on her shoulder. He traced his thumb along her jaw delighting in the silky feel of her skin. Her pulse raced under his fingers.

"Remember where we are," she whispered.

"I remember." He leaned down and brushed his lips against hers. When he slipped his arm around her back, her body curved against him, warm and welcoming. Her eyes opened, deep and dark in the glare of the classroom fluorescents. She drew a quick shallow breath between her parted lips, her heartbeat matching his.

"I thought we were friends."

"We are friends. We're very good friends." Jack curved his hand around the back of her neck, tangling his fingers in her long loose hair.

"Who do you think you are? Harrison Ford?"

He leaned down and kissed her again. Her warm mouth tasted like the punch she'd drunk at the dance. A deep rumble, almost a purr, started in her chest as he teased her lips open to drink more deeply. Caressing the deep curve of her back, he pulled her soft form tight against him. Every part of her molded to him the way he'd dreamed. Her light perfume surrounded them, reaching into his mind and clouding his thoughts. As he stroked his fingers through her silken hair, she shivered. Her arms wrapped around his shoulders tugging him closer, and lifting herself up to her toes. The heels of her shoes clacked against the tile as they slid off. Jack lifted his mouth from hers and kissed the corners of her lips. She had to understand now. They fit together. There was no need to fight this any longer. Didn't she know she was the perfect answer to all his questions?

"Jack," she whispered. She blinked, disoriented. Turning her head, she drew a deep breath and jumped backward out of his arms.

She slipped out of one shoe and landed badly on the other, twisting her foot. Jack grabbed her elbow as she seized on the chalk tray to balance herself. "Randy! What are you doing there?"

Jack turned to see Randy standing in the doorway with a push broom in one hand and a befuddled look on his handsome face.

"I saw the light," Randy muttered. "I thought somebody forgot to turn it out."

Katherine brushed her hair off her face, smearing her cheek with yellow chalk dust. The chalk dust looked garish against her embarrassed pink cheeks. "Well, your timing is impeccable. I'll take care of the light when I leave."

"O-okay." He swallowed. "Sorry. I didn't know."

"Don't worry about it." She turned to her desk, searching with her foot for the missing shoe, not meeting his eyes.

"Katherine," Jack said, reaching out to wipe the chalk dust from her cheek. He needed to touch her. To connect with her. He felt ripped in half.

She moved her head away. "Not here. Not now." Her long fingers clutched a slim green spiral bound book. "Are you ready?"

Nodding, he followed her out, switching off the lights as he passed. All the way to the truck she was silent and stiff. Only a few other cars still sat in the lot, and a police cruiser parked by the sidewalk. Katherine glared at it as they passed, but said nothing. Jack wanted to apologize, but he was afraid to speak. She had every right to be furious. He'd taken advantage of a weak moment and kissed her at her workplace where he should have known well enough to keep his hands to himself.

And those same hands still burned with the feel of her.

When he opened the truck door, he didn't put out his hand to help her in for fear of being brushed away. Walking around to the driver's door, he dreaded the lecture he knew he deserved. But she didn't say anything until they were out on the road.

"I'm sorry," she murmured. "I don't know what I was thinking. I should never have asked you to escort me to this dance. I should have known it would be too…" She paused and licked her lips. "Too emotionally charged."

"It's my fault. I shouldn't have kissed you at school," he said. Why she was apologizing? He instigated. All she did was respond to his ill-advised action.

"It was so stupid." With a soft sigh, she leaned her head back against the window. "I can't believe I did something that stupid. It's going to be all over school on Monday."

"You think the kids will know?" That had to be bad. He didn't remember ever hearing about a teacher getting kissed in a classroom, and there was probably a reason for it.

"No, but every teacher in the building will. Randy has such a big mouth. As we speak, the coach and the vice principal are hearing all about how he caught me in a clinch with my fireman. And knowing Randy, he'll enhance the story. Pretty soon he'll have caught us having passionate sex on the desk." When she squeezed her eyes closed and Jack saw a tear roll down her cheek. "They're all going to ask me about my new boyfriend. And I'm going to have to explain he's not my boyfriend, he's my tenant and my friend."

"Why can't you tell them I'm your boyfriend?"

"Because that would be a lie." She sounded pained.

"It doesn't have to be." Jack braced himself to say the words he wanted to say. "Katherine, I—"

"Not another word. Don't say it." Pulling her coat tight around her, she sat up. "You can't, because we can't, because I won't do that again."

"Won't do what?" Jack demanded.

"Won't be the widow of another hero."

Jack heard the word echo through the cab. The final piece of the mystery. The piece he'd been refusing to believe over all the evidence. She wasn't afraid of falling in love again, she was afraid of falling in love with someone like him. "Then something has to change." Jack stared out the windshield. So far he'd caught every light green when he needed a nice long red to talk to her. At this rate, they'd be home too soon.

"What do you mean?"

Jack turned at the corner of Jefferson. A few people hung out on the wooden porches of the apartment building there reminding him it wasn't that late, it just felt as if the day had lasted forever.

"I don't know yet." But he did know. All the time he'd been refusing to admit to the truth, he'd been thinking about it. He pulled in the driveway. "I could quit my job."

"No. I don't want that over my head."

Slipping the truck into park, he got out to open the garage door. Would he quit the department? It was the only job he'd ever wanted to do. The only thing that made him feel useful and helpful. It was more than his job, it was his life. When he put on the uniform, he felt so proud. Turning back to the truck he looked at Katherine through the windshield. Her head hung down and her hair draped around her face, hiding it. Would he feel as proud standing next to her for the rest of his life? After the way he'd seen her tonight with her student, he thought he could. She burned so bright, so alive. He couldn't live without that.

"You cannot quit the department for me," she announced in a low menacing tone when he climbed back in. "I won't allow it."

"It isn't your decision."

"If you quit for me, it is."

Carefully driving the truck into the garage, he shut it off, plunging them into darkness. "Then what do you want me to do?"

"I don't know." Next to her in the dark, he could only hear her soft breathing as she turned it over in her mind. "I know you would resent me, and I couldn't live with that."

"Funny, I've learned to love you, and now I can't live without you." Climbing out of the truck, he left her sitting in the dark.

Chapter 10

When Katherine pulled up the driveway on the last day of school, Jack was raking the backyard. It looked as if he'd tilled the entire thing, and as if he'd been at it all day. The garage stood open, so she only had to pull in, but he hobbled over to close it for her. He moved like an old man. How long had he been working to get that sore? And he was covered in dirt. She turned off the car and climbed out. Outside the door he stood looking at the asphalt, shoulders sagging.

They had never quite regained the uneasy-easy friendship they'd had before the dance. The day after, she'd stayed locked in her apartment, afraid to speak to him. Afraid he would say what she'd managed to stop him from saying in the truck. Katherine had been relieved when the last month of school was as chaotic as usual, because it gave her solid reasons to avoid Jack. He seemed to have found reasons not to be home as well. Roofing season was in full swing and he appeared to be picking up work doing that between his shifts at the station. Several days over the past month, she'd seen him getting into his truck in jeans and a flannel shirt to go to work instead of walking down the driveway, whistling. He didn't whistle when he went to his roofing job. So far the issue of his quitting the department hadn't come up again. Pam had agreed he would resent her if he did. Kitty had thought it was romantic that he would offer.

"Long day?" she asked.

"Yeah." He reached up for the garage door as she pulled a box of books and files out of the back seat of her car. "We had a couple of night runs last night."

"I heard." Now that she had her windows open she heard every time they went out, and it struck terror in her heart every time. "How come you're working on the back yard?"

"You said you always wanted to get to it and never did." His gaze stayed on the yard, avoiding her eyes. She couldn't tell if he was more emotionally or physically exhausted.

"When?"

"When you showed me the apartment in February."

"Oh. I forgot." She vaguely remembered mentioning the backyard when she showed him the apartment. Somewhere in her babbling, she must have, but it hadn't been important then. Why had he remembered five months later? Her heart clenched. He always remembered things like that. Little details to take care of her.

He shrugged. "I didn't. I got the soil tested, and I got a special kind of fertilizer to correct the Ph levels. The dirt is really acidic back here. It's the oak trees. Then I rented a tiller and tilled it in. The nursery said it would have been better if we'd done it last fall, but this will work. We'll have to decide what we want to do about grass."

Katherine shifted the box in her arms. It was a little heavy to be holding, but she'd barely spoken to Jack in a month. One of them was always headed out when the other came in. She had forgotten how much she missed talking to him. "What about grass?"

"We can put down turf and have an instant lawn, or we can sow seed and wait for it to grow. Turf is more expensive, but it'll definitely grow. Seed is cheaper, but unreliable. Birds eat it, it doesn't grow sometimes." He shrugged still not meeting her eyes.

Katherine forced a smile. "You studying to go into lawn care?"

"It's an option. Have to have some kind of job. It's interesting, too. Landscaping."

Her smile froze.

Turning away, he walked back to the yard. "Anyway, I want to get this finished before my whole body locks up. I should have waited until tomorrow to start."

"If you want, you can come upstairs and soak in my tub." She offered, willing him to accept. She needed to talk to him. About anything that would take away the pain she saw. Pain she'd caused.

"That's a bad idea." He picked up the rake without looking at her

"It can't hurt." The box was suddenly too heavy to support any longer so she leaned it against the fence. "If you're sore, a hot bath would be good for you."

"I have a buddy who has a hot tub if it gets bad."

"All right." Her heart crumbled in her chest. She missed the friend she'd had in him.

Christa Maurice

"Guess what?" she said, faking enthusiasm.

"What?"

"Three of my students gave me gift certificates to that big bookstore up the road. They're only five bucks each, but I can get two paperbacks." She bit her lip. It didn't look as if he was doing anything useful with that rake. More like he was stalling until she went away. "I was thinking about going there tomorrow. You want to come? We could have lunch at Wendy's."

"I've got to work."

"You're not on duty." Her calendar was still marked with his duty days and poker nights.

"The other job. It's peak roofing season."

She forced a laugh. "Get it? Peak roofing season?"

Jack shrugged and tried to smile.

Sucking in a deep breath barely forestalled a sob. "Well, I'm going in. Knock if you change your mind about that bath. I have all those pretty towels with the blue splashes on them."

His smile improved. "I'll let you know."

She started up the steps to her apartment and stopped. Turning around, she went back to the fence even though her arms were now screaming from holding the box for too long. "Jack?"

"What?"

"Why do I feel like I've got all the miserable parts of being married to you without any of the bonuses?" Tears gathered behind her eyes.

He looked up from his raking, meeting her eyes for the first time since she got home. His golden eyes were dull, but she didn't know if it was exhaustion or the conversation. "I don't know. I've never been married. Is this how the miserable part feels?"

* * * *

Jack waited until he heard her go inside. He been finished for an hour, but he'd known she would be home soon. Kevin thought he was out of his mind. That shouting argument in the parking lot this morning wouldn't help matters.

Was this how the miserable part of marriage felt?

They'd hardly talked since the night of the dance. The night he'd thought would be the best night of his life. When he'd thought he'd worked everything out. They hadn't been avoiding each other, things had just been very busy. At least that's what he wanted to believe. Katherine had a lot to do at the end of the school year, and when Mike Tomms called to ask if he wanted to pick up some roofing work, he'd jumped at the chance. The arguing with Kevin hadn't started until it got back to him through their captain that Jack had talked to Mike about joining his crew full time. The guys at the station had started leaving the room whenever Jack and Kevin were together.

Jack looked up at Katherine's kitchen window. She had forbidden him to quit the department for her. But she'd also told him in every way imaginable from the moment he met her that he couldn't have her and the department. It would have to be his decision which one he wanted more. Right now he wanted her more than he'd ever wanted anything.

Archer stood in the breakfast nook looking out the window. He didn't understand, but he knew something was wrong. Jack felt sorry for his dog. He missed Katherine, too, and he showed it by spending a lot of time sitting by the fence when he was outside and staring out the window when he was in.

Jack leaned the rake against the back of the house and went inside. He'd known what he was setting himself up for when he came home sore and tired from work and started working in the yard. Every muscle screamed. The hot bath sounded good, but spending that much time close to her sounded like agony of a different kind. He turned on the shower and took a couple of aspirin. Shoving back the curtain, steam billowed over him. School was out now. She'd be home more so he'd see more of her. Stepping under the flow of water, he wondered if that was good or bad.

* * * *

Katherine had been sitting in her living room listening for five minutes when she realized what she was doing. She heard Jack showering while she carried her box to her office. And he'd been shifting around in his apartment for a few minutes. She heard him let Archer out as she settled on the living room couch with a book. Then, the noises had stopped.

What was he doing down there? He hadn't turned on the television or the stereo and he wasn't cooking dinner. Could he have decided to take a nap? He didn't normally nap, even after a rough night.

Could he be sitting on his couch trying to figure out why she wasn't making any noise?

Intending to go to the kitchen and make a cup of tea, she stood up and crossed the room. Instead, she walked down the stairs, out her door and around to his front door. Once there, she knocked, for lack of any better idea. Looking down, she realized she hadn't even changed out of the blouse and jeans from in-service.

When he opened the door she noticed he looked a little less tired and a lot more wary. And he wasn't wearing a shirt. He leaned his right shoulder against the open door. "Yes?"

"I thought you might like a back rub." She held out her hands as if that would explain her presence. It sounded plausible.

"A back rub," he repeated. He reached up and massaged his neck.

She rubbed her hands together. The scent of Irish Springs soap surrounded her. "I thought after those night runs and the yard work, you'd be pretty sore." She could feel her throat tightening up and wondered how long it would be before she lost the ability to speak altogether. "You said you were worried about your muscles locking up. I thought I could help."

"Kate—"

"Please?" She stepped forward so she could block open the door if he tried to close it. Unfortunately that brought her much closer to him. Close enough to touch. "You did all that work. I owe you something."

"I guess. If you want to." He stepped back to allow her inside. "What do you want me to do?"

Katherine licked her lips. What did she want him to do? She wanted him to talk to her again. Like he used to. "Let's spread a blanket on the floor in the living room for you. I'll get it."

"No, I'll get it." He shuffled through the hall and into his bedroom.

Katherine went into the living room and slid the coffee table against the television to make a large enough space to work in. When he returned with the navy blue blanket from his bed, she helped him spread it on the floor.

"Lie down."

Jack stood warily on the far side. "You don't have to do this."

"I know. You didn't have to do the entire back yard by yourself today either. Lie down." She pointed at the blanket.

Jack stretched out on the floor groaning and Katherine knelt next to him. "Tell me if it gets too hard."

"What?" He pushed up on his arms as if he wanted to skitter away like a crab.

"If I'm pressing too hard. What… oh." She blushed when she realized how he'd taken her statement. "Lie down, and tell me if I'm hurting you."

She swallowed as the words came out of her mouth. Everything had two meanings. Of course she was hurting him. She'd been hurting him for months and couldn't seem to stop. He hadn't said anything. Instead he'd gone out and reconditioned the backyard. Brushing her hands across his muscular back, she oriented herself. Everything felt tight, as if he were holding his entire body rigid. "Are you relaxed?"

"No."

"I can't help you if you don't relax. I'm just going to hurt you more." She rubbed her hand down his spine. "Better. What made you decide to work on the back yard today?"

"It seemed like a good idea."

She worked in from his shoulders to his neck, feeling the tension in his muscles ebb further. "Are you upset about something?"

"No," he grunted. His shoulders tightened under her hands, revealing his lie.

"Are you sure? You tend to use physical activity to calm yourself."

"I do?" He sounded both amazed and alarmed.

"You do. I thought maybe that's why you took on a big project today." His entire back felt knotted even after he relaxed, but she suspected there would be a bad spot. She knew she'd found it when he groaned again. Up to then he'd been stoic and silent, even though she knew she had to be hurting him. There was a series of lumps in the small of his back where she expected. He was lucky he hadn't hurt himself working.

"So is there something bothering you?"

"Nothing I can't handle." He shifted his head to the other side, facing away from her.

"All right." She focused on the knots, admiring the light, even tan he'd acquired already in the roofing season. Occasionally he worked with his shirt off. She knew because she made a point of driving past his job sites when she could. Figuring out where they were required some detective work she wasn't proud of. She'd asked around school to find out who was having work done. Her coworkers were more than happy to tell her if Tomm's Roofing was doing a job in their neighborhood. The students required bribes, but the extra credit she'd handed out hadn't made a difference in their final grades.

She'd nearly convinced herself she was doing it so she wouldn't be surprised again, but hadn't been as successful with that as she had with the detective work. Still, it was hazardous for her to stumble on his work sites. She'd nearly totaled her car the first time, because she hadn't known he was working on a house on her normal route home from school. When she'd seen him strolling across the roof of a little bungalow without his shirt in the late afternoon sun, she'd nearly missed a curve and plowed into one of the stately elms lining the street. After that, any time she'd been able to glean where he was working, she'd made a point of altering her drive home, or taking a long walk before their work wrapped up for the day. It was all she saw of him now that they weren't spending half their free time sharing meals and splitting bowls of popcorn while watching a movie.

"Kate?" Jack turned his head again, and she realized he'd said something, and she'd missed it.

"I'm sorry. I didn't hear what you said." She felt her color rise again, glad he couldn't read her mind enough to know why.

"I asked how your in-service day was."

"Oh, the same. Getting grades done and turned in. Finishing the letters of recommendation a couple of the students asked for. I had lunch with the English department at Micelli's, and they harassed me all through it."

"Why?"

"They wondered what I'd be doing all summer now that I don't have to spend it in the basement," she lied. The entire lunch conversation had revolved around her and Jack. What would they be doing all summer? If they weren't dating already, when were they going to start? And why weren't they dating? Anyone who missed Randy's gossip and Kitty's enthusiastic observations had heard from a student 'Ms. Pelham brought a really cute guy to the dance.' She felt the amount of gossip surrounding her love life was an excellent indicator of how dull everyone else's lives were.

"That took all day?"

"Hey, if you can spend a whole day playing with hoses, I can spend all day playing with a calculator trying to figure out if Melina Diaz managed to scrape into an A." She nudged him with her knee and went back to work on his ribs. At least, she decided, she had learned to breathe and think while sitting this close to him.

"Did she?"

"With a little help from her teacher. She missed the honest A by about two points, but she's really picked up this last month of school, so I gave it to her." Katherine worked her way toward his shoulders.

"So, she got away from that little hoodlum?"

"Her mother said she doesn't think she's been running around with him since the dance."

"You fought pretty hard for that one, didn't you?" He sounded almost proud. Why would it matter to him if Melina Diaz managed to escape the cycle of poverty?

"I fight pretty hard for all of them, some don't rise to the challenge."

He took a deep breath, and she paused with her hands resting on his back. "Why?"

"Why what?" she asked shifting a little so she could work out the rest of the kinks in his lower back. His skin felt warmer and more pliable now. She felt warmer and more pliable, too.

"Why do you fight so hard? Why not give up?"

"And turn into Darlene McConikee? No thanks." Katherine shuddered, thinking about Darlene. Lately she'd been having nightmares about her between the nightmares about fire. Most of them involved suffocating.

"Isn't it possible to go in and do your job without forgetting what year it is?"

Katherine concentrated on searching for remaining knots while she sorted out the question. "I guess it's possible, but I still don't want to be that kind of teacher. It's not a job to me. It's my duty to do my very best for those kids even when they don't want me to. Especially if they don't want me to. Those are the ones who need me most."

"Duty," he repeated.

"Jack," she said. She started working along the last kinked muscle that swept from his lower back to the middle of his chest. "Let's not get into a semantic argument about your job, my job, and the true meaning of duty right now. Okay?"

He stiffened. "I'm not trying to start an argument. I never thought of it that way."

"It's okay. I guess I'm a little oversensitive today." She stroked her fingertips across his shoulders. "I lost one this year," she murmured hoping he wouldn't hear.

"Lost one?"

"Mark Hagood. Smarter than his grade,s but in the low functioning class. He could have been an honors student if he applied himself. But he had no intention of applying himself." She started tracing along his shoulder blade, picturing the boy. Bright blue eyes, unruly black hair, towering over her by at least six inches. Clever enough to make the tests believe he was stupid but not handicapped.

"What happened?"

"He dropped out three weeks ago. I think I drove him too hard." She remembered the first day Mark hadn't shown up, less than a week after the dance. She'd gotten a memo in her mail box telling her to remove him from her class list as she left that night. Jack had been at a roofing job, so she'd related the whole sorry tale to Archer. Archer had tried his best to be a lap dog and had licked her face, but that hadn't been quite what she'd hoped for. By the time Jack had come home, she'd recovered enough from her distress that she'd been too ashamed to abuse his friendship by crying on him.

"Did you drive him too hard, or did he not rise to the challenge?"

"Jack, you aren't going to make me feel better about this one. Not yet. It's too soon." She smoothed her hand down his back to the waist band of his jeans. His skin felt so warm and welcoming under her hand.

"So saying win one, lose one won't help either, huh?"

She smiled. He was trying awfully hard. At least two points extra credit worth. "Maybe a little."

"So can I ask you a question?"

"Sure." She traced her fingertips up his spine.

"Are you done?"

Katherine jerked her hand away from him. "I'm sorry. I wasn't thinking."

"I was starting to feel like the dog." Jack rolled over and sat up, rotating his shoulders. "Hey, that does feel better. You're pretty good."

"Thanks." She dropped her hands in her lap. "And thanks for reconditioning the back yard. I always meant to get around to it."

"To be honest Kate, I don't think you weigh enough to handle the tiller. There were a couple of spots back there where I thought I needed a jackhammer." He leaned against the chair, studying her.

Katherine watched his eyes linger on her face. He had been so solid, so patient. This handsome man who seemed to be willing to wait around until she made up her mind. She remembered when he kissed her in her classroom after the dance. The way his arm had felt tugging against her, lifting her off the floor. The taste of his lips against hers. The hollow clack of her shoes as they fell off. The heady wildness of being literally swept off her feet in the room where she taught every day, and her perfect willingness for it to go on and on.

Until Randy walked in.

She rose up on her hands and knees, leaning forward. Then she paused, analyzing his face for any discouragement. He looked puzzled, but otherwise at peace with her crawling toward him. She put one hand on his bare shoulder to steady herself and kissed him.

He drew a surprised gasp, but his arms wrapped around her, easing her into his lap. Her legs straddled his hips as she reveled in his soft mouth on hers. He pulled her tight against his chest. When she raised her lips from his she found she couldn't go far, and didn't want to.

"Why, Ms. Pelham, I thought we were friends," he whispered, keeping her tight against him.

"We are friends. Very good friends."

He wove his fingers through her hair. "You don't look anything like Harrison Ford."

"Lucky for you."

"Indeed." His grip on her waist relaxed, but she didn't move away. "There's no one here to interrupt us. Archer's even outside."

"I know." She brushed her fingertips down his chest, watching his flesh pebble. Her mind, for once, seemed to be functioning with perfect clarity. This, right here, was all she needed. Making it work seemed simple. His breath brushed across her cheek. The afternoon sun through the window picked up light stubble on his chin and his pulse throbbing against his throat. His eyes never left hers, devouring her.

His hand skimmed through her hair and down the curve of her back. "Do you have any idea how beautiful you are?"

"More or less beautiful than Harrison Ford?"

Jack traced his fingers along her jaw. Then he kissed her throat to the collar of her blouse. She sighed. When he leaned back again, he gazed at her. Heat rose through her body. His eyes seemed dark and serious. She wondered what he was looking for.

"Jack?" she whispered.

"Yes."

"What are you doing?"

"Just admiring you." He moved his hand around her waist until it rested on her thigh. The weight of it brought Katherine's temperature up a few more degrees. The fact that his thumb rested on the seam inside her thigh threatened to make her spontaneously combust. She knew he wasn't unaffected by their relative positions. His hard length pressed against her leg not all too far from where his thumb rested.

"Is that all you had planned?" she asked.

He paused for a long moment, looking at her. Studying her face and her body pressed close to his. "I'm not planning anything. I'm letting you lead."

"Oh. I didn't know." She reached for the buttons of her blouse. "Maybe you should have told me sooner."

His eyes seemed to get darker as he watched her undo her buttons. When she'd unfastened her blouse, she dropped her hands away, leaving it hanging closed.

Jack brushed her blouse off her shoulders, barely touching her. Closing her eyes and leaning her head back waiting for his hands to touch her bare skin, shivering as his fingers grazed her. He untucked it with agonizing slowness. Katherine felt the material sliding out of her jeans. He lifted her blouse away and dropped it to one side. Fortunately the lack of clean laundry had forced her to wear one of her fancier bras today. He stroked his hands over the lacy embroidered cups. Her nipples pinched under his touch. Then he reached behind her and undid the hooks of her bra, leaving it hang from her shoulders for the moment. "Are you sure this is what you want?" he asked.

"Yes, this is what I want." She leaned forward and kissed him again. He responded hungrily as her thighs tightened around his waist, his naked chest rubbing against hers. Carrying her with him, he stood up. She squealed and giggled. "Is this the firefighter's carry?" she asked.

"No, we'll try that another time." He carried her through the hall to his bedroom. Pressing her face into the curve of his neck, she breathed his scent and felt his powerful shoulders with her lips. For a long moment after he set her on his bed, he leaned over her, cradling her cheek in his hand before hooking his fingers around her bra strap and pulling it free. He knelt on the bed next to her, not touching her for a moment.

Katherine stretched in what she hoped was a seductive manner, raising her arms above her head. His eyes on her had the quality of a physical touch. She could see the effect looking had on him. His hands followed after his eyes, tracing her collar bone and down to cup her breast, sweeping his thumb along the edge of her areola. She moaned as the spike of heat shot through her body.

Jack leaned down, kissing where his fingers had caressed. She arched up to meet his lips, but he pulled back, working his way along her collarbone and down her torso with light, grazing kisses. Katherine gasped, clutching the sheets of his bed.

His lips found her nipple and, with one hand cupping her breast, he closed his mouth over the tense spot. "Please, Jack," she moaned, shivering.

As he lifted his head to look at her again, breathing in harsh gasps. He covered her mouth with his, probing and tasting. His hand closed over her breast, then glided down her body to the waist band of her jeans. When his fingers reached the closure he couldn't seem to close them over the button. Growling, he leaned away from her to try and see what he was doing.

"My dear, you seem to have your very own chastity belt courtesy of Levi's." He grumbled, still unable to get the button to slip through the button hole.

"I shall send them a letter of complaint." Reaching down she loosened the button. "Or maybe I'll just tell them my boyfriend has butterfingers."

"Butterfingers, hmm? Let's see." He eased her jeans and underwear over her hips and off her legs, flinging them to the far side of the room.

"How decisive of you." Katherine swallowed against what she first thought was panic, but then realized was raging desire. It had been so long since she had felt this much stark need and had seen the same desire in her partner that she didn't recognize it immediately. Closing her hands around his biceps, she tested them. Hard without being unyielding. There was some symbolism there too.

"Hmm." He leaned over her, trailing his hand down her body, leaving fire in its wake. His fingers roved down the outside of her thigh and up the inside.

* * * *

Jack watched Katherine close her eyes and draw a deep shuddery breath. He touched her in her most sensitive spot. She stiffened, making a breathy moan. Stroking her deliberately, he enjoyed the way her body reacted. Every inch of her ivory skin had developed a noticeable blush. Her auburn hair fanned out across his pillow and spread further with each helpless motion as she shifted against his hand. The scent of her desire coiled through his mind and only with a very tight rein could he keep command over himself.

When she crawled into his lap, it had taken every shred of control to not throw her down on the floor and make love to her. But he'd invested too many months and too much patience to screw it up now. He didn't just want her *for now*. He wanted her now *and* forever, but he still wasn't sure she wouldn't freeze up again. Even after all this time, after all his patience, he couldn't be sure she wanted this and she wasn't going to dart away. All the usual rules were off.

Heightening his pressure on her, he allowed his other hand to caress between her breasts, up her neck and along her parted lips. She took one of his fingers into her mouth. Her tongue glided around it as she sucked.

He took his finger from between her lips and covered her mouth with his own. Reaching for him, she ran one hand up his leg until it found his hard shaft. Her fingers worked on him through his jeans until he groaned against her mouth.

She turned to escape his insistent kiss. "Are you still waiting for me to lead?"

"What?" He paused, his fingers still pressed between her hot, slick thighs.

Her hand shifted to the waistband of his jeans, and she started toying with the button. "Are you still waiting for me to lead?" Her nimble fingers had no trouble unbuttoning his fly.

"Are you sure this is what you want?" he asked when his head had cleared enough to remember why he'd been letting her lead in the first place. There was still time to pull back. The shower was only a few feet away and there was plenty of cold water. He didn't want to hurt her any more.

"Make love to me, Jack. Please."

"Well, since you said please." He stood up and turned away, rubbing his hand though his hair in an effort to put order to his mind.

"It's much easier to do this when you're on the bed with me."

He looked back over his shoulder. She had sat up, curling her legs under her with her sunlit hair draped all around her. The motion didn't seem to be intentional, but that didn't matter. Jack's body reacted anyway. For a split second he almost forgot what he was looking for and went back to bed and to her. But if he'd moved away from her in the first place, it must have been important. Something so important he'd stopped touching her to walk across the room. But what was that important?

"We need a condom." Turning away from her, he was confronted by her reflection in his dresser mirror. He groaned. Had there ever been a woman so beautiful? Not sitting on his bed waiting for him. Forcing himself to look down at the drawer he'd pulled open, he pawed through his underwear and socks more irritated by the moment. It had to be here some place. He'd bought a new box when he moved in.

Katherine stretched sideways across the bed. "You're cold."

"No, I'm not," he mumbled. He'd always considered warehouse fires in August hot, but that had nothing on the heat he felt now.

"No, I mean you're not going to find them there."

"Why?" he asked. As he reached to open the drawer below it, he glanced in the mirror again. She had rolled over onto her back across the middle of his bed intuitively knowing which poses were most likely to drive him wild.

"Because they're in the built-in cabinet."

He growled and yanked open the door of the cabinet. The box sat in the back corner behind a framed photograph of his family, on top of a paperback novel. Grabbing one of the foil packets he turned back to the bed.

She waited with one hand out, still stretched across the bed with her hair wreathed around her face. "Let me help."

He swallowed to keep himself from whimpering. It had been a while. After four months of foreplay, he didn't have much control at all. The condom nearly slipped through his nerveless fingers and onto the floor as he passed it to her.

She sat up and hooked her fingers through his belt loops to bring him closer. Unzipping his jeans, she shoved the material out of the way. Before slipping the condom over him, she traced her fingers down his length, holding his eyes to hers while she did. A beautiful, secret smile played around her lips while she unrolled the condom over him. When she let him go, his knees buckled, and he had to catch himself on the bed.

But she had her arms around him, pulling him down on top of her. Her legs parted to welcome him and her thighs pressed against his hips. She moaned as he entered her. Covering her mouth with his, he moving inside her with long powerful strokes. He wanted to tell her he loved her and would take care of her. She would be loved, protected forever now. To promise her she would never be alone again.

But he was afraid.

He caressed her, memorizing the satiny texture of her flesh, afraid he would never again have the opportunity to feel her around him this way. This might be his only chance to drink in her throaty moans and cries, or watch her beautiful face transfix with pleasure. He drowned in the touch, taste and sight of her.

He thrust into her, glorying in the way her body moved with his. Pulling him deeper and higher. Drawing out need and desire, making them marvelous. He would never be able to survive without her now. Whatever happened after this instant, he was committed to her body and soul. Whether she would have him or not.

"Oh Jack," she whispered. The sound of her voice pierced him. Her body shuddered and her fingers dug into his back as she tightened around him.

His own climax crashed around him. He rode the tide of sensations until they beached him, leaving him exhausted and drained. For a few moments, he lay on top of her unable to think straight enough to move. When he did shift to one side, she made a mewling sound, following him and curling her body against his. He touched her hair, admiring the sleek texture of it and wondering what to say now. If he told her he loved her, would she run? If he didn't, would she be hurt?

"That was some back rub," he whispered.

"I'll say. It even relaxed me." She pressed herself against him, bending her knee and wrapping one leg across his. "Kind of amazing really."

"What?" Curling a lock of her hair around his finger, he admired the color of it.

"Well, how often is it you spend months dreaming about something and it ends up being better than you imagined?"

"Are you trying to butter me up for more yard work?" He kissed the top of her head.

She traced circles on his stomach. "You seem pretty buttery already. Butterfingers."

Sighing, she spread her hand against his skin. The pressure of it unfolded throughout his body. She sighed again and seemed to get a little heavier. After a moment her breathing evened out.

"Katherine?" he whispered.

No answer.

"Kate?" he whispered again.

Murmuring, she shifted. Her hair fell across his shoulder, tickling him. Her lips brushed his chest.

Asleep. He smirked. Aren't men supposed to fall asleep afterward? Jack hugged her. "I love you, Katherine."

She murmured again.

Jack stared at the ceiling savoring the weight of her body. Over the years he'd had what he considered pretty good sex. Sex that until now he would have called great sex. But this was a different thing altogether. Every time before had been more about biological urgency. Two bodies joining for the sole purpose of pleasing themselves. With Katherine it had felt almost spiritual. With Katherine, it felt as if a part of his soul had come home. He could never go back. There had to be a way to keep her. To convince her she needed to tear down that wall blocking the stairs and marry him.

That could wait. Right now she slept with her head fitted to the hollow of his shoulder and his arm stretched under her and around her waist, holding her close. Their bodies fitted together, warm and sated in the afternoon sun. He wanted to roll her over onto her back again and wake her with kisses before sliding back inside her. To be surrounded by her and to surround her again.

However, he didn't want to interrupt the incredible sweetness of her asleep on his chest. The feathery touch of her breath and the heat of her leg crooked over his. He wanted to sleep this way every night and wake this way every morning.

Closing his eyes, he relishing the sensation of her sleeping in his arms. She jolted upright with a gasp. "Oh God."

"What?"His mind seemed to be too relaxed to think. He tried to grab her but she scurried out of reach.

Then he heard it.

The approaching wail of a siren. "Katherine, it's just a police car." He tried to sound soothing, but her panic was infectious.

"I can't believe I did this. I can't believe I made it worse. I keep making it worse." She scrambled off the bed on all fours and grabbed her jeans.

"Worse? Katherine, what are you talking about?" He sat up. Cold dread washed over him. Even after all his patience and restraint, he'd been right. Katherine was leaving. "Where are you going?"

She got her jeans over her hips and headed for the bedroom door zipping them. "This is awful. I don't know what I was thinking. I'm so sorry."

Jack lunged after her. He almost fell off the foot of the bed, missing her arm by inches. "Wait a minute. Talk to me," he demanded. The fear in his throat turned it into a plea.

"I can't." She sobbed. "I can't be near you."

The police car screamed past the house.

"You said you wanted this," he protested. She had seemed willing. Had she lied? Had she slept with him for some other reason than her own desire? As he heard her run into the living room he got his feet under him.

"I did want this." She sobbed. "I wanted it too much. I'm so sorry."

"Kate!" he shouted. "Wait a minute. Talk to me."

"I knew I would pay for this. I knew I would keep hurting you, and now I've made it much, much worse."

Jack scrambled through the hall and caught her arm as she ran out of the living room buttoning her blouse. The force of her motion spun her against him. "Where are you going?"

"Home. I'm so sorry." She pulled away.

"For what?"

"For this. For us. For letting you have the apartment in the first place." She twisted out of his numb grasp and out the front door. The sound of the siren faded into the distance.

"What?" Jack skidded to a stop before he chased her outside naked. Running back to the bedroom for his jeans he hopped to the front door putting them on. Her footsteps thundered up the stairs and through her apartment. He ran around the house to her door and pounded on it. "Katherine! Open the door." One well placed shoulder and he could break it down. Get to her. Make her talk.

Archer started barking in the back yard.

"Archer, shut up," Jack shouted. He turned to see where the dog was and noticed the next-door neighbor standing in his own yard, a shovel and a flat of marigolds in hand, looking stunned. What was he thinking about the sudden spectacle? And what would he do if Jack broke down her door? Katherine's anger would be nothing compared to the arrival of the Arden Police. The arrival of Vince Howard.

Jack waved. "Hi."

"Hello." The neighbor leaned the shovel against his house and headed for his own back door.

Jack pressed his forehead against the house, cursing under his breath. There was no way he could have done it anyway. He couldn't break down her door any more than he could walk through a wall. It would frighten her, and he couldn't bear to do that. He couldn't be a brute even though the primitive part of him wanted to go in there and claim his woman.

But she was not his woman.

Everything hurt again. Parts that hadn't hurt before, hurt now. The last thing she said rang in his ears. 'For letting you have the apartment in the first place.'

She regretted every moment since February. Jack's heart shattered to a fine powder. Once, when he was about eleven years old, his family had gone to the beach and he'd gone body surfing. It had been exhilarating until he caught the wrong side of a wave. The water churned him around and dumped him face down , too disoriented to know which way the air was. He felt a lot like that now.

Nothing would ever be enough. She might not even give him the chance to start over. To win her friendship. To win her trust. She might cut him out of her life altogether.

And then what would he do?

* * * *

Katherine threw herself on her bed sobbing. Every part of her throbbed. She could still feel his rough hands dragging across her body and his lips tasting her. The deep, shattering contact still rang in her soul. Nothing before even came close, and she knew with terrifying certainty no one else would touch her that profoundly.

She hugged herself and discovered she'd forgotten her bra downstairs. Her underwear wasn't on so much as wrapped around one leg and shoved down the other leg of her jeans, leaving the seam of her jeans in close contact with her still tender womanhood. She heard Jack pounding on her door, but couldn't bear to face him. It was too soon. If she opened that door now, she would never again be able to close it with him on the outside. Archer barked in the backyard. Jack shouted at him. There was anger in his voice, but she also heard fear and bewilderment.

She loved him mind, body and soul. If that siren hadn't reminded her how dangerous it would be to commit to him, she would have. The sensation of her cheek pressed against his chest as she drifted into a contented half sleep haunted her. Had he said what she thought he had? It seemed quite likely and, without the warning of the siren, she would have told him how much she loved him too.

The risk was too high. She couldn't stand to be alone again.

But wasn't she alone now?

Chapter 11

Katherine rubbed her eyes. She had her box unpacked and everything put away for the summer. The gift cards waited on the newel post at the top of the stairs for her minor spending spree.

Yesterday, she'd cried herself to sleep. Jack hadn't made another attempt to get her to talk to him. When she woke up it had been dark, she'd had a throbbing headache, and she'd needed something to do, so she'd started unpacking her school box. It was a pretty thought-intensive project. At some point she'd closed her eyes to rest them and fell asleep on the floor of her office.

Jack woke her this morning when he closed the back door. She lay on the floor, stiff and aching from more than just the one bad night's sleep, listening to him open the garage, start his truck, back out, close the garage and pull out of the driveway. Then she'd gone to bed and slept until mid afternoon. After that nap she'd taken a bath, washing away his scent. Her soul felt as if it had been dragged for miles by a stampeding herd of wild stallions. She could feel their individual hoof prints.

Gary had never been like that. He'd never touched her that way. Seeing her late fiancé in Jack's shadow, he became smaller and meaner. She had more of a true marriage to Jack than she could have ever hoped for with Gary.

But she could not be married to Jack. Too much risk. If she had been shattered when Gary died, how would she feel when Jack died? *The Cambridge Sun* already had a lovely photo of her being carried out of Gary's funeral service. Would they get a better picture next time? Would she lose her mind completely? She could imagine that picture. On the front page of the newspaper, Jack's friends Kevin and Dan carrying her out of the church while she gibbered.

She picked up a book. The sophomore grammar book. With her free time this summer, she planned to try to work up some better lessons. As she put it on the shelf a note slipped out and flittered to the floor. In the middle of the page, in her own handwriting, it read, "Be careful at work tomorrow." Across the bottom in Jack's jagged hand it read, "I can't be careful. It's my job." She'd taped it to his door one night before going to bed and found it taped to her door the next morning.

Folding the paper in half, she jammed it in her pocket. She'd told Jack she was going to the bookstore today, and today had almost slipped away. On the way to the car, she dumped the empty box into the trash. Archer whimpered as she passed the fence. "Hello puppy, have you missed me?"

He put his front paws on the top of the fence and wagged his stumpy tail so hard she thought he might knock himself over.

She let herself into the back yard. The ground was still soft and uneven from the work he'd done yesterday. Jack's boot prints were still visible where Archer hadn't trampled them out. Archer bounded toward her with a tennis ball between his teeth. He dropped it and waited, poised to run. "So what is going on in your owner's mind, boy? Does he hate me? He should by now."

Archer yipped and nosed the ball toward her.

Picking it up, she tossed it toward the fence. Archer chased it. His feet sank deep into the tilled soil. Jack had even gotten the soil tested so he could get the right kind of fertilizer. He was always careful with her too. Thoughtful and gentle.

Archer brought the ball back and dropped it at her feet. He still liked the wrestle, but when they played fetch, he dropped the ball without a fight. To reward him, she threw it again. The sun would be setting in about an hour. The bookstore was open late, but Jack would be coming home soon, and she didn't feel up to another strange conversation like the one they'd had yesterday. Not after what had happened. She needed to get a little more time between herself and yesterday so she could think straight. A little more time for her body to forget. As if it ever could. "Time to go, Archer. I'll play with you more tomorrow while Jack's at work."

When she backed out of the garage, she noticed something under the windshield wiper. After closing the garage door, she pulled it out. It was a piece of note paper wrapped around a five dollar bill. The paper said, "Treat yourself" in Jack's handwriting. Tears came to her eyes, but she pulled back before it turned into a full on sob. If she didn't want to have a strained conversation with Jack, she certainly didn't want him to come home and find her sobbing over five dollars. She folded the note into the pocket with the other note and put the money with the gift cards in another pocket.

As she backed down the driveway, she flicked on the headlights because it was within an hour of sunset and according to the law drivers had to have their headlights on. It was one of the old Gary habits she'd never shaken.

She hadn't had the opportunity to shop for books in a very long time. It had been one of her great passions before Gary's death, but for the last four years, she'd done all her reading from the library or from her own collection. Choosing two paperbacks and a magazine she settled in at the coffee bar with a hot chocolate. For a while she sat watching the sky darken and remembering how it felt to be human again. Until the middle of February, she'd been like a robot going through the motions to keep at least her nose, if not her whole head, above water. And it hadn't started when Gary died either. There hadn't been money enough before, but something else had been missing too. Something that had been missing so long she hadn't noticed until the first time Jack looked at her. Even without touching her, they'd developed an intimate relationship of easy laughter and good conversation.

Then he'd kissed her, and she realized what she'd been missing all those years. The adoration in his eyes, and little things he did to please her—right down to an extra five bucks to blow on a nonessential. She touched her cheek where his hand had brushed her the night of the dance. The faint heat of his fingers still stained her skin.

And then there was yesterday.

Yesterday when she'd curled into his embrace after he'd kindled something she didn't know existed. One long glorious afternoon of touching and being touched. Healing and reveling in one another.

Until reality intruded.

And now that she'd had it, this felt like exile. Close enough to touch, but too far away to reach. He was Pandora's Box, and she'd opened him anyway and unleashed all the plagues of the world upon herself.

She sighed. The light had left the sky. Looking at her paperback novels she wondered if she should switch them for one self help book that would make her stop wanting heroes she couldn't have. If she could learn to settle for a nice middle manager or a teacher, she might be happier in the long run.

But would Jack? She'd hurt him. If she'd used a meat cleaver, she'd have done less damage. He was a hero, he wanted to protect people. While she was a wonderful victim of circumstance, losing her father and then her fiancé. Of course he would fall for her. She stopped pursuing that line of logic before it unraveled. She'd been attracted to Jack before she found out what he did, and he'd been interested in her from the first moment too, long before he discovered her history.

Picking up her cup, she put it in the bus tub before grabbing her books and magazine. She didn't feel attached enough to the fashion magazine to want to take it home, so she put it back on the rack. On the way out of the section, she noticed a magazine on display about fire trucks. Picking it up, she leafed through it. An entire magazine about fire trucks. Would he be annoyed or pleased when she used the money he gave her to buy a gift for him? She slid the magazine under her paperbacks and went to the register.

"I didn't know we had a magazine about fire trucks." The cashier picked it up and studied the cover. Her name tag read Jessica. "This is neat. Do you work for the fire department?"

"No, I have a...friend who does. I'm a teacher."

Jessica nodded. "Are any of these for classroom use?" She picked up Katherine's fantasy novel. "We have a discount program for books you plan to use in the classroom with the students."

"This is pleasure reading. But thank you. I'll keep it in mind." Katherine handed over her gift cards, pleased that she'd worked it out about right. She would walk away from this trip with a dollar and change.

"Here you are. Receipt's in the bag. Happy reading." Jessica handed over Katherine's bag.

"Thank you." Katherine headed for her car. The lot had been full when she arrived. She'd had to park in front of the computer store next door. Tossing her bag on the passenger seat she turned the key.

Nothing happened.

Katherine cursed, turning the key again and nothing happened again. Then she started feeling the controls, cursing more when the headlight switch shifted to the off position as she twisted it. She'd forgotten to turn her lights off, and they'd drained her battery while she sat sipping coffee and pondering the perversity of her fate.

She leaned her head against the steering wheel and considered her options. At one time, she could have called the police and they would have sent the nearest cruiser to get her on her way. But those days were gone, and there was no reason to dwell on it. If she felt cruel she could call Jack. He would do the husbandly thing without the benefit of being her husband. And then she would have to talk to him. She'd have to explain herself and make him understand why she couldn't marry him because he was a hero whether he worked for the department or not.

But she couldn't call Jack any more than she could call the police. She would have to pay for a tow truck. Inside the store there were a couple of customers ahead of her at the information desk, and she had to wait.

"Can I help you?" The woman on the other side of the counter frowned. "Didn't I just ring you out?"

Jessica. "Yes, you did. My car won't start and I need a tow truck. Do you have a phone book I can look at?"

Jessica reached to the side of the counter. "Is it a dead battery? Somebody here might have cables."

"Oh, no. I'll call—"

"I'll jump it."

Katherine jumped at the voice behind her. She noticed Jessica's eyes focus over her left shoulder so she turned to face the owner of that familiar deep voice.

Kevin stood behind her with his hands jammed in his pockets, looking gruff and capable. "I've got cables. Where are you parked?"

He didn't sound at all friendly despite the friendly offer.

"Is this someone you know?" Jessica asked, leaning forward so Kevin couldn't hear her. "Would you like one of the guys to go out with you and help? I can even come out if you like."

Katherine felt comforted by the offer. With Jessica around, she wouldn't have to have an awkward conversation with Jack's friend, but she didn't want to take the other woman away from her job just to save herself a little embarrassment.

"No. I know him." Katherine watched Kevin's eyes shift from her to Jessica and back. "If you don't mind. I'm parked out front."

"If I minded, I wouldn't have offered." Kevin grumbled, following her out the front doors. "Where are you?"

"Over there." She pointed. By this time, her car sat nearly alone in the lot.

"Go stand by your car. I'll get mine." He left her standing on the sidewalk.

She leaned on the back bumper looking through the darkened windows of the computer store until he drove up behind her. "Lucky for me you were here."

"Open your hood."

Swallowing nerves, she moved to obey. She didn't recall much from the two times she'd met him, but she didn't remember him being so angry. At the station he'd kissed her hand quite cheerfully, but maybe firefighters were like cops. Almost all the cops she'd encountered were happier working. They tended to view off duty hours as standing between them and their next shift.

"I saw you sitting in the coffee shop," he announced, hooking up the cables.

"I'm surprised you recognized me. We only met briefly. " She folded her arms.

"Oh, I recognize you."

Katherine swallowed hard and wondered if she shouldn't have asked Jessica for that escort. Kevin didn't seem at all happy, and his unhappiness seemed to be directed at her.

He walked over to her. "It has to charge." Standing in front of her with his ropy arms folded across his chest, he glared at her. "You know he's planning on quitting the department."

Katherine opened her mouth to speak and then closed it. Jack wanted to quit the department even though she told him not to, and Kevin blamed her.

"I never asked him to," she said.

"You didn't have to. You had to be afraid he was going to die like your fiancé did. Even though your fiancé died in an accident."

"What do you know about it?"

"I can read. The library has all the papers on file. The other officer was acquitted, you know. According to the paper it was an accident. A freak accident."

"I know." Katherine looked at the ground. She hadn't wanted to see Joe Mazoli convicted any more than anyone else. "Still, it's a logical fear."

"Is it?" Kevin unfolded his arms and reached into his back pocket. "Do you know what this is?"

Squinting, she tried to focus on the paper he held out for her, but the letters and figures blurred together.

"Occupational Fatality Report from the Bureau of Labor Statistics." Kevin pushed it into her hands to read, but she couldn't make out much in the low orange parking lot lights. "That's the 1990 report. I couldn't find anything newer. Take it. Jack wouldn't."

She stared at the paper. On the left side of the paper was a list of occupations and a ragged column of numbers.

"In 1990, thirty-nine firefighters died on the job. *Sixty* roofers died." He pointed at the paper, and Katherine assumed he pointed to the roofer line. "He talked to Mike Tomms about working with him regular."

"Mike Tomms?" Katherine's mouth went dry.

"Cap's brother-in-law. Jack worked with his crew today. Jack also said something about driving a truck. Look how many of them died in 1990. It makes burning buildings look safe."

Katherine tried to make out the number, but couldn't. She could see it was three digits and the first digit was a seven. It seemed both high and realistic.

"We know how dangerous the job is, Katherine. We're very careful all the time. We're rigged to the teeth with protective gear, and we're constantly training. We pay attention. I'll be willing to bet most of those roofers died because they weren't paying attention and fell. Or because one of their co-workers wasn't paying attention and left something where it didn't belong."

Katherine had a flash of Randy walking across the garage roof too casually and nearly falling when she yelled his name.

Kevin paused for a minute and ground his teeth as if this conversation wasn't going quite the way he planned. When he spoke again he was calmer, less threatening. "If he quits the department to get a safe job, he's going to be at a higher risk."

"I don't want him to quit," she whispered.

"Try your car." Kevin walked away.

She opened the door and the dome light came on full and bright. In its light she could see all the statistics. Truck drivers, seven hundred forty-nine. Police, one hundred seventy-four. The car started right up when she turned the key. Leaving it running, she stepped out. Kevin disconnected the cables and wound them around his arm.

"I don't want him to quit the department," she said with a stronger voice.

"Then maybe you need to explain that to him without using any big words, because he doesn't understand yet." Kevin dropped the cables in his trunk. "Katherine, I've known him a long time, and he's never been like this. Isn't it enough that he's willing to quit?"

"I don't want him to quit. I didn't ask him to quit."

"Then you're going to have to get over being afraid. He loves you, and it sounds as if you love him. You have to learn to love him as a firefighter, and believe he's going to come home every shift. You know when she opened Pandora's Box and let out fear and despair and misery, all that stuff. The last thing in the box was hope. That was the thing she shut the box on."

Kevin got into his car and drove away. Katherine stood for a long time in the parking lot listening to her car run and looking at the paper she couldn't read for the tears in her eyes, wondering why Kevin had mentioned Pandora's Box.

＊ ＊ ＊ ＊

Katherine sat bolt upright in bed before she even knew the siren woke her. The room was dark and her alarm clock said 3:56. Everything hurt because she'd been playing over energetically with Archer yesterday, which she wouldn't have been if she'd been able to summon the courage to talk to Jack that morning. She'd been up half the night poring over the fatality report Kevin had given her, preparing her speech, but when the time came she hadn't been able to make herself go down and give it.

So instead, she spent the entire day lavishing attention on his dog as penance. She had even considered walking to the station to talk to him in the afternoon, but decided she didn't want to have that particular conversation with an audience.

But what if he got hurt tonight? What if he got hurt on this run, and she never had the chance? She could end up a widow without ever having been a wife. Again. That thought paralyzed her for a moment. Kevin, in his garbled way, had been right. The last thing in Pandora's Box had been hope.

Katherine scrambled out of bed, pulled on the first clothes she found and ran out of the house. As she locked the door Archer started barking.

"You can't go," she shouted at him. She winced as her voice rang off the neighbor's house, reminding her it was the middle of the night.

She had sprinted down the driveway and halfway to the corner before she realized not only was it the middle of the night, but they could be out for hours. Until they returned, she would be waiting alone. Deciding she'd be better off with the company of a big dog, she doubled back to the house for Archer. Before she could take the dog, she had to get keys to Jack's from her apartment so she could get Archer's leash out of the back room, and then she had to search for the leash in the dark because she didn't want to waste time turning on the light. About ten minutes later, she headed up the road with the dog at a more sedate pace.

＊ ＊ ＊ ＊

"Hey Conley, why is your landlady here with your dog?" Lew asked. He'd been twisted around in his jumpseat looking out the windshield.

"What?" Jack turned, jostling Lew out of the way.

Katherine crouched against the telephone pole across the street with Archer curled around her feet. Her hair was loose and wild but he couldn't make out much else because the rising sun had left her in shadow. He shrugged off his turnout coat which, ten minutes ago, he'd been too tired to remove. As Kevin stopped the engine to back it into the bay, Jack jumped out and crossed the street.

"What are you doing here?" he asked before he reached the center of the lane.

"I heard you go out." She stood up using the pole for support. "I was worried."

"So you got out of bed and walked up here in the middle of the night?" Stepping up on the curb he looked down at her. She looked as if she might have been crying earlier, but she'd stopped. A few stray dog hairs stuck to her cheek. He longed to brush them off, but knew he wouldn't stop there. One little touch would lead to him burying his hands in her hair and tasting her lips. Smelling her shampoo and her skin. His turnout pants didn't have pockets so he put his hands behind his back.

"I wanted to talk to you, and I chickened out this morning...yesterday morning."

Jack felt a chill creeping down his back. It couldn't be good news if she'd walked up here in the middle of the night to tell him and waited two hours for him to get back. "Yeah?"

She fidgeted. "What does Kevin know about Pandora's Box?"

Jack flushed. He'd asked Kevin about the reference after she'd mentioned it. Kevin had loaned him a tattered book of Greek mythology with the story marked, but Jack had read the book from cover to cover. "I don't know. You want me to ask him?"

"No, that's—never mind." She waved her hand. "You can't quit the department."

Jack stepped back a pace. It wasn't the bad news he'd feared, but he didn't like the direction anyway. "I thought we'd had this conversation."

"No, this is different." She reached for him and caught one of his suspenders. "I talked to your friend, Kevin. He gave me some information."

"When did you talk to Kevin?" Jack wanted to take another step back. To put some distance between himself and her, but she had hold of him and he had nowhere to go. Archer walked behind him, trapping his legs with the leash. She had the dog on her side.

"At the bookstore."

"I got the magazine you left me," he said. "Thanks."

"I thought you'd like it." She frowned. "You probably were a terrible student."

"Why?"

"You're trying to get me off the subject."

Guilty as charged, but willing to give it another go. "Don't you wear that sweatshirt the other way? I thought the seams went on the inside." He plucked at her exposed shoulder seam.

Katherine looked down and back up. "Stop that. I didn't walk up here at four in the morning and stand around in the cold for two hours waiting to have a silly conversation with you." Then she bit her lip. "Jack, you know I'm afraid of you getting hurt on the job."

"You have every right to be. It's dangerous."

"Less dangerous than roofing."

"So I've heard." Jack looked over his shoulder at the station. He couldn't see the faces watching them, but he guessed the whole gang was out by now, even Dan and Mark Davis, the other paramedic. Both of them had probably been asleep until somebody woke them up and told them about the show outside.

"Look." She placed her palms on his chest, garnering all of his attention. "I got engaged to a self-centered guy who worked in a dangerous profession, and it isn't fair for me to punish you for him. I was trying to avoid being in a relationship with you, and I ended up in one. I tangled myself up in an emotional bond and in trying to escape from the intimacy I needed, I became aware of how much I needed it."

Jack felt pretty sure she meant the word intimacy in a different way than he thought, but it made his temperature rise anyway. Even without that distraction, he doubted he would have understood a word she had said anyway.

"Wow, you want to say that again? I'm just a dumb firefighter."

She sighed. "You are not dumb. Stubborn, maybe. I'm trying to say I love you and I'll either learn to sleep through the siren, or we'll move. Besides, I think the dog wants us to stay together."

Jack looked down. Archer had wrapped the leash around both of them and when Jack stepped forward, Archer pulled it tight. She seemed unsteady, but he could put that down to leaning on a telephone pole for two hours on very little sleep. When he stroked his thumb along her jaw, she leaned into his touch. Her eyes drifted half closed as if she wanted to focus on their contact. The steady burn he'd felt since yesterday when he found the gift she'd left for him, flared up threatening to consume him. "So does this mean you're not going to evict me?"

"Goodness no, I was planning on extending your lease so I could torture myself by eavesdropping on you through the heating ducts." She smiled her secret smile that never failed to shorten his breath.

"Is that what you do up there? It seemed quiet." He touched his lips to hers and she rose up on her toes, wrapping her arms around his shoulders. Her body melted against his, her pulse throbbing in time with his. When her fingers dug into his back, he curled his arms around her waist. She gasped as he lifted her off the ground.

"What are you trying to do?" she asked.

"Knock your shoes off again. It was fun the first time."

"They're tied on this time."

He smiled. "I'll have to try harder then."

She giggled. "I thought we were friends."

"We are friends. Very good friends." He kissed her again.

She slipped her tongue between his lips, tasting sweet as always. Her hair brushed over his hands. Heat spread through his body when she moaned against his mouth. He slipped one hand down her back, feeling her respond to him and wanting more of it.

"Jack," she said, dropping back to her feet and pulling back. "We have an audience."

"I don't care." He kissed the corner of her left eye. There was soot on her face, and he remembered that he hadn't had a chance to wash yet. It felt as if hours had passed since the last run, but the sun was still barely over the horizon and his world had changed again. Hopefully the change would stick this time.

"You will when it becomes the subject of humor." She planted her hand on his chest, gaining a little space. "We'll talk more at home."

"Anything you want."

Kate raised an eyebrow at him. "Anything?"

He smiled and watched her eyes go dark and soft. "I don't think you're thinking about talking."

"Maybe not. Does that bother you? We can have a nice long conversation if that's all you want." She traced her fingertip in circles against the base of his skull.

"Well, I don't get off duty for a couple of hours yet so why don't you let me consider my options?" Two weeks ago, he'd barely been able to stop her long enough to say hello. Two days ago, she'd seduced him and then run out hysterical at the sound of a siren. In two hours, when he got off duty and got home, would she still be this willing?

"You're not going to change your mind are you?"

"Change my mind?"

"Katherine, I love you, and I don't want to see you hurt. Are you sure this is what you want? You're not going to change your mind like you did the other day?"

"The other—oh." She shook her head. "No, Jack. I had a long time to sit here in the dark waiting for you to come back. If I were going to change my mind I would have done it sometime before sunrise when a police car went screaming down the block."

Jack pulled her tight again and pressed his cheek to the top of her head. He wanted to believe her, but he didn't think he would until he had some kind of commitment out of her. Something permanent and binding. He stood holding her, considering the future. The question came so easily to mind, but would she say yes?

Behind them the alarm tone rang. Katherine stiffened in his arms, and Jack growled. "I have to go."

Slipping out of his arms, she lifted her chin. "Be careful."

He kissed her nose as he stepped out of the leash. Then he jogged across the street. Kevin was already pulling out by the time he reached the truck, Lew popped open the door when Kevin came onto the street. Jack watched her as they pulled out. She stood by the telephone pole, unwrapping Archer's leash from her legs and seemingly not paying attention to the engine, but when they slowed again at the corner he saw her look up. Her face looked as serene as it had been in the newspaper photo of Gary's funeral, so he knew what her mind was doing.

* * * *

Katherine watched the engine disappear around the corner and sucked in a deep breath. She had stopped breathing about the time the tone sounded. The dizziness passed with the second breath. "Come on, Archer, let's go home."

Forcing herself to walk down Worcester, she returned the way she'd come. The other route would have followed the path of the engine, but by doing that she would be going out of her way to no good purpose. Following him to the fire wouldn't help. She'd told him she would learn to sleep through the siren, so following the engine was off limits too.

People were waking up and going about their morning routines. Making breakfast. Getting the paper. Letting the dog out or the cat in. She ducked under the arching rose vines near the corner, pausing to inspect for buds. Maybe over the summer she would make a habit of walking Jack to work. The entire path always looked pretty. She turned on Washington and followed the crook in the road to Judge. A woman stood on the porch of the brick house on the corner watering her plants. She called a cheery hello, which Katherine returned. The short block of Judge she needed to follow to get to Jefferson was tree shrouded and quiet, but a police cruiser had parked at the stoplight, blocking traffic from going down her block.

"You live here?" The female officer called when she reached the corner.

"About halfway down the block. What's going on?"

"Apartment fire."

Katherine went cold. "That big building on the corner?" Three stories, red brick, weeds in the yard and a rickety wooden porches attached to the sides.

"Yes." The officer was distracted by traffic.

Katherine started down the road. She could see two engines parked in the road and hoses already snaked from the hydrant across the street. A crowd huddled on the sidewalk in various states of morning attire. Katherine walked faster and faster along the sidewalk until she was running. Skidding up her driveway she wrapped Archer's leash around her wrought iron railing. "Just stay."

Archer leaped after her when she ran down the drive, but the leash brought his bark to an abrupt end.

Katherine's heartbeat thundered in her ears, nearly blocking out the hungry growl of the fire. This couldn't happen. They were sorting things out. Her life was showing a glimmer of happiness. She leaped off the curb and over a hose, skirting the hysterical, stunned mob of apartment dwellers and headed for the nearest engine. The top floor on this side of the building was fully involved and orange flames licked up over the roof.

The first engine she passed was a pumper not a ladder truck and had a twelve stenciled on the side. Swerving around it, she headed for the ladder truck. She'd passed the cab when a strong arm caught her around the waist, lifting her off her feet.

"I don't think so."

"No. You don't understand." She jerked in his grasp, twisting far enough to recognize the face.

"I'm sorry, Katherine, but you've got to stay out of the way," Vince said. "You know how this works."

"I have to know if he's okay." She sobbed. "You can't do this to me."

"He's a professional, and he'll work better if he knows you're safe." Vince's grip on her loosened when she stopped struggling, but he kept his arm around her. "That's better. You need a Kleenex?"

She shook her head. "I need to know where he is."

"I know. You stay right here, and I'll see if I can find something out, all right? What's his name?"

"Jack." She pressed her hand over one eye. Panic pounding through her brain. "Jack Conley. He's with nine."

Vince looked at her and pointed at the ground. "Right here."

She nodded and leaned back against the engine before her knees gave out. Her ingrained police wife training kicked in, and she felt her face forming a mask. Always stay calm for the public. Keep your head in a crisis. Your emotions come later, in private. Never let the photographers get a picture of you falling apart. *They already had one of those.* She looked around for the cameras of the local paper. They, at least, wouldn't run the awful ones.

"Katherine?"

She looked to the left at the firefighter working the controls in the side of the ladder truck. By the time she looked at him he'd turned back to the task at hand and it took her a moment to place his profile. "Kevin?"

Kevin glanced over. "He said you'd show up."

"Where is he?" She took a step toward Kevin before she remembered she'd promised to stay where she was.

"Third floor."

"What's he doing up there?" Katherine tried to control the squeal of panic slipping into her voice.

"That's where the fire is." Kevin gestured at the side of the truck. "Take a seat on the running board."

Katherine eased down. Her knees felt like jelly, and she didn't know if she would ever catch her breath again. Fire seemed to be everywhere, flickering in the puddles on the street, and roaring through the air. She drove past this building on her way home from the library. It was considered an at risk location by the police. Why did it have to burn down now?

Vince came back. "He's up on the third floor, and he just reported in so he's fine."

As the words left his mouth, Katherine, who had not taken her eyes off the building, rose to her feet. A whimper escaped her. Vince and Kevin both turned to see what she was watching. Vince reached for her.

A firefighter had backed out onto the wooden porch. Katherine watched with frozen fascination as the supports broke away, causing the porch to tilt. Grabbing for a handhold, the firefighter fell backward through the railing, dropping two stories to the hillside. He tried to catch himself with one arm when he hit the ground and that arm twisted underneath him. The paramedics ran forward, but Katherine never moved. She stood watching with one hand gripping the edge of the cab, not breathing. After a moment, they helped him to his feet and he followed them to their truck.

Katherine walked toward them, shaking. It had to be Jack. Since he'd walked away, it couldn't be bad. They positioned him on the running board of the paramedic truck. One knelt in front, immobilizing his wrist with an air cast.

"Just a tip," the man working on his wrist said. "When you're falling from a height greater than your feet, using your hand to stop yourself is a really bad idea."

Katherine looked down and realized the paramedic was Dan, who had helped Jack move in and fixed her garage roof. Jack took off his helmet. His face was dirtier now than it had been a little while ago but he had a band of clean skin where his helmet rested. She fought the impulse to lean down and kiss it. They had an audience. Some of the crowd had turned from the drama of the burning building to the drama of the injured firefighter.

She swallowed hard and tried to breathe. Whole, hale and healthy except for the wrist. His eyes met hers, and she thought she saw him cringe a little.

"Look," he said with a forced cheer. "All in one piece."

"Yes. I saw. It was a lovely dive. It won't get you out of your lease, but I give it an eight point five. Next time try to do it into a pool. How bad is it?" she asked Dan. She felt Vince and someone else stop behind her. A glance told her it was Jack's captain.

"He can't even break anything right. It looks like a bad sprain."

"Really? Hey, I'll be out for a while with that." Jack grabbed Katherine's hand. "Wanna get married?"

She sighed. "You're broken now. I don't accept damaged goods."

"I'll get better."

"That won't get you out of the lease either." Katherine felt herself start to smile.

"I know. I want to sign a longer one. A permanent one. I want to marry you."

Someone in the crowd shouted, "Come on, marry him."

Katherine frowned. Her heart had started to slow down. Marry him? Was he joking? She'd watched this lunatic fall two stories from a fire. His fingers squeezed hers while his golden eyes searched hers for an answer. A real answer. "Well, okay."

She heard a shutter snap close by and looked up. A reporter stood nearby grinning. She knew his face. He worked for the *Arden Journal*.

Maybe she would be able to convince them to run the picture with the wedding announcement. Some of the apartment dwellers started to cheer.

Jack pulled her down next to him and draped his uninjured arm over her shoulders. She leaned against him and closed her eyes. Maybe being married to a hero wouldn't be so bad after all.

Epilogue

Archer paced around the foyer. From Jack to the bottom of the stairs and back. He knew they were leaving, and he got the impression he wasn't going. In the nine months since they had married, he hadn't gotten to go a lot. The wedding had been fun. A bunch of people and a couple of other dogs in the park. Then they'd added a whole second floor to the house. But since then, things had gone downhill. Sometimes they even locked him out of the bedroom. And about six months ago, her scent had changed, which worried Archer at first. The last time that happened, he'd gotten a new owner. That had worked out, but Archer didn't feel like training another new owner.

"Are you ready?" Jack shouted. "We're already late."

"Hey! If you were six months pregnant I'd give you a break once in a while." Katherine started down the stairs. Archer stood at the bottom of the steps watching her hopefully. Maybe she would relent and let him go. She stooped to pat his head as she passed him.

"I'm never going to be six months pregnant, so it's all speculation, isn't it?"

Katherine handed Jack her coat so he could help her put it on. "I can't believe you're taking me to Wendy's for Valentine's Day dinner."

"You suggested it." Jack slid her coat up to her shoulders.

Archer sat on the floor and watched them. Something fishy was going on in the room at the top of the stairs. It had been repainted and re-carpeted. New furniture kept showing up.

She leaned back against his chest. "Oh, I forgot."

He put his arm around her middle and kissed her cheek.

"I thought you were worried about being late," she scolded.

"I was. I'm not any more. It's Valentine's Day, let's stand them up."

"You are evil. Lew needs our support, and if the whole gang doesn't show, he might chicken out and then where will you be? Your grandmother will not be happy." She turned out of his arms.

"All right, you nag. Archer, back room," Jack ordered.

Archer flattened his ears to look as pathetic as possible. If they wouldn't take him with them, they could at least let him stay in the house.

"Let him stay in. It's cold back there, and we won't be gone long." Katherine scratched his ears. "You'll be good, won't you?"

Archer licked her hand.

"You are so gullible." Jack opened the door. "Archer, guard the house. Don't let anything happen to the baby's room."

Katherine walked out first followed by Jack, and the door locked from the outside. Archer ran to the kitchen window and watched them get the truck out of the garage. Archer ran to the foyer window and watched the truck back onto the road and drive away.

They'd done it again. They'd left without him. Archer walked up the stairs and turned into the room at the top. There was a sink and a counter on one wall and a tiny refrigerator under the window. On the other wall sat a crib with a rocking chair beside it. The curtains had flowers all over them. Archer lay down in the middle of the floor. He liked to sleep in this room when they locked him out of the bedroom. It was quiet here. And he didn't mind much that they locked him out, because since they started sleeping in the same place, they both seemed happier. Archer groaned and rolled over on his side. He could sleep until they got back.

Meet the Author

For my seventh birthday my brother gave me The Eagles' *Hotel California* and I was completely enchanted by the title track. No clue what it meant, but I loved it and my fate was sealed. Unfortunately, as a hard core introvert, performing onstage in any capacity was off the table as a career choice. So I turned to writing and spent many boring college lectures detailing the adventures of Touchstone in the margins of my notebooks. Years later I decided to do something with them and wrote what became *Heaven Beside You*. These things do tend to get out of control with me. A fun side project that kept me entertained while I was teaching English in Korea turned into a series that I was working on through a stint in Chile, the US and the Middle East. And I'm not slowing down.

When not writing, I like to travel so much that I recently had to have pages added to my passport. I also enjoy eating, reading and listening to music. Often simultaneously.

Also by Christa Maurice

Drawn to the Rhythm Series
Satellite of Love
Heaven Beside You
Twenty Flight Rock
Let Me Be the One
Keep Coming Back to Love

Arden FD Series
Three Alarm Tenant
Struck By Lightning
Spark of Desire

Weaver's Circle Series
Secrets Everybody Knows
Long Memory

One Ring to Rule
Melody Unchained

www.ingramcontent.com/pod-product-compliance
Lightning Source LLC
Chambersburg PA
CBHW022153260626
47155CB00017B/1859